RESCUED DREAMS

LAST CHANCE
· FIRE AND RESCUE ·

RESCUED DREAMS

LISA PHILLIPS

sunrise
PUBLISHING

Rescued Dreams: A Last Chance County Novel
Last Chance Fire and Rescue, Book 8
Published by Sunrise Media Group LLC
Copyright © 2025 Lisa Phillips
Paperback ISBN: 978-1-963372-55-7

For more information about the author please access her websites at
www.authorlisaphillips.com

Published in the United States of America.
Cover Design: Ana Grigoriu-Voicu, Books-Design

LAST CHANCE
• FIRE AND RESCUE •

Expired Return

Expired Hope

Expired Promise

Expired Vows

Rescued Duty

Rescued Faith

Rescued Heart

Rescued Dreams

Last Chance Christmas

ONE

WHOEVER SAID THE TRUTH WAS LIKE A FLAME got it wrong.

Lies were the real fire. One moment there was a tiny flicker. Then it grew and spread, destroying everything until there was nothing left but ash.

From that destruction, Amelia Patterson had rebuilt her life. Come hurricane or high water, she was determined to do whatever it took to keep it.

No one was going to take from her ever again.

"Single file. Keep it steady." Amelia stood on the landing between two floors, ushering residents of this fourplex down to the ground floor.

An older man stumbled. His shoe slipped off a step, and he started to fall.

She braced her weight in a squat and caught him, bringing him up to standing height. "You good?"

"Thank you." His face flushed, a little embarrassed.

"It's my job." She led him to the next set of stairs, where he grabbed the rail. "Everyone keep it steady."

A young mother and her little son came down, moving fast.

The woman had a stuffed-full tote bag over one shoulder, despite the fact they'd instructed everyone to leave their belongings. Even the kid had a tiny suitcase behind him, decorated with a children's cartoon about puppies. Amelia said nothing.

At the top of the stairs, one of her firefighters emerged from the apartment to the right. Four doors, two on each side that faced each other. Della Nixon said, "Lieutenant, apartment 2-A is clear."

The other female on the team, Zoe Lewis, came on the open radio channel. "1-B is clear. Working on the others now."

Amelia's radio hung between the open sides of her turnout coat, clipped to a strap that went from one shoulder to the opposite hip. "Copy that." She pointed across the upper floor, and Della nodded before heading there to clear the apartment and make sure no one had stayed behind. "Collins, status."

Izan, the only guy now on Truck 14 after years of Amelia having mostly guys or all guys, was clearing the area where the fire had originated. A hot pan of frying oil had caught alight, burning the resident trying to cook their chicken.

The ambulance at the curb had the injured victim inside already, the EMTs of Ambulance 21, Trace and Kianna, treating their patient.

They wouldn't be here long unless something else happened.

"Collins!" she called out, shoving the front door of the apartment. It bounced back toward her, and a man emerged, moving at speed. Had he jammed the door shut? She caught sight of dark facial hair and a thick hood in the split second before he shoved her and she went down onto her backside.

Amelia cried out. "Hey!"

She could only watch him race away, the wind knocked out of her. What had that guy been doing inside the apartment that was on fire? And where was Izan?

Amelia clambered to her feet and headed for the door again. She stepped into the hallway of apartment 1-C. Black smoke had filled the air, rolling along the ceiling in the hall. She turned and ran back to the truck, tore off her helmet, and crouched to get her air tank and face mask on. Radio situated.

She replaced her helmet as she pushed off the ground, launching from the crouch, and went back to the apartment. "Izan! Dixon, Lewis, on me. The fire is spreading! Get me foam extinguishers." A grease fire wasn't going to be put out by water, and this one had kicked things up a notch. She shoved through another door to the kitchen. "Collins!"

Izan had come in here less than ten minutes ago, armed with a fire extinguisher, to subdue the small fire. Now the thing was close to being out of control. Where had he . . .

She spotted a boot and the hem of a turnout coat leg. "Izan!"

To her left, the fire raged on the stove, now spreading across the floor, melting the linoleum where the grease had splashed. Flames licked up to the ceiling, scorching whatever popcorn texture had been sprayed up there by the construction workers. Now it was dripping onto the floor.

She ran an assessing eye across the room as Dixon and Lewis ran in. "Get the fire smothered. I'll get Izan out. The gas should be off, but I'll check it."

"Yes, Lieutenant." Della aimed the fire extinguisher hose at the base of the flames.

Amelia went to Izan, unconscious and lying on the floor beside the breakfast bar counter. His fire extinguisher had rolled under the dining table.

She ducked her head, lifted his upper body, and stood with him over her shoulder. Amelia gritted her teeth and headed for the door. She walked through the entryway and out to the grass in front of the apartment building, where she deposited Izan on the soft, muddy earth. She ripped off her helmet and air tank. "Medic!" She shouted as loud as she could. Trace stopped what he was doing and ran to her. Amelia sat back on the grass, breathing hard. "We need another bus."

Trace stuck a stethoscope in his ears so he could listen to Izan's breathing. "Give yourself a second."

This was supposed to have been a routine callout, but fire was never routine. Things could go wrong a million different ways. One moment, a fire extinguisher was all it took, and evacuating residents was only routine. The next, she'd have to call for the hose.

Behind her, the fire boomed, blowing out the windows of apartment 1-C. Everyone in the vicinity ducked, covering their heads. Someone screamed. An older woman tripped trying to walk faster, and a young man moved to help her up.

Amelia switched her radio to the dispatch channel. "This is Truck 14." She gave the address. "We need backup."

She listened to the dispatcher's response in her earpiece while she replaced her mask and helmet. "Copy that." She ran back to the apartment. The natural gas line had to have caught the flame somehow and gone up. It should've been off. What on earth had happened here?

She shut off the analysis she could save for her report, wondering how the hyperawareness that meant she saw the worst coming was even supposed to be helpful. It wasn't like she could've stopped it in time.

Useless.

How many times had she been called that? As many as it took for that word to sink into her bones. For it to become a part of her.

The Christians at the firehouse kept telling everyone to pray, but God had never shown up to save her before. Why would He start now?

Amelia shouldered the door to the apartment open.

The manager ran over between the buildings. "Hey! What's going on?"

She yelled from behind her face mask. "Keep everyone back."

Amelia ducked inside the apartment. She spotted one of her firefighters in the hallway on the floor. She grabbed Zoe Lewis under the arms and dragged her out the door, across the concrete to the grass.

Rescue squad pulled up, but they weren't close enough. She left Zoe on the grass near Izan, who was now stirring as he woke up. Trace moved over to assess the downed female firefighter.

Amelia ran back to the apartment.

Inside, she could barely see her hand in front of her face. She clicked on the light on the side of her helmet and pressed into the dark. Searching for her friend.

"Nixon, call out!" She found the base of the fire, but the main blaze of the oil pan had been extinguished. Flames in the living room came from the gas fireplace and an open line. The buildup had caused the explosion, but now the running gas was coming out, keeping the fire going. The front of the unit had blown off, and the blaze swept up the wall and across the ceiling now. Moving fast, toward the hall. Seeking out fuel. Destroying everything in its wake.

"Nixon!"

She went back to the kitchen, trying to figure out where—

A heavy hand dragged her shoulder back. "We've got this."

Bryce Crawford. Twin to Logan. Ladies' man turned one-woman good guy. Penny was a blessed lady. Bryce was a good lieutenant.

Amelia considered him the brother she'd have preferred to the one she actually had. But his family, the Crawfords, were all over-achievers, and she had to fight for every inch just to measure up, so belonging to the Crawford clan would never have worked.

Besides, there was only one guy at the firehouse she would even consider dating. The rest of them . . . she knew too much personal stuff about them. And their locker room smelled like a high-school gym.

"Get clear." Eddie Rice tromped in after Bryce, followed by Zack Stephens, whose wife was pregnant. He spent every spare moment at the firehouse reading baby books.

"We'll find Della," Zack said.

Then Ridge was there in front of her. "You good?"

Every word they said would be heard by everyone on the comms channel. All the firefighters on scene, and the EMTs as well, if they switched over to hear what was happening.

He stared down at her, close enough their face masks were nearly touching. She saw his eyes scan her face. Checking if she was all right. His dark gaze held hers, those brooding eyes that always seemed to see far too much.

Until he got too close and she had to tell him to back off. Give her some space.

Amelia squeezed his elbow. "Find her," she said into the comms channel. "I'm going outside to check on the others."

She tromped out, partially irritated that rescue squad had to swoop in and save their bacon—even if she'd been the one to call for backup. She and her Truck 14 crew wouldn't hear the end of that one for a while.

As she approached, Amelia saw Izan had sat up. Zoe pushed away Trace's hand and did the same.

Amelia deposited her helmet, mask, and air tank on the grass, then sat and leaned against her gear. Fists tight on her knees.

Cops had arrived, easing people back from the scene.

"Another bus?" she asked Trace, sweat rolling down the sides of her face.

"Almost here."

"How is the patient?" She tipped her head to his ambulance, asking about the resident caught in the initial blaze.

"She needs to get going." Trace's expression held a shadow.

"So go. We're good."

Zoe said, "Go."

Izan nodded. "Get the patient to the hospital."

Trace grabbed up his gear. "The other ambulance will be here in a minute. No one gets up until they're cleared. Got it?"

Amelia lifted her hand and gave him a salute.

Trace ran for his ambulance.

Zoe said, "Did you see Della?"

Amelia shook her head. "Looked like the gas fireplace exploded."

"No way." Izan frowned. "I turned the gas off from outside before I went in."

Amelia shrugged. "It blew."

"That makes no sense."

Zoe turned to watch the apartment. She had a smudge line of ash on the shoulder of her turnout coat and sweat on her hairline at the back. The dark-haired state women's hockey champ two years running had two brothers who were Marines, and she'd married a US Army soldier—much to her brothers' dismay. Her husband had been deployed for eight months and wasn't due back for at least another year. Her mother pitched in to watch their two kids, aged four and seven, while Zoe worked long shifts.

Izan hadn't had a girlfriend in a while. Amelia got the feeling he had a thing for Olivia Tazwell, but since Amelia had her own unrequited thing going on, she wasn't going to get into it.

Eddie was first out the door, Zack on the other side of him with Della between them. They held her upright, walking at a rapid pace.

Amelia stood, shielded her eyes with her hands, and waited for them to get close enough. "Where was she?"

"Behind the dining table. She's awake, just dazed." They set her down on the grass, laying her back. The EMTs who had just arrived ran over.

Amelia wanted to sink back onto the grass.

"Takes two of you to bring out one of us?" Izan grinned. "Amelia dragged me out on her own, then went back for Zoe. She got us both out." Izan brushed imaginary lint from his shoulder. "But that's Truck versus Rescue for you, I guess."

Amelia bit the inside of her lip so she didn't smile. She lifted her brows.

Zoe twisted around. "You really did that? Never mind, of course you did."

"We go back for each other," Amelia said. "No matter what."

Zoe nodded. "No matter what."

Izan reached over and squeezed her shoulder.

Amelia watched the EMT assess Della like it was just another day on the job. But when someone could die at any minute, when a routine callout could go wrong in a thousand different ways and an innocent could get a call that their world would never be the same . . .

Amelia couldn't let go of her focus for even one second.

She'd been right to tell Ridge that she couldn't get into a relationship. Not when being a lieutenant meant everything to her and, with one tiny flick of the hand from Whoever was in control up there . . .

She could lose it all.

No, it just wasn't worth the risk. Not when any day now, her carefully constructed life would come crashing down.

She didn't have the strength to rebuild it all again.

TWO

RIDGE DUG HIS AXE INTO THE DRYWALL AND tore out a piece, confirming the fire wasn't in the walls. The fact that the axe had embedded a little harder than it should have was . . . unsurprising. She'd dumped him, and there was nothing he could do about it. What was the point in going around and around and never making progress? Spinning his wheels because she wasn't about to change her mind.

He keyed his radio. "I think we're clear. The fire is out in the living room."

"Copy that," Bryce responded. "Same here. Let's clear out and work on cleanup."

"Meet me by the gas valve outside," Eddie said over the radio. "Got something to show you, *Lieutenants.*"

Ridge grinned, but on the open comms channel, he'd have to hope Amelia hadn't heard that, or maybe she'd figure Eddie had misspoken. Ridge had passed the test a couple of weeks ago and gained the rank of lieutenant. But considering there were currently no open lieutenant spots with Last Chance Fire Department, it was almost a moot point. He hadn't even told the other firefighters outside rescue squad.

He and Amelia were technically the same rank now. They no longer worked on the same engine, and he was no longer her subordinate.

Another situation that had a resolution, at least partially. He could've used it a year ago, when she'd been open to a relationship—for a hot second—until she'd realized he wanted her to let him into her life. Then she'd shut it down, and he was out in the cold. Figuratively.

"You coming?" Bryce shoved his shoulder.

"Yeah, yeah, *Lieutenant.*"

Bryce grinned. Ridge followed him out, peeling off the helmet and face mask as they went.

Life had always frustrated him. He'd never gotten what he wanted. After this series of disappointments, he'd thought finally dating Amelia would help him amass some hope in his heart so he could start to believe things might be different. It had been a year since that failed attempt at dating. He just hoped going for a lieutenant spot wasn't going to end the same way.

After years of being officially "dead," living under the radar, his cousin Kane had been able to resurface. Not that they'd never communicated. Kane had figured out how to stay in touch the whole time.

Kane, his girlfriend Maria, and his Delta Force buddies had been wildland firefighters for two summers, but now the Trouble Boys had resolved the reason their Delta Force team had been forced to go underground. Kane and Maria were headed here so they could all spend some time together. In fact, Ridge was expecting them later today.

So what he'd figured he would gain from a relationship with Amelia had, in fact, come from Kane showing back up in the land of the living.

Hope, but still it was wrapped in disappointment.

Probably written all over his face.

"Seriously, bro." Eddie shot him a look, his dark eyes flashing.

Ridge and Bryce were supposed to have met him by the shutoff valve, but Eddie had met them just outside the front door instead.

In time to catch the look on Ridge's face that Bryce had missed. "I suppose I have every reason to be thankful. It's a beautiful day. The sun is shining. No one was seriously hurt." Ridge shot Eddie a look, then pointed at him. "You're dating a movie star. Bryce is engaged. Zack and Naya got married, and now they're having a baby in a few months."

"And Ridge is still single." Bryce clapped Eddie on the back of the head. "Have a little compassion, bro. He's the last domino to fall."

Eddie shrugged. "Okay, but he's so sad. He's bringin' down the mood."

Ridge walked away, not toward the other firefighters on the grass. He carried his SCBA face mask under his arm and set his helmet back on his head. His hair probably stuck out everywhere, but he didn't care enough to fix it. He went to the valve, and the others gathered around.

Eddie said, "The gas was on when I got to it."

And he'd shut it off, from the look of this. "Let's go find out what happened." Ridge swung around in time to see both Eddie and Bryce snap a salute.

"Yes, Lieutenant." Both of them spoke at the same time.

Ridge rolled his eyes, but it was pretty funny. They were proud of him. His boys, his team. Zack was over with the others, crouched by Della Nixon. Ridge tried not to look at Amelia, but he scanned all of them. She looked tired—and frustrated. *Join the club, honey.*

Probably not frustrated about the same things he was though.

He hung back and let Bryce take the lead. The rescue squad lieutenant held out his hand and helped Amelia to her feet. Bryce said, "You guys shut the gas off?"

"I did." Izan got to his feet, holding his hand out for Zoe. Della sat on the grass, sipping from a water bottle. The EMT was packing up his gear.

Ridge caught Amelia's gaze. "You good?"

"Just got the wind knocked out of me when that guy ran out of the apartment." Amelia looked around, and he followed her gaze, seeing a black-and-white police car pull onto the street.

Ridge saw her swallow, an indication she was nervous. Interesting. "Izan, did you see anyone in there?"

"The gas was off when I went in." Izan rubbed a hand through his thick black hair. "I was about to start with the foam when someone knocked me out. They came from the hallway. Maybe they ran out in time to slam into you?"

Amelia shrugged. "I didn't get a good look at his face."

"The door was cracked," Ridge said. "I figured it was you guys that opened it."

Amelia's dark-blonde brows drew together. "Someone deliberately targeted us. Or the apartment."

"I'll go fill in the cops. Get them to talk to witnesses and see if anyone saw anything." Bryce wandered off toward the officers on crowd control.

Ridge said, "I'm going to walk through the apartment."

"I'll go with you." Amelia peeled off her gloves and left them with her helmet and SCBA on the grass. That left her in turnout pants and a T-shirt, suspenders over her shoulders. Hair pulled back in a low bun so it didn't get caught in anything. Wisps of blonde that had come free hung on the sides of her face.

She was gorgeous, and half the men in the fire department had been in love with her at one point or another. Too bad she was so determined to succeed in Last Chance County that she didn't notice the attention. But her determination made her an incredible officer. He wanted to be as good a lieutenant as she was. It was a large part of what had driven him in his training and studying to pass the test.

Not only that, but his life had changed in the last year, and he needed a greater income now that he had two mouths to feed at home.

Ridge went into the apartment first, then stepped aside and let her pass so she could go into the kitchen. She hit the living room instead.

Amelia stood in the middle of the room, now a bunch of black, scorched furniture surrounded by black walls. She stared at the fireplace, her hands on her hips. "The gas must've built up and then blown."

"The pilot light probably caught with the fire." He went over and crouched in front of the fireplace unit. "There isn't much that comes out to make the flames in a fake-wood unit like this, but if the gas built up behind the face plate . . ." He looked at the switch on the wall—where it was supposed to be, anyway. "I wonder if whoever shoved Izan turned the fire on and opened the valve. These things have safety features. They're not supposed to just blow."

"Gas doesn't turn itself back on, and there's no question Izan turned it off if he says he did."

"So our conclusion is that whoever was in here messed with it and deliberately caused the accident." He blew out a breath. The same person had knocked her down. "Thank God no one was badly hurt."

His faith was new, or old, depending on how he looked at it. But all his conversations with Kane the past couple of months had led him to dig his Bible out of the back of a cupboard in his town house and even darken the doors of a church a few times.

Amelia said, "Mmm."

Whatever that meant. Ridge wandered to the kitchen to look around.

"Hey, listen. I didn't really come with you so we could look at the scene. I need to talk to you."

He turned. "What about?"

She stood in the kitchen doorway—what was left of it. Amelia lifted a hand and brushed hair back from her face, tucking the errant strands behind one ear. "I got a call. From the Benson Fire Department. A guy I used to work with—Julio Espinoza-Vasquez—called me."

"Coda." Ridge nodded. "We met him when we went to Benson last year to help them out after that huge fire downtown." They'd been scheduled to go there for training as a collaboration between the two departments, but given what had been going on, they'd quickly switched to pitching in.

"He asked me to provide a reference on a prospective applicant." She kept her expression blank, making her face unreadable. "You made lieutenant?"

"A couple of weeks ago."

Hurt flashed in her eyes, but it disappeared quickly. "And you applied to BFD?"

"There are no open lieutenant spots in Last Chance County." He shrugged. And they'd broken up—so what reason did he have to stay? Even his sisters were on board with the idea. Tentatively. "And they have a few positions. I'm still deciding."

"Julio was nice about it, but he told me you should put someone else's name on your application." She winced. "I didn't leave Benson under the best circumstances. To be honest, I have zero credibility there."

"They asked who my former superior officers were. That's all." Nothing personal—just the way she liked it. Ridge was trying not to get cynical, but it was hard. "Sorry you got dragged into it."

"I just wanted you to know why my opinion won't help you in Benson. But I'm sure Crawford gave you a glowing reference."

Ridge took a couple of steps toward her. "What happened to you there? Why'd you leave Benson?"

She shrugged, but the weight on her shoulders didn't move. "I needed a fresh start. Fire is fire. Doesn't matter where you fight it."

"You've said that to me before." Now it seemed a little too rehearsed. "But I've lived in Last Chance my whole life. Maybe it would be a good change to go live somewhere else. The Benson FD seemed like some really solid people. It could be good." He stopped before he repeated himself again.

She said, "They're solid now."

"Now that you're gone?"

She flinched. "I wasn't the toxic one."

He took another step toward her. "What happened?"

"I left. That's what happened."

"Why?"

"I wanted a *change.* Why are you interrogating me?"

"Because if I keep doing it, eventually you'll tell me the truth."

Her eyes flared. "What does it matter?"

She already knew the answer to that, so Ridge just stared at her. Wordlessly willing her to figure it out on her own.

"Whatever. Leave." She shrugged. "See if I care."

"Is there a reason I shouldn't go to Benson?"

"Not anymore."

Ridge dipped his head and tried to catch her gaze. "If you don't want me to go, then ask me to stay."

She twisted to face him. "Do whatever you want."

Then she whirled around and walked out.

Ridge watched her go, trying to figure out why it amused him to rile her up. Probably he just enjoyed torturing himself with what he couldn't have.

Bryce appeared in the doorway. "That went well."

"Swing and a miss." Ridge mimicked holding a baseball bat.

Bryce chuckled. "Pressing her buttons isn't exactly the tactic I'd have gone with."

"I don't need any more advice." Ridge swiped at his forehead and realized too late he still had his gloves on. "Just tell me that the truck crew aren't in danger. That they aren't being personally targeted. Then there's a hope I'll be able to get some sleep tonight."

Bryce said, "I guess we should figure it out. I happen to know a private investigator."

"Fine, call your girl. Tell her we'll pay whatever she charges." He needed to know if their friends were at risk.

Because if Amelia's life was in danger, there was no way he would leave Last Chance County.

She might have given him up. But he wasn't going to lose her.

THREE

AMELIA DROVE THE FIRE TRUCK BACK TO THE firehouse since she was the one with the least injuries. The quiet in the cab, everyone thinking—or overthinking—or relaxing for a moment, gave her time for her thoughts to wander. She gripped the wheel and swung Truck 14 into the engine bay of Eastside Firehouse ten minutes before the end of their shift, more than ready to hand off the rig to the incoming crew.

Thinking about Benson always got her way back in her head. She didn't need that. Now she resented Ridge for bringing it all back up. The captain from Benson—Coda, because he was the child of deaf parents—had been nice about it, but he knew the story.

Amelia didn't want the past invading her life here. She was just going to shove it from her mind the way she'd been doing ever since she got back. Not that there weren't plenty of problems in her history based here in Last Chance County, but at least those were all dead. Or in jail.

Izan rolled his shoulders, sat over in her spot in the passenger seat. "Gonna shut the engine off?"

The two women on her crew had hopped out.

Amelia put the rig in Park and shut the engine down, leaving the keys in the ignition. "Interesting day."

"I'll say." He hopped out. "Pretty much a miracle we're all mostly unscathed."

They'd all been checked out by the medics on scene, and no one had needed to be taken to the hospital—which meant not only was everyone good, but Truck 14 was still in service. Going out of service was a necessity sometimes. They couldn't respond to a callout if they were tied up at the hospital and had the fire truck with them.

She jumped out of the truck and rolled her shoulders, feeling the pull of her sore muscles. A good day of hard work. Tomorrow she would hit the gym where she was a member and use the sauna—get rid of the tension. Until then, she needed a hearty meal and a strong cup of tea.

Amelia got her gear stowed away and slipped her feet into running shoes she kept at the firehouse. She pushed through the double doors into the hall that stretched from the engine bay to the front door. The kitchen was to the left about halfway down one straight hall, off which was a U-shaped corridor with the bunk rooms, the gym, officers' quarters, chief's office, and the conference room so that the building was a square. On slow days, they made the rookies race around the hall doing laps, and when they were bored and the chief was gone, they turned it into a relay with obstacles and those guns that shot foam darts.

She took the quiet hall past the bunk rooms to her office in the south hall, able to hear the chatter from the kitchen and living area on the north side of the building. Her counterpart for the next shift was already in the office, logging on to his laptop.

She knocked and entered. "I just have to grab my backpack."

Lieutenant Morris was pushing fifty, heavyset with thick dark brows and not much hair on the top of his head. He took off his reading glasses and turned, making the chair creak. "Sounds like it was an eventful shift."

"Excitement is better than sitting around waiting for the bell to go off." She hated feeling antsy with too much energy and nothing to do. "How about you? Do anything interesting on your day off?" She swiped her book from the nightstand and dropped it in her backpack.

"Not really. The kids had a track meet, so I went to that. Chief James wants to talk to you on your way out."

Amelia frowned. "Any idea what it's about?" She'd been planning to change and head out, not get sucked into a meeting.

Morris shrugged. "I didn't ask."

She swung her backpack onto her shoulder. "Have a good one."

He muttered something, but she ignored it. Personal and work didn't mix. She knew that better than anyone. She didn't have to work the same shift as Morris, and she liked it that way. Amelia and Bryce had a friendly rivalry. Morris would have been forever trying to undermine her just to make himself look better.

Something she'd had enough of for a lifetime.

Amelia was going to keep things professional with everyone, even if it killed her. Considering the alternative nearly had, she knew the stakes, and she was okay with doing her job to the best of her ability and then going home to her echoey house. No one could ask more of her than that.

She knocked on Macon's door and heard a muffled "Come in."

"You wanted to see me, Chief?"

He sat behind his desk, a gold ring on his left hand. A Styrofoam container on his desk that smelled like Italian seasoning. "Shut the door, Lieutenant." His expression shifted, but she didn't know what it meant.

Amelia eased the door shut. "Should I sit?"

"That might be a good idea." His frown lines deepened as he sat back in his chair, his wide shoulders almost as broad as the seat. "I was going through the personnel files recently and discovered that yours doesn't seem to have your rank qualification report included. Any idea why it's missing?"

Amelia held herself very still. "From your files?"

"The system indicates the files were paper, not electronic. They were never scanned into the database by the admin pool, and I can't seem to locate the paperwork. Until I can, you're technically not able to work as a lieutenant, as I only have the firefighter qualification for you. Nothing after you passed the initial training."

She swallowed. "So it went missing? Or someone took it?"

Amelia needed to seem surprised, maybe confused. She was only confused about why it had taken him this long to realize there was a problem. *Ridge.* Macon had gone into the files to update Ridge's rank and discovered the discrepancy in hers.

"I need a copy of your lieutenant paperwork, Patterson. ASAP. You have to get it to me by next shift, or you won't be able to lead Truck. Put in a call to the Benson FD and have them send it over. I'm sure you'd rather not have Foster take your spot until this is cleared up, so get it figured out. Got it?"

"Yes, sir. Is that everything?"

The chief nodded. "See you Thursday."

She got up, moving as easy as she could, keeping things smooth. No jerky movements. "See you later, sir." Amelia closed the door to his office. She walked sedately to the front door. The receptionist who worked during the day on weekdays said something, but Amelia didn't hear the words. It sounded like garbled whomps.

Then she was outside, and all she could hear was the rush of her own breath in her ears.

Amelia practically ran to her pickup truck, then slid in behind the wheel. She grasped the steering wheel while rain dropped on the windshield. She hadn't even noticed it was raining. The sky was heavy with dark gray clouds.

Ridge walked by her truck, his duffel bag over his shoulder. She spotted Eddie and Izan walking together.

Amelia turned the truck on, shoved it into Drive, and peeled out before Ridge could open the passenger-side door and try to talk to her. Someone honked, but she didn't know if she'd cut them off or simply had a taillight out.

She ignored everything. Shut off the music on her radio, tuned to the local country station. She drove to Main Street in town and pulled into the parking lot behind Bridgewater Café.

Amelia keyed in the code for the back door, letting herself in the employee entrance. Meg Andrews, the owner, had been Amelia's best friend in high school. Back then, Amelia's father had . . . She didn't want to think about him.

Steven Hilden had run the town like a tyrant until local cops and first responders had exposed what he was doing a handful of years ago. He'd been the fire chief at the time—and he was responsible for Meg's father's death.

On the wall of the back hallway in the café hung an old photo of Meg's father in his firefighter uniform. In the picture, he stood beside another firefighter with short blond hair and dark-brown eyes. *Dad.* The sweet man her mom had remarried when Amelia was five, Matt Patterson.

They'd both died on the same shift.

Not just because the fire had overtaken their position, leaving them with no way out, but also because the chief had known they disliked his extracurricular activities. For the crime of believing a firefighter should be working to save lives and prevent fire— not working for his own personal gain through any and all illegal means—they'd been left to die.

She remembered fondly this man she had loved, who had doted on her. Amelia lifted her fist and knocked it against the frame of the photo in solidarity. But with how shaken she was, it rattled a little too much.

Meg stuck her head out of her office. "Whoa. What happened?"

Amelia shook her head. "It's fine."

"Fine enough you look like your cat ran onto the freeway." Meg rolled her eyes. "Get a soda and get in here."

Amelia went to the refrigerator in the kitchen and grabbed a diet plus a drink for Meg. She set Meg's on the desk in her tiny office—mostly covered with textbooks for the college courses she was taking. Her friend was trying to get her degree in all the masses of spare time she had after running the café.

"Don't tell me it's fine. Tell me what *it* is." Meg sat back in her chair and took a sip of her drink.

Amelia wanted to throw her drink at the wall, so she put it on the desk and turned to pace. "Macon asked for my lieutenant paperwork. By next shift."

"Oh boy." Meg paused. "We knew this could happen eventually."

She wanted to explain that Ridge would get her spot on Truck, but that wasn't even the point that made this whole thing so huge. "We knew it would blow up in my face." She turned back to pace the other direction and shrugged. "Now it's over. I'm done."

"You're not done until you quit."

"I might as well quit." She lifted her hands, then let them fall back to her sides. "What's the point pretending I'm not an impostor?"

"You're a fire department lieutenant."

Amelia stopped pacing. "One who bribed the old fire chief to let me have the job because of what we knew he used to do for Steven Hilden . . ." She couldn't say "my father." Not out loud. She had to pause just to breathe. "I coerced him to hire me as lieutenant when I have no official standing for this job."

"You passed that test fair and square. It was just that . . ." Her words descended into muttering. "He—"

"I know what he did. I was there."

Meg leaned forward in her seat. "Maybe you should say it out loud for once instead of burying it or pretending you've forgotten. What did he do to you, Amelia?"

"He—"

"Use his name."

Amelia let out a sound of frustration. "Nicholas Danielson, Benson FD captain." She shot Meg a look and saw her friend nod. "He wore me down until I agreed to date him, using his position as my superior to get me to cave. Then when things didn't go his way—"

"Or when you succeeded at *anything*."

Amelia continued, "—he was vindictive, abusive, and undermined me."

"And convinced all your coworkers that you were unhinged because he was *drugging your coffee*."

Amelia closed her eyes. "There's no paperwork. He destroyed it."

"You earned that rank fair and square."

She opened her eyes. "Doesn't matter now. I'm done. My career is over."

Meg held her gaze with a steady stare. "It's only over when you say it is."

FOUR

RIDGE PARKED HIS JEEP IN THE NUMBERED SPOT for his town house, and a glance over at the guest spot told him the twins were home. He grabbed the bag of food he'd picked up from Backdraft off the front seat and his duffel from the back.

He'd been thinking about what had happened today the whole way home. The fact that it seemed like firefighters had been the target of a deliberate attack. The cops hadn't had enough time to ascertain anything, so there was no new information.

Okay, fine, he'd been thinking about the look on Amelia's face when she left.

Whatever she'd talked to the chief about had upset her, but Ridge had no idea what it could be, and with a whole forty-eight blissful hours off work to look forward to, he wasn't going to get an answer on that anytime soon either. Not unless he tracked her down outside work—which he'd never done.

They'd gone on exactly four dates. She'd always gone with him from the firehouse or met him at a restaurant or movie theater. He'd never picked her up from her house and had no idea where she lived. Then again, no one from the firehouse had been to his town house since he'd moved in.

Rescue squad used to come over sometimes to watch a basketball game, or they'd all go to Bryce's to watch football. But with the guys getting into relationships, that happened less now.

He and Amelia were just private people, and he didn't want the twins all aflutter because of a bunch of firefighter guys and gals in his house.

He doubted Amelia would answer the phone if he called.

The door opened before he even reached it, and one of the twins appeared in the doorway. Maddie always tracked his phone, and when the app said he'd arrived, his sister always met him at the door. "Take this bag, will you? Dish up and I'll go shower real quick."

Now that she was seventeen and on the cusp of being a gorgeous woman, keeping her out of line of sight of firefighters was a good plan. They had enough drama with boys at school. Even if he trusted his friends implicitly, he didn't like the idea of personal tangling with professional—unless it came to Amelia.

Maddison had long brown hair with a wave that came nearly to the small of her back. She wore wide-leg jeans low on her hips and a shirt that didn't touch the waistband. As long as there wasn't a belly-button ring in her navel. At least, not one he hadn't been informed about before she got it. He was going to keep his mouth shut and pick his battles.

"You should put your laundry on. Your duffel smells like Josh's car." She took the bag and wandered to the kitchen counter. "He's on the football team."

A person could stand in the middle of the kitchen, reach out and touch all the counters plus the fridge without stretching too far. The little square space was barely big enough for two people, let alone all three of them at once.

When they'd moved here, the twins had replaced his black-and-white highway print on the wall in the hallway with a vintage *Casablanca* movie poster. Six months ago it had been replaced with a poster for *Trek of the Osprey,* a sci-fi show he'd watched as a kid, which they called "vintage" and insisted on watching over and over when all three of them were home.

"Hi." Ella burrowed under his arm and squeezed his middle. Slightly smaller than Maddison, she had the same hairstyle but wore a floral top and a pair of skinny jeans. Aside from their sense of style and Ella's more introverted personality, the girls were mirror images. Most people couldn't tell them apart.

He put his arm around Ella. "Good day?"

She shrugged, still holding his middle with her slender arms. He rubbed a hand across her shoulders. "Maddie, how do you know what Josh's car smells like?"

Even though her back was to him, he knew she winced. Ella let out a little giggle. Maddie twisted around. "Did I say Josh? I meant . . . uh . . . we went to the library. That's how I know what his car smells like. We studied. At the library." She shot wide eyes in Ella's direction.

"That's where I do all my studying," Ridge said. "At the *library.*"

Ella laughed aloud, and it was about the best sound Ridge had ever heard. Up there on his top five favorite things, along with Christmas carol services sung by a children's choir, a hot dog at a ball field, and Amelia's smile.

Ella disconnected from the hug and went over to slump on their cushy sectional. The one they'd made him spend two hours picking out because they had to sit on *every* couch in the entire store. Twice. And okay, it had been worth it. Not that he'd admit as much to them.

"I guess I should pay more attention to that tracking app. See where you're going." He watched Ella curl up with a calculus textbook and her math notebook, sliding the pencil out from behind her ear.

"Right now I'm in the kitchen, doing what you told me to do."

"Is Josh still a thing?" He'd learned Maddie switched out flavors of the month like an ice-cream shop, but he'd rather she just have a lot of friends so he wasn't worrying about her getting hot and heavy with some guy while he had an overnight shift at the firehouse.

Maddie shrugged. "Ella didn't like him."

Despite their differences, the girls' instincts were sacrosanct for decision-making. If one had a vibe, it was law. Thankfully, when their mom had remarried eighteen months ago and their stepdad Gary didn't want to be tied down with kids, they'd had the feeling Ridge would be great to live with. So the twins called a family meeting and announced their plan to have Ridge adopt them.

Gary had been thrilled.

Considering Ridge never would've left the girls in the lurch, he hadn't even given it time so he could think it over. He'd said yes immediately, and they'd been living with him as their guardian since.

At the time, Ridge had been in a one-bedroom apartment on the rough side of town, saving for a down payment on a house. He'd taken that money and put a deposit on this place. The girls got the main bedroom upstairs because it was bigger—and had two sinks in the bathroom. He had a small room he used a few days a week, and the third room was an office with a pullout couch.

Maddie put a full plate of food in the microwave, then took the container of salad and two packets of plasticware and went to sit by her sister on the couch. Ridge got the breadsticks and ate two on the way to the shower.

He rinsed off, set his clothes in the washer, and headed back to the kitchen in sweatpants and a T-shirt. While he'd been in the bathroom, he'd received an email from Chief Macon James, asking him to come in early next shift. He responded, acknowledging the request, and set his phone on the breakfast bar.

"I made you a plate. It's in the microwave." Ella didn't look up from her math.

Maddie nudged her.

Ella looked at her sister, then at Ridge.

"Whatever it is, let me eat first. I'm starving." He went to the microwave and pulled out the hot plate of sausage pasta. His stomach growled. Ridge went to the armchair. He ate one bite, then said, "Okay, hit me with whatever it is."

Ella smiled.

"Okay, well." Maddie shifted on the couch, curling her legs up so her knees were almost in her sister's lap. "We've been talking about Benson, Washington."

"About you getting a job there," Ella said.

"And we don't want to move."

"We wanna stay here."

Both of them stared at him.

Ridge said, "There aren't any open lieutenant spots in Last Chance County."

"We're in our senior year. We shouldn't leave before graduation," Ella said. "It would be too much of an interruption to move mid-year."

"I know." He'd been dragging his feet for that exact reason. He'd also called his mom and talked about her coming home for a few months. "But they have a good college there." He knew they'd been applying around, finding somewhere they could both land.

Ella said, "They already accepted us."

Maddie nudged her. "But so did three other schools, so it's not like we're locked in."

"We could all move." Ridge set his plate on the coffee table and leaned his forearms on his knees. "Get a house there. You guys could go to school in Benson and get your degrees."

Maddie stared at him, her expression almost brittle. Like it was about to shatter. "This is our home. We didn't want to leave before, when Mom left, and we don't want to leave now."

"I know, kiddo." Ridge sighed.

"Be a firefighter here. On rescue squad. I thought you liked it."

He glanced at Ella. "There are some things you don't understand."

"You don't want to work with *her*," Maddie said. "Because she broke your heart."

Ridge shook his head. "It didn't get that far."

"But she dumped you."

"That's not—"

"Now you wanna run away. Like when Eric asked Stacey to prom, and I wanted to die . . . or switch to the high school across town because I couldn't stand to see either of their faces." Maddie winced, her eyes glistening with tears.

He'd been home for those two rocky days before the summer, when Maddison had been in bed in tears with a gallon of ice cream and a bag of chocolate chips. No one wanted to relive the Great Eric Firestorm all over again. Considering Ridge's ankle injury at the time, he hadn't been able to work out and couldn't leave the house without Ella driving him. They'd all been trapped with nowhere to go, but they'd survived.

Before he could respond, she continued. "I worked through it. And you need to do the same thing." She nodded, certain she was right. Her composure back in place. "So we can stay."

Ella looked at her phone, then at her sister. "They're here."

"Who is here?" He scooted to the edge of his seat. "Who else do you have on that location app?" It had better not be more Joshes. "Ella?"

She lifted her chin. "We also can't leave because this is where our family is."

They only had Mom and . . . "Kane?" He glanced between them. "You convinced Kane to back your plan to stay here?"

Maddie's expression matched her sister's. "We knew you were serious, so we decided to get serious."

Ridge strode to the front door and opened it in time to see Kane and his girlfriend Maria coming up the front walk. "So this is a setup?"

"Nah." Kane grinned. "Just here to tell you we're engaged."

Maria lifted her left hand and wiggled her fingers. She looked as happy as anyone had a right to be, a smile spread wide across her face. The woman was gorgeous, all dark features and Hispanic coloring.

Ridge grinned. "Congratulations." He gave Maria a hug, and she stepped in. He held out his hand to his cousin Kane, and they slapped each other's backs. "I'm glad she said yes."

"Me too." Kane chuckled, twisting between Ridge and the doorframe. "How are my two favorite girls?" He spread his arms wide, and both twins came over to hug him. They hadn't seen Kane since they were little, and barely remembered him. But since Kane had come back from the dead, and back into their lives, a couple of months ago, he'd become an ally. Even Maria seemed to be part of their little group now.

Ridge said, "All right. Sit, all of you. I still need to eat." He pointed to the kitchen. "There's more if you guys are hungry." He grabbed his plate. "I'm not talking about anything else that's serious until I'm done with my food."

Maddie rolled her eyes and looked at Maria, who smiled. Kane's fiancée said, "My father was the same way after work."

Maddie leaned against Ella's shoulder and asked Maria, "Did you figure out your jobs here yet?"

Maria said, "We spoke to a guy in town, Tate Hudson."

Maddie looked at Ridge, who said, "He's a private investigator," then took another bite of pasta. Kane sat on the floor with his back to the couch, handing Maria one of the two bowls he carried.

"Thanks, this smells good." Maria said, "He's closing his business and handing off a lot of cases to others. He's shifting his job to more of a support role, but I'm not sure if investigating is what we want to do. I have a remote job consulting also, and that takes up a good chunk of my time. Working together might not be the right answer. We just don't know yet."

Kane swallowed a bite of food. "We're actually talking to some friends of friends about joining a search and rescue team." He glanced at Ridge. "They work out of Benson, where they have a whole K-9 team."

Maddie said, "Benson?"

Kane winced. "I know you don't want to go, but Maria and I need the right jobs for *us*. Her consulting gig isn't full-time, and I need to feel like I have my thing."

"And Ridge gets the right job for *him*." Maddie stood. "And no one cares what's right for us." She stepped onto the coffee table so she could get out of the sectional area.

"Maddie—"

"I *know*." But she didn't stop walking until she was upstairs, where she slammed the door.

Ridge winced, glancing at Ella. "Is that how you feel as well?"

Ella scrunched up her nose. "I want to pass this calculus class. I want Mom to come to our graduation, but she said she 'isn't sure what her plans are.' Maddie doesn't know what she wants her major to be, so how can I pick a college?" Her voice hitched.

Ridge's heart squeezed in his chest. This wasn't just about them all moving, it was about all the things the two teen girls in his house were dealing with.

"And I want that woman we shall not name to un-dump you."

"Don't worry about that."

Ella shrugged. "You can't tell me not to worry about you. She made you so unhappy you're leaving town, and now we all have to go."

"Ella—"

"I have a test tomorrow." She gathered up her books and left the room.

Ridge set his plate on the coffee table and ran his hands down his face, groaning.

Kane said, "Is this a bad time to ask if it's still okay that I stay here for a while?"

Ridge lowered his hands and looked at his cousin. The guy had been given back pay for his time serving the Army and his pension owed during the time he was supposedly dead, and Maria had been cut a check from the CIA for services rendered.

"Maria is going to get an apartment."

Ridge shrugged. "Sure, whatever. We can work it out tomorrow."

He almost laughed, even though there was nothing funny about this. He needed to do something about . . . everything. Before the girls decided to ignore their schoolwork and try to fix things themselves. Before he got a real job offer in Benson and had to make a final decision.

Kane set his bowl on the coffee table. "In that case, I'll go get my overnight bag."

Maria stood. "I'll go with you."

Ridge sat alone in his living room, trying to figure out how to fix the mess that was his life. Preferably before something else happened.

FIVE

AMELIA WALKED INTO THE FIREHOUSE JUST AFTER five in the evening, almost an hour before her shift was due to start. She cleared the entrance, and down the hall to her left, Ridge emerged from the chief's office.

Great.

Just what she needed when she'd come early specifically to talk to Macon.

He lifted his chin. "Hey."

Keeping it professional. The way she needed it to be—the way she wanted. "Hey." Amelia had to clear her throat. "You're in early." She didn't want it to sound like she was fishing for information, but it was what it was.

"Yeah, Chief James wanted to talk to me. He said there might be a spot for lieutenant open in the department soon, and he wanted to give me a heads-up just in case." He shifted, a little nervous almost. "Not sure who's getting fired or what."

"I guess we'll find out soon enough if he felt like he had to give you a heads-up." She'd been deflecting attention and questions since moving here.

His cell phone chimed in his pocket. He smiled at the screen and replied to a text.

Her heart squeezed in her chest. "New girlfriend?"

Great. She was blurting out everything today. Amelia winced while he wasn't looking at her.

Ridge lifted his gaze from his phone. "No, it's my sisters. Kane and Maria showed up in town, and Kane's staying at my house. They're making something for their dinner, and they needed to know where I keep the apple cider vinegar." He shook his head, smiling.

That was more than either of them had ever said about their personal lives. "Oh, that's nice." So, no girlfriend?

When she'd broken it off with him—not that it ever really got going—she'd had the feeling he was holding off introducing her to his family. Probably waiting until she passed muster, some kind of test to make sure she was good enough for his people.

They'd never made it that far.

He'd made his little sisters seem like a big deal in his life, and she wanted to meet them. But that was exactly why she shouldn't. They had to keep things surface level, casual. Professional now. Getting to know each other outside of work brought a boatload of things she didn't want to address.

Like where she lived.

And who she was.

Plus everything else.

"I need to talk to the chief about something, so I should do that before everyone else gets in." Amelia took a step back and moved around him.

"Is everything okay, Amelia?"

"Sure." She glanced back, trying to smile—hoping he believed it. "Why wouldn't it be?"

She'd only spent forty-eight hours trying to rest. Giving up and going for a run instead. Nearly getting run over by a crazy driver over by the greenbelt path. Eating potatoes with every meal because it made her feel better. And trying to fix the leak in one of the bathrooms in the big house.

Amelia knocked on the chief's door and, when he answered, stepped inside.

Chief James looked over from his computer monitor. "Good. You have the paperwork?"

"No, I don't, Chief." Amelia stood in front of his desk with her hands clasped behind her back. The worst part of all of this was that this chief was the first one she'd ever respected, and now she was letting him down.

He laced his fingers together on the desktop. "And if I call Benson FD and ask for a copy?"

She caught the look in his eye. *He knows.* She was certain he'd already called and found out—which meant he'd know if she lied. "They won't have it, but I'm sure they'll tell you an interesting story."

"They did." Macon nodded.

"I took the lieutenant's test in Benson and I passed. I would never lie about that." She respected the job far too much, despite the leaders she had worked under, and her father, who had tried to raise her as a child. Or any guy she'd made the mistake of falling for.

Another great reason not to get too deep with Ridge. She would find out the truth about him, something she never wanted to know. It would ruin everything to learn he wasn't who she wanted him to be. The man she believed he was. If he turned out not to be a good guy, she wasn't sure she would be able to handle it. But if she fell for him, then there was no way he was decent. Her life didn't work that way.

The chief shrugged just a little. "I need to have the paperwork to prove it, and while they have firefighters who say they heard you took it, no one can find a record that you ever passed the lieutenant's exam. Thankfully you qualified as a firefighter in the first place in Last Chance County, because I at least have that."

She'd worked here for six whole months before moving to Benson because she couldn't take it anymore.

She'd moved back for the same reason. Because she'd hoped things were different here with the former chief dead.

Macon continued. "There were some other things mentioned as well."

"I don't want to hear them. Not again." She fought to maintain her composure, clenching her fingers behind her. "I came here for a clean slate, and I've more than proven myself as a firefighter *and* a lieutenant."

"I know that, Amelia. But this is a legality issue. The department can't have a lieutenant with no official paperwork leading a team."

"So you're giving my truck to Ridge? Is that it?"

"Until you can either produce the paperwork or requalify as a lieutenant, you have to step down."

"Am I being suspended?" She nearly choked on the word.

"I don't think that's going to be necessary, and we can keep all of this in-house. Just until we get things straight."

Which would be never, considering her paperwork probably hadn't ever been created. And if it had, then her ex had destroyed it. And *that* meant she was going to have to retake the test.

This was humiliating.

"Go get squared away for shift. I'll tell the crew at our briefing to keep this to themselves." He paused for a second. "This isn't the end of the world, Amelia."

"Right. Of course not. Thanks, Chief." She headed for the door.

Thankfully he didn't order her to stick around. He let her go so she could grab the couple of things she kept in the truck lieutenant's office and take her backpack to the women's bunk room. She sat on the edge of the bed and sent a text to Meg.

The reply she got said,

Meg

Not getting fired is a good thing, right?

Amelia wasn't too sure she could agree with that just yet. But at least he hadn't taken away the one thing she had. The thing that defined her.

Della and Zoe came in, Zoe in the lead. Mid-sentence, she cut off whatever she was saying and stopped in the doorway. "Uh . . . Lieutenant?"

They passed her, going to their bunks. The four beds in here were plenty for the two of them and Kianna, the EMT. Now they'd have Amelia in here cramping their style.

She bit her lip. "We're switching things around for a few shifts." Or who knew how long. "The chief will explain at the briefing."

Ten minutes later, she took her usual spot at the end of the middle row of tables and chairs. The chief stood over at the whiteboard. Ridge sat by Bryce on the far side. Izan took a seat by Eddie. Zack closed his book and put it on the tabletop. Della and Zoe came in with coffee, and Trace and Kianna—their EMTs—stood at the back.

Her head swam through his whole introduction. Right up until he said, "For the foreseeable future, Ridge Foster will be the lieutenant on Truck 14. Zoe Lewis, you're on rescue squad."

Everyone looked at each other, and for a second, no one was looking at Amelia.

This is a disaster. She wasn't unaccustomed to being the center of attention for bad reasons, but it hadn't happened since she'd moved back to town.

She needed to email the testing center and find out when she could be requalified.

Hopefully as soon as possible, or she'd be giving up her role to Ridge of all people. Sure, he'd be nice about it. But it was still humiliating.

Chairs scraped across the floor, and she realized they'd been dismissed. Amelia tuned out the loud chatter and ignored the questions tossed her direction as she went to the kitchen. They all came in after her.

She should have gone to the bunk room.

"Coffee done yet?" Eddie strode past her.

Zack got pasta and jars of spaghetti sauce out of the cupboards. Ridge went to the coffeepot and grabbed half a dozen mugs out of the cupboard above it. He reached over to his right and flipped on the electric kettle. "Coffee, everyone?"

He moved one mug over to the kettle, dug in the little box, and put a teabag in the mug.

A peace treaty.

He knew how she felt—or he thought he did. And he knew she didn't want to talk about it, but she would want a strong cup of tea. She hadn't drunk coffee since . . .

That wasn't something she wanted to think about right now, when this was all *his* fault. Her ex didn't need to take up any space in her mind.

When the kettle boiled, she poured hot water over the tea bag.

The speaker up in the corner of the ceiling chimed. "Truck 14. Ambulance 21. Residential fire, persons trapped."

Everyone except rescue squad dropped what they were doing and headed to the engine bay. She dragged on her turnout pants, slid her feet into her boots, and shrugged on her jacket. Grabbed her helmet.

Amelia reached for the front passenger-side door.

Ridge grabbed the handle and opened it.

She realized what she'd done. "Habit. Sorry."

He was the one who looked sorry.

Amelia got in the back, beside Izan. Della fired up the engine, and Ridge pulled up the address on their dashboard computer.

Izan tapped her arm.

When she looked over, he mouthed, *Are you okay?*

She gave him a look like, *What do you think?*

"This too shall pass?"

"Let's just fight fire, yeah?" But she wasn't the lieutenant anymore. Somehow, she would deal with that fact.

Amelia rolled her shoulders. This would be fine. She just had to remember she wasn't in charge. The change in duty would give her a little perspective. Remind her what it was like to be the underling. Not to mention give Ridge the chance for some command experience before he . . .

He was looking for a lieutenant position somewhere else.

Now he had hers, here. Everyone probably thought it was better this way, that he was the lieutenant on Truck. After all, no one here wanted to lose Ridge. Things could change, and people sometimes left, but this was Ridge.

Della pulled the truck into a residential area, behind the middle school on Wiltern Drive. Amelia's stomach clenched. She used to live in this area.

In fact, she used to live on this street.

"What's the address for the fire?" She leaned forward and patted Ridge's shoulder.

"Number fourteen, Wiltern."

Amelia sucked in a breath.

"What is it?" Izan leaned forward, looking out the front window.

Sure enough, number fourteen was on fire. A woman out front waved her arms, and Della pulled over to the curb.

"What is it, Patterson?" Ridge asked.

"I used to live in that house." She pushed the door open and jumped out, going to the frantic woman. "Is this your house?"

Ridge appeared by her side, shooting her a look.

Amelia took a step back.

"It just exploded." The woman gasped. "My daughter is in her bedroom. You have to save her!"

SIX

RIDGE TURNED TO AMELIA. "YOU WANNA—"

He saw the look on her face. She wanted to find that child. In fact, she already had her tank and mask on.

"Yes." Amelia took off running toward the house. So maybe it was better for him to be the lieutenant right now.

If she were in charge of this scene, she would need to stay outside and be the commander on site.

Something about this being her childhood home meant she was on alert. Everyone wanted to find a missing child, a tender-age victim, but her knowing the layout of the house would be an asset.

He turned to Izan and Della, already hooking up the hose. "Get water on the front rooms."

"Ask her what happened. Ask where the kid will be hiding." Amelia's breathy voice filled his comms earpiece.

Ridge turned back to the mother. "Can you tell me what happened?"

The mother had curled blonde hair that hung past her shoulders, and she looked to be about forty, maybe a little older. Slacks and a blouse, over which she had pulled a wool sweater with the collar of the blouse flipped over the neck. Flat black shoes. Smartwatch.

She sucked in a shaky breath. "I was walking around, picking up before we left for Karlie's piano lesson. Waiting on her to grab her other shoes. There was a boom. It was so loud, and I ran out the front door. The windows shattered. There were flames everywhere. Karlie isn't answering her phone."

Ridge looked at the house with its wide bay windows downstairs. Manicured lawn. The kind of place that had an above-ground pool out back in the summer. Brand-new-looking white van in the drive and a basketball hoop.

This was where Amelia had lived?

He wasn't sure what he'd expected, but it probably wasn't this. He hadn't grown up destitute, but he certainly hadn't lived in a neighborhood like this.

Amelia said, "I need the room." Her breath washed over the channel. "I'm almost to the end of the hallway."

"Copy that." Ridge turned to the homeowner. "Which room is Karlie's, and where would she hide?"

"The last room on the right." The mom pressed her fist to her lips for a moment, then said, "She makes forts in her closet. Or she'll be under the piano in the den, if she made it that far. Sometimes she kicks off her shoes under the piano, so she might've gone to the den to find them."

Ridge turned away slightly. "In the closet in her room, last on the right. Or under the piano in the den."

The mom frowned. "Don't you need to know where the den is?"

Ridge said, "The firefighter who went in knows the layout of the house."

She shook her head. "How could she know that?"

Amelia interrupted what he'd been about to say with, "I need to focus. This chatter is distracting."

Ridge watched Della and Izan fight with the hose, spraying the blown-out front window to the right of the door. Smoke poured out of the left side. He turned back to the mom and said, "Hang here."

She nodded, likely too distracted by her child being in danger to worry why a firefighter knew the layout of her house.

Ridge strode across the lawn, still unsettled by the fact that Amelia had lived here. This place was where people who had brand-new leased cars, went on cruises every year, and skied all the time in winter lived. He didn't mean to be prejudiced about people with the money to enjoy their lives, and he didn't resent that some had more than others—it was simply the discrepancy between this place and Amelia.

But then, when they'd never seen even a glimpse into each other's private lives, why wouldn't he be surprised by what he found?

"*Lieutenant.*"

Amelia was back on comms.

Ridge said, "Go ahead."

"I have her. Back door is the closest, so I'm coming out that way. If you're not busy right now."

Ridge frowned. Amelia and her abrasive edge. He knew it was a front and she felt deeply. She treated the job with the utmost respect because she cared so much. She only got mouthy when someone's life was on the line and they were able to do something about it.

When the situation turned and there was nothing they could do, when saving a life was impossible, she would get very, very quiet.

That worried him more than her hard edges, which he'd been determined to soften with a relationship. Only, she hadn't let him. She'd shut it down because it was safer for her to live in her little protected space where she called the shots and everyone was better because she held them to a high standard.

"I'm coming around." Ridge picked up his pace and jogged

around the side of the house, using the gate to make his way back there. A dog greeted him with barks and suspicion.

Ridge held his gloved fist out for the dog to sniff and closed the gate so the Lab didn't get loose.

When the dog calmed a fraction, he rubbed the animal's flanks and assessed him for injuries. "You seem okay. Come on, let's go find them."

The dog understood his intent. The animal led the way to the back patio with his tail wagging. At the corner, he glanced back at Ridge, who was a couple of steps behind him.

The dog would still need to be checked out by a vet, even just for smoke inhalation. It hung thick in the air like a cloud, coming out of all the vents in the walls and the crawl space.

He climbed up the stone steps to the back patio and spotted the above-ground pool. Not where he'd have put it, but no one asked his opinion about that stuff. He slid the patio door open and spotted Amelia in the smoke, coming toward him with a tween girl in her arms.

The dog went inside.

Amelia stopped walking. "Get that dog out of my way."

Ridge whistled. "Hey, puppy. Come here." He waved the dog over. "Come on. Outside."

The dog came out, turning around to watch Amelia leave. She walked tentatively, like she was scared the animal would attack her.

"Give me the kid. I'll take her."

Amelia snapped out of it. "I've got her." She stepped outside and headed around the house with Ridge following. He glanced back at the dog, but movement at the end of the yard caught his attention.

"Get her to the ambulance."

Amelia was already out of earshot, but he heard her "Copy that" in his earpiece.

The dog turned, his ears pricked. He darted across the lawn to where Ridge had seen the movement, then disappeared into the trees. Ridge ran over.

He heard barking, then a yelp, like the dog had been injured. Kicked.

Ridge chased after him. Two of his team members were fighting the fire, and another had rescued the victim. While he was running for . . . what?

He might not have worked on Truck for a while, but he'd been on rescue squad for more than a year, and coming back hadn't been a demotion. He was in charge.

Qualified. Trained.

Why did he feel like he had no idea what he was doing?

He'd been certain he would be fine. He knew how to do this. Amelia wasn't mad at him. At least, he didn't think she was, when in reality, she had every right to be furious that her position had been taken away and given to someone else.

The dog scurried out of the trees, limping slightly.

Ridge slowed. As he reached the rear of the yard, he spotted a guy disappearing over a fence behind a line of trees. Just a flash of dark clothing. Considering Ridge had his turnout pants and coat on, it wasn't surprising the guy had escaped. In this getup, he'd never beat someone wearing civilian clothes in a footrace.

The dog lay on its belly on the grass, ears up, panting hard.

Ridge left him and went back around the house. It would be faster to walk through the structure and see the state of the fire, but he didn't have his air tank or mask. He'd wind up with early retirement and a list of health problems a mile long if he didn't follow procedure and take the necessary precautions to keep himself safe. If he was injured or incapacitated, he couldn't save anyone—and he couldn't effectively lead a team.

A guy in a suit stood by the mom, close to the back of the ambulance. Ridge jogged over. "Your dog is in the backyard. He's okay for now, but he needs to get checked out. How is Karlie?"

The guy put his arm around the mom. "She's being treated. You guys saved her life." His eyes were a little glassy. His dark hair, streaked with gray strands, was mussed as if he'd run his hands through it.

Ridge said, "We'll take care of securing the house. You guys only need to focus on Karlie, all right?"

The mom barely nodded. Dad turned away to the back of the ambulance. Ridge watched them start to climb inside and then turned away. "Nixon, Lewis. How's the fire?"

He found himself face-to-face with Amelia, flushed cheeks and anger in her eyes.

Instinct had him reaching for her elbow while Della said, "This is Nixon. We've got it under control."

"Copy that." To Amelia he said, "Are you all right?"

"What took you so long to get back to the front of the house?"

Ridge said, "There was a guy in the yard. The dog spotted him first."

She flinched.

"Are you . . . afraid of dogs?"

"I can do my job. Don't worry about me." She lifted her chin.

"It *is* okay to admit when you're scared of something."

"Then tell me what you're afraid of."

Ridge walked himself right into that one, didn't he? "Old orange juice. Once, when I was a kid, the juice had gone bad, and I took this giant mouthful and it was fizzy." He made a face because it made him nauseous just thinking about it. "I hesitate every time I drink some now." He shuddered. "You saved that girl."

Amelia stared at him like he'd grown two heads.

"You found the closet okay? No problems?" He scanned her face. *Just another day. Just another callout.* Except *he* was the lieutenant now. Why did that give him an odd sense of satisfaction? It was what he wanted, but not at the expense of her job. He didn't like that it had been taken away—even if it wasn't him who'd ousted her.

Okay, so there was a whole lot to unpack there. But was she going to give them the chance to talk it through, or was she going to ignore it and pretend things were fine?

Amelia shrugged.

"When the shift is done, can we go get something to eat? Or just get coffee, or tea, somewhere?" It would be six in the evening, so dinner seemed like a normal, casual thing to do at that time of day.

"Really?" Her expression hardened. "You're my boss now, big-shot. We can't *date*."

The only way to fight fire was with . . . okay, not fire. But it fit right now. "Who says it's a date? Unless you *want* to go on one?"

She let out a bark of laughter. "As if I have time to worry about having a love life. I've got to study for the lieutenant's exam."

"Why did you lose your rank, Amelia?" He softened his tone. "Macon didn't really say why you're not a lieutenant anymore."

"It's my business. Why don't you just worry about your job, and I'll worry about mine."

Ridge shook his head. "You should know by now that's not how this works." He motioned between them with his gloved finger.

"There is no 'this' between us." She took a step back. "Never was. Never will be."

She was a little too emphatic, almost like she was trying to convince herself. That was the only thing that gave him a semblance of hope that things could be different. But she was so determined to keep him out of her life that she was practically shoving him out of the door to take a job in Benson.

Ridge was about to rethink his entire life. Which would start with who was going to be the truck lieutenant when she got her rank back.

And where that would leave the two of them.

Because whether she liked it or not, she'd have to deal with having him in her life.

After all, the girls didn't want to leave. He wasn't sure he wanted to fight them when it seemed like he had everything he wanted.

Amelia turned and stomped away. Ridge caught Della and Izan looking at them and saw flashes of smiles shared when they glanced at each other.

Great.

His first day as truck lieutenant was going just great.

SEVEN

AMELIA STEPPED OUT OF HER TURNOUT PANTS, feeling the ache of spending a couple hours working at that house. Making sure the fire was put out. Cleaning up enough that the family could get in and out when they came back. And boarding up the doors and windows that had been destroyed. No one wanted some enterprising thief going through the house and taking what they wanted.

"That's twice now, right?"

She glanced over at Ridge. Trying to make small talk—about work—when he'd practically asked her out before. Amelia didn't know what to say to that. Or what to do about him and the fact he was her boss now.

She managed to say, "Twice now, what?"

It was more than triggering having him in a position of authority over her. The awareness of him was in her bones. She'd made peace with that and had come to terms with working together.

She didn't even care that he might be the other firefighters' choice.

The simple fact was that her feelings would cloud her judgment. And with him as her lieutenant, he could use that sway over her. He could use it against her the way her ex, Nicholas, had.

"That we've seen someone run off from a scene." He stepped out of his pants and waited for her to gather up her coat and pants.

She walked to the coat room with Ridge right behind her. "I didn't see the guy's face, did you?"

"I only saw a flash of dark clothing," he said from down the aisle where rescue squad kept their things in cubbies. She stood in the Truck 14 section. A nice arrangement, their things separate from each other, which meant she'd occasionally worked a whole shift without thinking about him. Doing her job, sticking to her office.

Now she would see him every time she got in the truck. Taking the lieutenant's test again would put things back to rights, but would she get her position back, or would Chief James conveniently find her a spot somewhere else—like Westside Firehouse?

She shoved her boots onto the shelf. "You know, when I get my bars back, I want my seat back as well."

Ridge glanced over. "I filled a gap in the lineup in a pinch, that's all. Rescue squad has had two lieutenants before."

"That doesn't mean I get my seat back. That's a justification for me staying in this seat while you have mine. Long-term."

"I don't want your job, Amelia." He took a step toward her, rested his palm on the wall and braced himself like that. Taking up the whole aisle with the breadth of his shoulders—or it seemed like that, at least.

"Good, because you can't have it."

"If I'd turned Macon down, he'd have brought in a lieutenant from another house or found a float to fill the position. I didn't want that to happen."

Amelia said, "Well, thanks. I guess."

"No one is trying to take anything away from you."

She sniffed. "Good, because I don't have anything to give."

Ridge let go of the wall and came closer. "Why do you think that's true?"

"Because I'm not a liar."

"Amelia—"

She knew that look. "Can we not do this? I'm not a challenge you need to best. I'm not a problem to solve. I just want to do my job and then go home—" Her voice broke. She cleared her throat. "Home."

Home was the firehouse.

She had to shut this down before he said something else. "I don't need any help from anyone. I can deal with this. I don't need to talk, and I definitely don't need coffee."

She might miss coffee, but she didn't trust it. Not ever. She wasn't going to touch another drop again the rest of her life after what her ex had done.

Ridge frowned, that strong jaw and those concerned eyes nearly making her want to stay. But she wasn't going to spend the shift in this closet. "What happened to you? I know it's something."

She flinched. "It's none of your business or anyone else's. Don't ask me again."

Amelia ducked around him and hurried out of the coat room to the girls' bunk. She closed the door behind her and heard the slight sound of crying. Someone sniffed. Amelia moved farther into the room and saw Della sitting on her bed.

"Oh, hey." Amelia had no idea what to do. She was used to her office and having her own space. This was going to be a nightmare. "Is everything okay?"

She might not want to talk about her business to anyone, but she figured she could listen pretty well. It just meant keeping your mouth shut, right?

Della swiped at her cheeks and shoved a folded paper under the edge of her blanket. "Hey, Amelia."

"Did you get bad news or something?" The other woman seemed almost scared.

Della had a mixed heritage and lived with her grandmother, who was from India. Her dark hair was curly, but she kept it pulled back the way they all had to while they worked. She usually wore a little makeup but not much. She bit her full bottom lip. "It's fine."

Now Amelia knew how Ridge felt. "If you want to talk . . . I can listen."

"Thanks." Della stood, and Amelia spotted a fake lily in a slim vase beside the bed. "I'm going to see how dinner is coming along."

Amelia nodded, staring at the lily and wondering what had made Della choose that flower. Lilies had been Amelia's favorite flower. But her ex had used any kind of romantic gesture as a way to curry favor. To get her to do things she never would have done otherwise, until she realized she'd humiliated herself and wanted out of the relationship. But it was too late because the damage to her reputation had already been done.

When she went to her superiors in the Benson Fire Department, she was told not to spread rumors about an officer with good standing. Then her behavior had become erratic, thanks to whatever substance he'd laced her coffee with. From there, things had descended into a situation where she'd had to cut ties and run in the middle of the night.

If she'd stayed, Amelia wasn't sure she would have survived.

She was barely surviving now, but at least she got to do the job she loved. She'd gone years without anyone questioning her sanity. Blissful years of working and resting and then coming back for another shift. Saving lives. Protecting the town the way firefighters were supposed to. Not the way her father had, using it as a cover for his sick crimes. The old man had kept the town in a stranglehold.

Amelia slumped on her cot and pulled the blanket over her head, too tired to eat. She slept a few hours, awakened by a call for rescue squad. They took the incidents involving trapped people or equipment failure in warehouses and factories. Other industrial accidents. Elevator failures. Truck didn't get another fire call until the morning, and that was thanks to a cigarette tossed into a dumpster.

Back in time for breakfast, Amelia headed right to the kitchen. The smell of coffee drew her. But she'd made a promise to herself that she'd never be vulnerable again, so she hit the button on the kettle to make tea. Strong black tea with milk, robust enough to wake an elephant.

The other firefighters moved around her, getting breakfast set up. She had to clean the women's bathroom later, before the shift ended at dinner time, and she wasn't on cooking duty until next shift. Trace sat at the table, reading a worn paperback novel.

Amelia had just sat down when a guy stepped into the doorway. She said, "Can we help you?"

He had a broody face, dark-blond hair, and the build of someone who did the kind of work they did. Strong and capable. "I found him." The man's face split into a smile.

"Kane!" Ridge jogged over from the fridge and practically jumped at the guy. The two of them hugged. The others came over, and Ridge stood with Kane beside him, his hand on the guy's shoulder. "Everyone, this is my cousin. Kane Foster."

Amelia sipped her tea while the others shook Kane's hand. A couple of the guys had obviously met him, given the way they greeted him. He was so excited to introduce them all to his cousin that she couldn't help watching the look on his face the whole time, seeing his affection and the pride he had.

She had cousins. She hadn't spoken to them in years and didn't care enough to text. If they showed up, she definitely wouldn't act like he was.

"And this is Zoe. Her husband is Army—he's deployed." Ridge said to Zoe, "Kane was Delta Force."

"Wow." Zoe shook his hand and said something that made Kane laugh.

"Yes, ma'am."

Amelia nearly rolled her eyes. He was one of *those* guys. The kind who said "ma'am" like it was normal. Who held doors open for others and gave an older person their seat on the bus. Given how Ridge acted, she wasn't entirely surprised. But Ridge had never mentioned his cousin before. He barely spoke about his sisters.

She was better off thinking about hooded men running from fires, the fact she'd been shoved the other day, and her childhood home burning down yesterday.

"This is Kianna."

Kane shook another hand.

"And over there is Amelia Patterson. She's, uh, another fire-fighter here."

Thankfully Ridge caught himself before he said "lieutenant," saving them all from having to hear the whole explanation.

She let go of the mug and waved. "Nice to meet you, Kane."

"You too." Broody guy studied her a little too long.

Yeah, no thanks. "Who's cooking breakfast?" She moved to get up.

Zack said, "It's ready," and set a casserole dish in the center of the table on a hot pad. Cheese bubbled around the edges, and she spotted sausage and potato.

Amelia eased back into her seat. Plates were passed around, and each person took a turn getting a portion. Across the table from her, Eddie squirted far too much ketchup on the breakfast casserole.

Ridge looked at Kane, now seated beside him. "What brings you here?" He took a bite of breakfast.

Kane said, "Actually, I think I might do the tryout to be a fire-fighter here in Last Chance County."

Amelia got herself a slice of the meal and set it on her plate. She grabbed her fork, hesitating as always. Looking around like she needed something. Waiting for a few of the others to eat a couple of bites. That way she knew it couldn't possibly be spiked with something.

It wasn't like she could personally supervise what went into every meal.

This was the only way she could get close to being sure it wasn't going to send her into a tailspin because it had been dosed with a drug that had no business in her system.

After no one reacted to it right away or watched her too closely, she took a small bite.

Ridge said, "Thought you were looking at search and rescue."

"That's the problem." Kane shrugged. "I kinda have no idea. It's driving me crazy, asking God and asking again and hearing silence." He shook his head and took a bite.

Kane's attention came to Amelia, too fast for her to look away.

She ducked her head. They seemed like brothers. More like Bryce and his twin Logan in Alaska. Logan had recently suffered one too many blows to the head and now worked at the jump base up in Copper Mountain as a coordinator for the Bureau of Land Management. He wasn't ever going to fight fire or jump from a plane again.

If anyone knew what it was like to lose everything they'd built, it was Amelia.

She just had to get her rank back, then she'd feel like she had her equilibrium again. That was all. Then Ridge would have to give her spot back.

Amelia wasn't going to go down without a fight.

She lifted her head and looked at Ridge and his cousin, feeling all the frustration of her entire life bubble up inside her. "Hey, maybe I'll get fired and then Kane can have my spot." Her fork clattered onto the plate, and Amelia strode from the room. She didn't stop in the hall but pushed through the heavy front doors and stepped outside.

Trying to get some air.

She heard a car door slam, but that was the only thing to enter her awareness. Amelia looked up at the wide expanse of sky, tinted orange with the rising sun. Hands on her hips. Breathing hard. So what if the best part of her life was falling apart?

It didn't mean she would just let it happen, roll over and say nothing.

Pounding footsteps approached her from behind. Amelia twisted around just in time to see two men run over. Both had hoods pulled up to disguise their faces. "What do you—"

They didn't stop but slammed into her, knocking her to the ground.

Hands grabbed at her.

Amelia's back pressed into the ground, and she cried out.

A gruff voice said, "Where is it?"

EIGHT

MELIA'S WORDS ECHOED IN HIS EARS. THE breakfast tasted sour in his mouth, and a few of the others shot him glances. He knew she'd gone outside.

Kane nudged him. "You aren't going to figure it out unless you talk to her."

They'd gone over the entire relationship in the past few days. Kane knew more than anyone, because his cousin was his best friend and more like a brother. Even when he'd "lost" him when Kane had supposedly been killed in action, he hadn't let the other man go. They'd found a way to communicate.

"I know. Thanks." Ridge pushed his chair back and went to the entrance. Did *thanks* even cover it? *Thank You.*

Sandra, at the front desk, pointed to the door. "She went outside."

Ridge went that way, not sure how this would go. Amelia was mad, and there was nothing he could do about it when he was part of the problem. It could seem more like rubbing salt in the wound.

He pushed open the door and heard an odd, muffled cry. She was on the ground with two guys on her. "Amelia!" Before the door closed, Ridge yelled, "Call 911!"

He ran for the two men on top of Amelia, who were holding her down. "Hey!"

He kicked at one, who stumbled back. The other guy dragged his buddy to his feet.

The door behind Ridge swept open and more than one person ran out, their footsteps pounding on the concrete.

The two assailants turned and ran.

A group of firefighters—and Kane—chased them. Ridge raced over to Amelia, who was already trying to get up. "Stay where you are. Don't get up." He touched her shoulder and crouched. "Let Trace check you out."

He wanted to pick her up in his arms and carry her inside. Did she need the ambulance to take her to the hospital?

Ridge looked at her face. She had flushed cheeks, and her gaze didn't quite focus on him. Her breaths came fast. "Where are you hurt?"

"I'm not." She took a breath. "I just got knocked over."

He frowned.

Amelia reached up and pushed hair back from her face, got some small pieces of gravel off her hand, and brushed off her palms. He spotted a tiny wince.

"Trace and Kianna are going to check you out anyway. Whether you're injured or not."

Amelia pinned him with a stare. "Is that an order, Lieutenant?"

"It's an order from your chief." Macon stood behind her, his arms folded across that massive chest. The guy looked like a battleship standing like that.

Ridge felt like a tugboat being pushed out to sea. She didn't want him to help her. Or she was so stubborn, so unwilling for anyone to see her as less than a hundred percent capable, that she refused to admit weakness. Or injury.

Amelia flinched, her shoulders curled in a little and her expression blank.

Ridge didn't know what it meant, but it sure wasn't nothing. He couldn't ask because Trace dumped a duffel beside Amelia and crouched. "Make some room."

Ridge got out of the way and wound up pacing a few steps. He spotted Kane and a couple of the others coming back, looking disappointed.

Kane shook his head. "They jumped in their car and took off."

"Your bro here nearly jumped on the hood to stop them." Eddie grinned.

"I did not."

Eddie lifted his chin. "You thought about it."

Kane didn't deny that. Instead, he said, "Is she okay?"

Ridge made a face because he didn't know. It was the same thing he'd been dealing with for months. Amelia's inability to admit when things were less than optimal. Or that she had any kind of problem. *Or* that she had any kind of personal life whatsoever.

He'd thought he was making inroads a couple of years ago when she agreed to dinner and a couple of other dates. Now that he looked back, it was more as if she'd been testing the waters. Testing him. Seeing if she was comfortable. Baby steps.

As if she'd been hurt in the past and wasn't confident enough to open up and risk it happening again.

Now that he'd seen a little more over the past week, he thought it might be something far worse. Whatever it was could very well be the reason it seemed like Truck 14 was suddenly the target of attacks. Or even Amelia herself.

If she hadn't been demoted, he would probably have never seen beneath the surface. She'd cracked a little the last few days, and he didn't like it. He wanted to help her. But Ridge couldn't try to swoop in and be her savior. That was the Lord's job. *Help me figure out what to do. How to help her.*

Kane stepped close and spoke low. "What did you see?"

"Two guys." Ridge folded his arms. A few of the others had

gathered around. Bryce and Eddie, Della and their chief, Macon. "They had her on the ground. One of them spoke to her, but I don't know what he said. She was pretty freaked."

Macon said, "The cops are sending a couple of officers. I'll go check the security feeds and see what we can see."

Bryce nodded. "I'll meet the cops, and we'll find you. What are we doing about Truck? They still have eight hours on their shift."

"I'll call and get a floater to replace Amelia for the rest of the shift. She's done for today." Macon wandered off, looking as unhappy about this as Ridge.

The others dispersed.

Kane didn't move. "She's in danger?"

"You were looking for a job."

Kane grinned. "Protection detail? Turns out I've got plenty of experience with that."

"She's never gonna go for it."

"Maybe she doesn't have to know."

Ridge winced. "That's not a good idea."

"Maybe you don't have to know."

"I know."

"You do? I'm leaving." Kane clapped him on the shoulder. "I'll see you later, maybe. Gotta do a thing. See a guy . . . about the thing. Find my girl. Hang out."

Right. "I know what you're going to do."

Namely, sit in his car until Amelia left for the day, and then follow her so he could watch out for her. Gather intel on Ridge's coworker. The woman he'd had a thing for all this time. For far too long.

Ridge shook his head. "Maybe I should've given up the idea of me and Amelia a long time ago. Hanging on like this isn't healthy. I'm spinning in circles, putting my life on hold for a woman."

"Hmm. Turns out I know what that's like as well." Kane stuck his hands in his jeans pockets, his elbows splayed out. "Hanging on, friends for years. Working together. Wanting more but knowing it's not the right time."

Ridge said, "I know you do."

"'I wait for the Lord, my whole being waits, and in His word I put my hope.'"

"I'm not waiting for Him," Ridge pointed out. "I'm waiting for Amelia."

Kane smiled. "But where is your hope? Is it in her, or is it in Jesus?"

"Ouch. Fine." Ridge blew out a breath. "Do whatever you're gonna do. I need to finish my shift."

Bryce walked over from the curb with Anthony Thomas, a local PD officer, and Olivia Tazwell.

"Don't worry, I will do whatever I'm gonna do."

Ridge wasn't sure it was the best plan, but there had to be a reason he had all these resources in his life. Trained former-military soldiers. Operators. Spies. Investigators. Why not use what God had given him?

He had a feeling that before this situation was over, they might need all the help they could get.

"Hey." Officer Thomas held his hand out, and Ridge shook with him. He would've introduced his cousin, but Kane had slipped away, remaining anonymous. "Tazwell is going to speak with Patterson. I'd like you to run through what you saw happen."

Bryce said, "They took Amelia to the Truck lieutenant's office, so you can use mine."

"Thanks." Ridge showed Officer Thomas the way. By the time they were done talking, Amelia had already left. He found Zack in the kitchen, cleaning up. "Is Trace around?"

"The ambulance got called out. The floater is here, in case Truck 14 gets a call."

"Thanks." Ridge didn't care what the implication was, he just spat out the question. "How was Amelia?"

"Shaken up, not that she'd ever admit that." Zack tossed the wipe he'd used on the counter in the trash and washed his hands. "Bruises. Trace didn't give a lot of detail, but he wasn't happy. No one was. Probably because it happened right under our noses."

"What about surveillance? The chief said he was going to check the cameras."

"Can't see their faces. But there were two guys, and they shoved her down." Zack got two water bottles from the fridge and tossed one to Ridge as he came over. "Let's hit the gym. You look like you need to bench-press something heavy."

"I really do."

Ridge worked off his frustration with the barbell, focusing on the physical strength he needed for this job until his shift ended. He ignored his phone, prayed for Amelia, and then set aside everything his mind wanted to go around and around on. When the twenty-four-hour shift ended, he walked outside to his truck and checked his phone once he was in the driver's seat.

A text from Kane came first.

Kane

Dude. Followed her to her
house. Dude.

A series of GIFs followed it, images of rich people in their houses. Lying by a pool. Wearing fancy clothes and drinking cocktails.

Ridge called his cousin and pulled out of his space, onto the street. When Kane answered, Ridge said, "What are you telling me?"

"I'm going to send you the address."

Ridge hit the turn signal. "Why would I need it?"

"Because you're gonna come over and talk to her."

"Why—"

Maria cut him off. "Ridge, she has a piece of particleboard. She's trying to board up a broken window, but she keeps having to put it down so she can clutch her side, like she's in pain."

And they didn't want her to know they were watching her, so they hadn't gone to help.

"Fine. Send me the address." They had to be exaggerating about the fancy house. That didn't fit Amelia at all. He highly doubted she lived in some rich neighborhood.

"Good," Maria said. "She needs help, even if she won't admit it."

"She won't like me showing up." He pulled up to a stoplight and tapped the address, which opened the app for directions. "She might send me packing and never speak to me again."

"So be charming," Kane suggested.

Ridge frowned. "I'd rather hear from Maria what worked for her."

He heard Kane's girlfriend chuckle quietly. "Well, Kane is *very* charming."

"Thank you."

Ridge smiled, heading for Amelia's neighborhood. He knew that area but didn't go there much. It was on the edge of the coverage area for Eastside Firehouse.

Maria said, "He stuck with me. We were friends for two years, and I can't imagine spending that much time with anyone else. When it came to falling in love, it just seemed . . . inevitable."

"Is that how you feel about Amelia?" Kane asked.

"The question is how she feels about me." Ridge already knew how he felt about her. That wasn't the issue here. Nor was the fact that staying in Last Chance County because she gave him a reason to would solve the twins' problems as well as his. So not the issue. Seemed like it would work out great for everyone.

But was him—and the twins—sticking around the best thing for Amelia?

"If she lets you help her," Kane said, "then we'll take off. But we'll stick around a bit just in case she kicks you out."

"Thanks, guys." He didn't want them to put their lives on hold to help him, but he was grateful they'd given up one day to make sure Amelia was safe. "I appreciate it."

"Bro, we're family." Kane hung up the phone.

Ridge spotted his cousin's car but drove by and pulled into the driveway for Amelia's house.

Scratch that.

Amelia's *mansion*.

His foot slipped off the gas halfway down the long drive, and the car slowed while he gaped at the stone structure. This house had belonged to the former chief who had terrorized the town. This place was where high school kids came to cause trouble, daring each other to sneak in after dark. As if the house might actually be haunted or something ridiculous like that.

What was Amelia doing living here?

NINE

AMELIA HEARD THE CAR BEHIND HER AND STIFF-
ened so fast she dropped the piece of wood from her hands. She
jumped back so it didn't land on the toes of her tennis shoes.
Getting knocked onto the concrete drive in front of the firehouse had
left her achy and bruised.

The piece of wood she'd been about to board up the window
with hit the bare planter, which was nothing but dry dirt and
weeds, and fell toward her. She kept backing up, so it landed flat.
Her back and hips hurt. She had abrasions on her elbows, and her
head didn't feel great.

She turned to see Ridge climb out of his car and rolled her eyes.
Of course he'd come over. Determined to rescue her from . . . he
didn't even know what.

"Are you okay?" He raced over, concern in his features.

As if she needed compassion after the day she'd had. What she
needed was to be left alone. And that included being left alone by
the people who had ransacked her house while she'd been at work.

"I'm fine, Ridge. I don't need help." She had to say that. It was
the principle of the thing.

But she knew he'd be determined to do the work for her, so

she strode to the grass and lay down, all out of the energy to care which one of them actually nailed the board to the frame around the broken window. She settled onto the grass and stared up at the stars.

Ridge grabbed the wood off the ground.

She bent her elbows and supported her head so she could watch him. Of course he was going to help her. Amelia rolled her eyes again.

With nails from her tin now in his pocket and her hammer in his hand, he braced the wood and nailed the four corners in place. Once it could hold its own weight and not fall down, he added more nails.

Her side hurt. Despite what Trace and Kianna thought, she didn't need an X-ray for her ribs when it was just a bruise.

Amelia wasn't going to explain how she knew the difference between a bruise and broken ribs.

Not even to the police, especially not when they had zero leads and no evidence. Just her statement and whatever Ridge claimed he'd seen.

She'd told them what had happened, been checked out, and left. Only to come home and discover her front door ajar. Broken windows. Inside, there were busted walls, and her things had been scattered all over the floor in her room.

Too late, she realized Ridge was done. Now he towered over her, hands on his hips. "We need to talk."

She groaned and slumped back on the grass again. Closed her eyes and let out a long sigh.

"But first I'm calling the police about your broken window."

"Nope." She sat up, shaking her head. "Don't waste their time."

"How did it break?"

Amelia pulled her hair tie out, because the ponytail wasn't helping her headache, and ran her hands through her hair.

"Amelia." He sounded choked.

She looked up at him. "What?"

She had no idea what that look was on his face. Was he just going to stand there staring at her?

"You're purposely distracting me. You need to answer the question."

"Distracting you?" She shook her head. "I didn't ask you to be here. I don't need your help."

If he needed her to, she would keep saying it over and over again. *Don't want your help. Don't need it.* Not just for his sake. It also helped to keep her own thoughts in line. The promise of whatever could be between them was a wasted daydream. She had work to do, and her life hardly had room in it for a relationship, even if she was interested in taking a risk like that.

Ridge turned and sat by her on the grass, enough space between them that he wasn't crowding her. "I've never seen you with your hair down."

Amelia frowned. "And it's distracting?"

He scanned her head. "It looks good loose."

She pulled it back and secured it in a messy bun, just to get it off her face. "This isn't about my hair. I have a headache."

He opened his mouth to say something but changed his mind. Shook his head. Said, "Are you hungry?"

Not what he'd wanted to say, but she didn't feel like challenging him right now.

"I have cleanup to do inside. I'll eat after." Or she would fall into bed exhausted and eat tomorrow. There were probably some leftovers in the little fridge she kept in her room.

"Like glass from the window?"

She nodded. "The door was open when I got home. There are a couple more holes in the drywall than there were when I went to work." She sighed, climbing to her feet.

He caught her elbow and helped her the rest of the way up.

"I'm fine, okay? It's just a bruise on my side where I landed on it. That's all." She didn't want him to bench her. "I can work tomorrow."

Having to stay home because of injury was about the worst thing she could imagine. How could she do the work she was supposed to do and save people's lives if she wasn't up to the job? Kiss of death.

Ridge walked with her to the front door. "What did the cops say?"

"You mean about how the firehouse surveillance cameras don't even show their faces? They told me after they watched it." She sighed. "I wasn't going to watch myself get tackled. I already felt it."

He scanned the door frame, split a little close to the strike plate. "Someone broke in?"

"Not the first time. Won't be the last." She lifted a hand. "Don't bother calling 911. If no one saw anything and they left nothing behind, then the police can't find the culprits."

Ridge frowned. "I have so many questions, I don't know where to start."

She could kick him out, but that would never satisfy him. What she could do was give him some time and *then* kick him out. "Order a pizza delivery from Backdraft, and I'll sweep up the glass. I'm not saying I'll answer everything, but you can ask."

Ridge pulled out his phone, watching her. Probably wondering what was up with her since she was suddenly being accommodating.

Amelia wandered inside and left him to his confusion—and their dinner order. She found the broom in her hall closet, and her footsteps echoed down the empty hall to the sitting room. Whatever this one would've been called. More of the same bare floor. Nothing on the walls. No window coverings or furniture.

Glass had shattered across the floor under the window where a metal radiator would've provided heat to the room generations ago. She'd disconnected it all because it was far too expensive to heat the entire house.

Besides, her room had its own fireplace.

She got all the glass in the dustpan and turned to find Ridge in the doorway. "Guess you think you know all my secrets now." She straightened and realized … "How do you know where I live? I've never told anyone. The address in my file is a PO Box." There was only one way. "You followed me?"

"Kane and Maria, his fiancée." Ridge didn't seem to feel guilty about it at all. In fact, he leaned against the wall like this was a casual conversation. "I asked them to keep an eye on you until the end of my shift. Just in case those guys came back for another try."

She flinched and wasn't able to stop it.

"What happened here? And how come you live in this house?"

"Who says I live in this house?"

He looked at the dustpan and broom, then lifted his gaze to her face.

"Move out of the doorway so I can go dump this in the trash."

He followed her, his boots a dull echo on the floor behind her. That's why she hadn't added rugs, even though the floors got cold. No one could move silently through this monstrosity of a house.

"If you must know"—at least for the sake of not dragging it out—"this is a family house." Amelia stepped on the foot lever, and the lid of the trash can flipped up. Empty kitchen, just like the rest of the house. The backsplash was way outdated. She watched enough home decor TV shows to know that. But the wide farmhouse sink was a work of art.

"Where's your fridge?"

Amelia said, "Not in here."

"Can you please start explaining?"

She set the broom aside. Problem was, if she started talking, Amelia was worried she might not stop. "It's my life. No one else needs to worry about it. I can take care of my own problems."

"I'm not gonna argue with that. But sometimes even the most capable person needs help." He continued before she could respond to that. "I know this house belonged to the former chief. The one who was a criminal. He held this town in a chokehold, he and his buddies. I've read all those stories, even if it was a long time ago."

"Welcome to the real, in-person next installment. Hopefully it's the conclusion, because I'm so over having this house broken into." Amelia sighed. "I've put it on the market half a dozen times, but no one will buy it because he lived here. I get three or four calls a week in September and October, people asking if they can use the house for a Halloween party or some kind of haunted house where they're going to charge way too much for people to walk through and have the business scared out of them."

"A family house." He kept his expression impassive. She could tell he was burning with curiosity.

"You've never told me much about your family," she pointed out. "I've never seen your house, and I don't know where your apartment is."

"I moved a while back because my sisters came to live with me. I live in a town house now."

"See." She lifted her hands, then let them fall back to her sides. "I didn't even know that."

"What's your point?"

Amelia leaned her hips back against the linoleum counter. "I'm supposed to tell you everything about my personal life, but the fact is, you don't share any more readily than I do."

They were pretty well matched as far as she could see. If he got her to tell him all about her family and who they were, or the whole of what had happened in Benson with her ex-boyfriend—which was another story entirely—then was he going to reciprocate?

Would he tell her what made him guarded so that he didn't want to let people into his personal life easily? It wasn't bad or wrong to be a private person. Nor did it have to be about self-preservation or boundaries put in place after trauma. Could just be how he wanted to live. Separating personal and professional parts of his life.

But she wanted to know it all.

The same way he seemed to want to know about her life, even if it was only about making sure Truck 14 was good. That the team was safe. Enabling the police to stop whatever was happening to them.

He didn't want to be part of her life. Not anymore. She'd ruined any chance they might've had by cutting things off last time. This was only Ridge doing his job.

If she did let him in, she would either learn he wasn't worth it, or she'd discover he was and fall for him all over again.

Amelia didn't know which one of those would be worse.

Either way, she'd wind up more heartbroken than ever. Because she really liked Ridge and respected him as a firefighter—even as her lieutenant. He was the kind of man who was worth loving, barring the revelation of any horrible secrets in his life.

This was about survival for her, with no margin for error. If she trusted the wrong person, the slipup would cost her life. She knew as much from personal experience. This was life or death.

She had to keep her heart guarded.

"Patterson isn't my original last name. It's the name I took when my mother remarried." Just the facts. "This was my father's house. I inherited it. No one will buy it. People think it's fine to break in and trash stuff. Not that there's anything to break, because I have nothing in the main house."

She took a breath and continued. "They come by thinking he left something sordid, but I cleaned the whole place out after he was killed, and there was nothing like that. They're looking for a payout. He's supposed to have hidden money . . . somewhere in the house."

TEN

RIDGE SHOT OFF A TEXT TO KANE AS HE WALKED back from the front door with one pizza. He'd left the other on the doorstep for his cousin to grab. Maria and Kane were going to hang out regardless of whether Amelia thought someone would show up to harass her tonight.

He was rapidly assimilating information he'd never known about her and trying to get his equilibrium back. Amelia was the daughter of the former fire chief—the one who had been exposed as a dangerous criminal. Someone who had profited off the misery of others.

She had been raised by him.

He couldn't imagine what that must have been like. His childhood hadn't all been sunshine and bike rides in the park, but he had no idea what she'd endured. No wonder she didn't let people in easily. A firefighter who was the daughter of that man?

Ridge found her at the back door, waiting for him. "Kind of chilly to eat outside, isn't it?"

She said, "Come with me."

The back patio had some old furniture, just metal frames of

chairs with no cushions and a table that had been knocked over. Wrought iron, lying on its side.

"Nice yard." It resembled a park, wide and deep. Trees around the edge blocked it from view of the neighbors. A white stone pool to the right had been emptied long enough ago that it was now lined with leaves from the neighbor's tree.

"It's pretty good for running sprints up and down if I need to work out on my day off and I don't have time to get to the gym." She walked with her back to him, striding ahead, down to the end of the yard. Not looking back, just assuming he would follow her.

He was curious enough to do it. "I bought the town house a year ago. The complex has a clubhouse with a little gym that has enough equipment I can do what I need to do."

She ducked under the limb of a tree and kept going, into the shadows between the trees.

"Pretty spooky back here. You don't live in a tent, do you?"

She chuckled but didn't say anything and still didn't look back. "It's not a shed . . . exactly. More like a storage hut. I worked on it, made it into a kind of clubhouse. Or a she shed. No one knows it's back here."

He spotted it between the trees.

"He probably used it to store lawn equipment or pool supplies." She slowed her approach. "At least, I hope that's all he used it for." She looked back at the house with a smidge of distaste on her face.

"You grew up there. You probably heard, or saw, all kinds of things he got up to."

Amelia clicked the metal keys on the door lock, a ten-digit combination that unlocked the cabin. She'd cleaned it up nicely, though it could do with some brighter paint than the sandy color on the outside. He saw a spigot at the bottom of the wall on one side with a bucket beside it.

But then, improving the exterior would make it more noticeable.

She was hiding.

Amelia clicked on a switch by the door, and fairy lights strung up inside the cabin, all around the top of the wall, illuminated.

"Wow." He stepped inside and looked around. Single cot, lots of blankets and pillows. A space heater. She also had a wood stove in the corner with a funnel that went up to the roof for the smoke. No sink, but she did have a refrigerator and a camp stove, a coffeepot plugged into a power strip. And one of those tower water-cooler things that dispensed hot and cold water.

He frowned. "Wait. You don't have a toilet or sink—or a shower?"

She shrugged. "I either shower at the gym or at work. I actually have a little outhouse out back, since there's no water at the house."

"An outhouse?" He imagined the twins being told they had to pee outside.

"Camping toilet. Super clean. I made it cute, which I'm sure you'll fail to appreciate." She dragged a second chair from the little desk over to a tiny table in the corner, where the back of the chair leaned up against the edge of the bed.

"Why not just get a condo, or a house?"

"Can't sell the house. But the government keeps reminding me that the taxes and fees for owning it are my responsibility, along with everything else I inherited. Like constant break-ins and the need to hide my original last name."

He set the pizza down and took a seat. "Constant?"

She shrugged. "I've called the police a few times. They can't do anything because I can't ID the perpetrators. They say I should get cameras in the house, or a security system, but the one time I did that, someone ripped it all out. No one in town wants to work on this house. Even with the warranty I asked for on the cameras, they wouldn't come back and install new ones."

She slumped into the chair. "I don't want to talk about this. I'm hungry and exhausted, and my side hurts."

Ridge bowed his head for a second and said grace silently to himself, quickly asking for her pain to ease.

"I don't want to be the sad tale. I don't want pity. I just want to do my job and have people leave me alone."

"I don't pity you." He'd rather help her. "My mom got remarried a few years ago."

She frowned, her mouth full of hot and spicy pizza.

He continued. "Her new husband isn't the kind of guy who wants to be tied down with kids. The twins, Maddie and Ella, were fifteen at the time. Gary—my mom's husband—wanted to get an RV and hit the road. The girls were in their freshman year of high school, and Mom isn't the, uh . . . homeschooling kind."

Amelia swallowed her bite. "What did they do?"

"I moved from a one-bedroom apartment to a two-bedroom town house, and they moved in with me." He shrugged. "It isn't something I talk about much. They don't need to be at a firehouse, and they have school. Homework. Jobs. They're busy with their friends when they aren't working. Now they're seniors, and they turn eighteen after Christmas. I got a town house so they can have more space in a nicer place." He was probably talking about them like a proud parent. "They're great kids."

She smiled. "Thanks, in a big part, to you."

He ducked his head and grabbed a slice. "Maybe some. They make it easy. Most of the time, anyway."

Amelia sat across the little round table from him. She wiped her hands on a napkin, tipped back on her chair, and opened the refrigerator in a move so smooth he knew she'd done it plenty of times before. She pulled two flavored soda waters out and handed him one.

She said, "Didn't take long for my mom to realize what Dad was. You'd think him being the kind of man he was, he'd have put up more of a fight to keep her, but maybe she and I were cramping his style. Getting in the way." She put her palms together, her hands between her knees. "She left and got her own place. As long as I can remember, she was dating other men on the side. I don't know when she and Steven Hilden got divorced, but I was in elementary school when she married Matthew Patterson. After that she was a one-man woman, at least as far as I know. And I took his name as soon as I could."

"They're the ones who raised you?"

She nodded. "I always knew who my dad was, but she kept me away from him as much as she could. At least, until the court ordered I spend time with him in the summer and some holidays. Matthew was a firefighter."

"He worked with Chief Hilden?"

Another nod. "Matthew died on the job. Hilden left him and another firefighter cut off from assistance, trapped so they had no way out. He waited until they were dead and then sent the others in to recover them. He never attempted to rescue them. He wanted them to die."

Ridge's heart squeezed in his chest. "I'm sorry you lost your dad, Amelia. That's tragic."

"Mom wasn't ever the same. Eventually her heart gave out. I tried to honor Matthew's memory by becoming a firefighter here in Last Chance County, but it was too hard. I transferred to Benson in the first year, and I figured it would be better there."

He had a feeling the story didn't end with her move. That there was more because it hadn't necessarily been better.

She'd lost her family. Whatever the criminal actions of the former chief had cost others in town, it had cost Amelia far more.

Ridge said, "Are you okay back here, on your own?"

"I don't need a guest. There's no room." She waited a beat, then smiled at him.

"Good, because the second the twins see this place and how adorable it is, they're going to want to move in."

Her smile widened and she laughed.

Ridge loved that she'd set him up with the chance to lighten the moment. Things were heavy for her, and that wasn't going to be solved with one conversation. This was her life. The way it had turned out might not seem fair to her, but from his experience, life wasn't even close to fair. It hadn't been for him.

She took another bite of pizza, color in her cheeks now.

"If it's okay with you, Kane is going to hang out in the house overnight. So that you have someone close by who can offer protection in seconds if you need it. Rather than you having to wait five minutes for the police to arrive." He figured Maria would likely stay in another room. Ridge half wanted to camp out in the mansion as well, just to be near in case those guys came back, but they didn't need to bombard Amelia with all of them.

"I'm so tired, I doubt I'd notice if there was anyone in the house."

"I need to ask you about what happened at the firehouse. But there's something else I need to say."

She frowned, switching back to being wary of him. Which he didn't like.

He said, "Before you went outside, you said something about your spot on Truck being given to Kane." Ridge had to tread carefully. "No one is going to fire you, Amelia. You're a great firefighter, and everyone knows it. Especially the chief."

"I just spoke without thinking. It doesn't mean anything."

"I'd love to work with my cousin. Kind of like Bryce jumped at working with Logan. But not at the expense of losing you." He leaned forward over the table, planting his elbows beside his napkin. "Don't leave."

"I'm not going to. But I might not be able to stay."

"A realist. Why am I not surprised you're a stone-cold pragmatist?"

She shrugged. "Why live in a dream world? I'd rather live in the real one, even if it sucks."

"Why don't we try and see if we can make it suck a little less for you?"

Amelia chuckled. "That's one way to put it."

"What do you say? Is that the kind of enticing invitation you can't refuse, or what?"

She was still laughing.

"I'm in for the ride. Are you?"

"Okay, stop," she said, laughing. "If it gets you to stop, then fine."

"I'm not trying to take over your life, Amelia. I just want to help as much as you'll let me. That's all."

She studied him from across the table, the lights around them casting her in a soft glow. He thought he heard a phone vibrating but ignored it. He needed this moment. Close to her. Building rapport and convincing her to trust him.

He had a feeling they were going to need it.

ELEVEN

AMELIA STEPPED OUT OF THE CONFERENCE room and turned to the right. *Wrong way.* This direction would take her to the office *formerly* known as hers.

She'd realized her mistake too late, and everyone would know it.

Ridge appeared beside her. "Going my way?"

Amelia had rolled her eyes plenty lately, and she wasn't going to do it again right now. "Fine. I could use the steps." A circuit of the hall would get her to the women's bunkroom eventually.

She set off toward his office.

"Not often rescue squad gets a callout right in the middle of the briefing."

She glanced over at him, half expecting him to use what she'd said to him the night before against her. Maliciously. She'd spilled her heart. Told him more than anyone else in her life knew—except Meg.

Instead, he seemed to be more interested in small talk.

Nicholas, her ex, would have used the information she'd spilled to have the upper hand. Strategically waiting until exactly the right time to use her vulnerability against her.

Ridge stopped at his office door. "I'm just trying to keep things light. You've had a rough few days."

"I don't need special consideration." She was about to walk away when he moved fast, showing up in front of her. "What are you doing?"

His expression shifted, his demeanor pure innocence, and he thumbed over his shoulder. "Wanna go get some coffee? *Right.* You don't drink coffee. Why don't you drink coffee?"

The way he tipped his head to the side was adorable. She wanted to stand here and appreciate it. But when had attraction ever helped a person get their work done? When had it created quality productivity?

Time for more confessions. Amelia stuck her hands in her pockets. "I like coffee just fine."

He frowned. "Then why don't you drink it?"

"We could be training or waiting for the last shift to bring back the truck. You want to talk about getting coffee?"

"Humor me."

She fought the urge to roll her eyes again. "I love coffee. I just had a . . . bad experience."

Two guys came around the corner at the end of the hall, behind Ridge. The smell of ash and burnt wood preceded them. Lieutenant Morris and one of his truck firefighters.

Amelia wrinkled her nose.

"What's up, Lieutenant?" Sean, a firefighter on the shift that came in before them, asked the question with sarcasm in his tone. "Never mind. You're not an LT anymore. Guess that's Foster's office now." He lifted his chin. "Lieutenant."

Sean made a point of practically ignoring her.

Lieutenant Morris followed him over. "Gotta grab my stuff."

Ridge nodded. "No problem. We just finished our briefing."

Now these guys would hand off Truck 14 to Ridge and the rest of them.

"I'm gonna go get some coffee." She eyed Ridge. He knew she had no intention of getting coffee, just not that her life had been upended by drinking it when it had been laced with something that made her lose her grip on herself.

Sean got in her way. "Heard about your demotion. How long were you gonna keep it a secret that you've been lying to the department? Pretending to be a firefighter."

"Who's pretending? You and I were in the same training class." Amelia lifted her chin. "Or did you hit your head so many times you forgot?"

His eyes narrowed.

"Okay, this has been informative." Ridge wanted to shut down the conversation? She didn't blame him.

Amelia eased around Sean and headed down the hall so her lieutenant and Sean's could deal with him, maybe even reprimand him over that comment. She had no idea what they would say to Sean. Or if he'd actually be reprimanded for getting in her face. What she didn't want to do was stick around to hear them laugh like the joke was funny.

That had happened too many times.

She could have chosen to get angry at Sean, but what would that achieve? She knew better than anyone that outbursts of emotion didn't change people's minds. They believed what they wanted to believe, no matter what she said.

"That was uncalled for."

She heard Ridge continue behind her but didn't catch what he said. She turned the corner without looking back. Not being in charge right now was a benefit.

She went into the women's bunk and closed the door, leaning back against it. He'd listened last night. He hadn't used the information against her—yet. Now he was standing up for her.

What on earth was she supposed to do with Ridge Foster?

"Hey . . . Amelia." Della shifted on her bunk. "It's weird not calling you Lieutenant."

Amelia smiled and headed for her bed, on top over the other side. "It's weird for me too."

She dug in her backpack and pulled out a paperback she'd been reading lately. Fantasy, because it was way better than real life. The cover had a moon and stars, and a guy in furs with a sword. *Lord of Winter.* Amelia intended to get lost in that world later if the shift was quiet. She tossed the book on her bed. "Everything okay?"

Della shifted quickly, moving a paper beneath her own book. On the cover of the book was a hand-drawn image of an orange sky, green grass, and a pink-and-white lighthouse. *Where I Found You.* "Everything's fine."

There was definitely something off with her teammate.

Amelia might never have noticed if she'd been a lieutenant, still in her office. She wouldn't see Della in the women's bunkroom, because she had a cot in the office. Only by being here did she get a good impression of how things were with her colleagues. Which made her wonder what else she had missed while she'd been lieutenant.

Amelia leaned her shoulders back against the bar under her mattress. "Will you let me know if there's anything I can do? If there is something that will help you."

Della looked a bit nonplussed. Finally, she said, "Sure. I can do that."

"Great." Amelia didn't exactly make friends at work. She kept things professional because it was always better that way. But she didn't want Della to suffer with no one to talk to.

Amelia said, "I should go see if there's an update on how things are going with rescue squad's callout."

She was almost to the door when the chimes went off.

From the speaker high in the corner of the wall, she heard, "Truck 14, Belleview Junior High. Person trapped."

Amelia grabbed the handle and flung the door open. They shucked on their gear. Della ran for the driver's door, and Amelia climbed in the back.

Della pulled the truck out of the engine bay onto the street and flipped on the lights and sirens.

Ridge hit the keys on the dash laptop and said, "Dispatch reports a kid is missing. They were told by friends that he climbed up into the ceiling to hide from a teacher."

"So one of us is gonna climb up between the ceiling panels and order him to get out?" Izan said, "If it was my brothers, they'd get down quick. It ain't as good as Zoe's mom voice, but it works for me."

Amelia glanced at him and grinned. "I've heard that voice. Got the sudden urge to clean my room."

Izan laughed.

Della pulled into the school parking lot. Several teachers and other staff members stood outside the front doors wearing office attire of slacks and shirts or blouses. Name badges on lanyards around their necks.

Della parked, and both Amelia and Ridge jumped out. Amelia hung back a second as he approached the staff and said, "You have a child trapped?"

"I'm the principal, Stacey Wallace." The closest teacher shielded her eyes from the sun, up at a forty-five-degree angle as it made its way to being overhead. She had curly hair in tight red spirals around her head. "He was hiding from a math test. Apparently the kids go up there when they want to skip class."

"And he won't come down?" Ridge asked.

Principal Wallace nodded. "He has some allergies, and it's dusty up there. Maybe he can't breathe." She worried her lip between her teeth. "He isn't answering us, and we can't get him down."

"Show us the way." Ridge turned back. "Nixon, Lewis, grab the med bag and tools."

They had no idea what they needed until they got a look at the problem, but Amelia grabbed a fire axe because the kids would be impressed, and she'd get more cooperation than if she didn't have it. She swung the axe onto her shoulder and steadied her helmet. "Lead the way."

She caught the edge of Ridge's smile, because he knew exactly what she was doing and why.

Amelia followed him and the teachers inside the building, and as soon as she did, it hit her. The smell. The feel of it. The sounds and sights of middle school.

One of the teachers glanced over at her. "Middle school. We never outgrow the trauma."

Amelia's eyes widened. She must've given away her reaction. "Is it me, or did I go here?" She'd actually attended a junior high across town, she was pretty sure.

"All the junior highs in the school district were constructed from the same basic floor plan," the teacher said. "Been in one, been in them all."

Amelia shook her head. "I guess I know how to find my way around, then. Though it's been a while." She spotted a couple of kids in the hall and called out, "Get back to class, guys."

The teacher up front turned into the library. "According to the student's friends, they climb into the ceiling from the top of this stack." She stopped in the corner and pointed up at the ceiling, where a square panel had been slightly dislodged. "He had a math test and didn't want to take it, so he snuck up there. One of the kids climbed up when he showed us, but he couldn't get Ernie to respond."

And no one had been able to get him back down.

"He didn't answer? You're sure he's up there?"

Principal Wallace nodded. "The student saw him."

Amelia was used to hearing a story more than once. If the details didn't change in a way that aroused suspicion, they didn't need the police. Assuming nothing criminal had occurred.

"Patterson, care to do the honors?" Ridge glanced around.

Amelia spotted a shoe print on the shelf about waist height, where the child had climbed up.

"I'll give you a boost." Ridge laced his gloved fingers together and held his hands out.

Amelia set her axe on top of the bookshelf. She grabbed Ridge's shoulder and spotted Della and Izan entering the library, followed by a few kids. Amelia put her boot in Ridge's hands and grasped the top shelf.

He lifted her up, and she wedged herself to sit up there by her axe.

Amelia pushed the panel aside and wiggled over to stick her head through the opening. "You said his name is Ernie Halstead?"

The principal nodded.

Ridge said, "Did you call his parents in?"

Amelia clicked on her helmet light and lifted up on her knees while Ridge took care of the particulars. She looked around in the ceiling and spotted a form. Clothing and the color of skin. He'd crawled pretty far through.

She scanned the area. They might need to go up a different panel, from another classroom. They could lower the kid down near where he lay now if they accessed from the other side of him.

She heard the teacher say, "His mother is an accountant across town. Her office said she's out at a meeting, but they're going to track her down. I wasn't getting an answer on her cell phone. Mr. Halstead is an anesthesiologist. He's in surgery and will be here as soon as he's finished."

Amelia got her elbows through the opening. "Ernie? I'm Amelia. I'm a firefighter. Can you hear me?"

The kid didn't respond or move.

She spotted a flash of skin that had to be his forehead. Clammy, dotted with sweat. Knowing Ridge would hear her over the comms, she said, "We'll need the med kit, but I wanna get him down where he's at. Which might be the next room."

"I'll call for the ambulance," Izan said.

Ridge continued talking in her ear. "You see him?"

"He's unconscious." Amelia knelt on the top of the bookshelf, her upper body through the opening.

She looked around so her helmet lights lit up the space between the drop ceiling and the roof. Barely three feet above her, a lattice of triangular openings in the beams spread a couple of feet apart presented a problem.

Amelia wiggled off her jacket and dropped it back through the opening.

She moved from the first beam to the next. Each beam stretched in front of her from left to right, trusses that held up the ceiling. Her turnout pants snagged on a metal plate with screws, depositing some of the material behind her.

"Ernie?" Amelia grabbed a truss with both hands and used the wood beams to brace her as she wiggled over a ceiling tile that definitely wouldn't hold her weight.

The student didn't move.

She wormed her way closer to him. "It's hot up here," she said in the comms channel. "We're going to have to get him out before we can give him medical attention. He might be over the next classroom."

She'd climbed up here close to the corner of the library. Now she was several feet beyond that wall. What was the next room? "Lieutenant?"

Ridge responded, "We're in the next room. Knock on a tile."

"I'm more likely to bust through it. These things don't hold any weight." She gritted her teeth and shifted so she could have a free hand to knock and let them know where she was.

"Be careful."

That was interesting.

She didn't need to be distracted by him when a kid was potentially in medical distress. But it almost seemed as if Ridge cared about her.

Did he actually feel about her the way she felt about him?

TWELVE

RIDGE SLID AN ARM UNDER THE KID'S KNEES. Amelia lowered him from the ceiling through one opening, sitting on a truss with her legs through the space where the neighboring ceiling tile should've been.

Trace and Kianna took the student from Ridge and laid him on the stretcher they'd wheeled in. Over by the classroom door, Izan and Della held back students who wanted to see what was going on. He'd heard one of them say "No, put your phone away" more than once.

Trace and Kianna got to work, assessing the unconscious child. The boy had sweat through his shirt, and his hair was matted to his forehead.

"Coming down." Amelia lowered herself through the hole.

Ridge stood on the table under the opening. Her boots and pants lowered, and her hips came through the hole. Then her waist. She gripped something above her, like she was lowering herself down from doing a pull-up.

He wound an arm around her hips and held on to her until her face came into view and she let go of whatever she was holding. "Okay?"

She winced very slightly, something only he saw. "I'm good."

Amelia's hands landed on his shoulders. He hadn't put her down on the table, more reluctant to let go than he wanted to admit to himself. Face-to-face. Her cheeks had pinked, and a few loose blonde strands framed her face. He'd never been this close to her blue eyes or seen the freckles on her nose from up close.

"Is she your girlfriend?"

Ridge jogged out of his Amelia daze and set her down before he turned to the door, where one of the kids leaned around Izan to stare at them.

Amelia jumped off the table. "Don't you have a math test?"

The kid frowned.

Ridge climbed down and saw Kianna grinning to herself—and listening to the patient's heart rate.

"It's steady." She looked at Trace. "He needs fluids."

Trace nodded. "Let's get moving."

Ridge headed for the crowd by the hall. "All right! Everyone back it up, they're coming through. Make a path. Clear the space out."

He waved as he spoke, motioning them all—including the firefighters—back from the door. They parted to either side of the hall so Trace and Kianna could get the kid to the ambulance and off to the hospital.

Ernie had an oxygen mask over his mouth and nose and a blanket over his body.

"Well?" The same kid stared up at him, almost to Ridge's shoulder. Red hair and a thin face. "Is she your girlfriend?"

"If she isn't, are you going to ask me to get you her number?"

Someone else snickered.

The kid's face scrunched up. "It's just a question."

"She isn't my girlfriend." Much to his dismay, if he was going to be honest.

Amelia eased up beside him. "He's my lieutenant. Which makes him my boss. Which means no dating."

The kid just looked confused, but she'd succeeded in ending the conversation.

One of the kids was crying.

Amelia looked around. "Did we all just learn a valuable lesson about not climbing up into the ceiling to get out of tests?"

Several nodded.

"Good." She headed off down the hall.

Ridge grabbed his clipboard and headed for the principal, trying not to be mad that she'd told the truth. Amelia was stating facts. She dealt with the truth, even if it was painful. He respected that about her. She didn't beat around the bush or try to manipulate people.

For a while there, with them on different engines, they'd have been allowed to date.

Same with him becoming a lieutenant, making them the same rank.

Now they were back to having a roadblock of procedure between them. And just when he was getting somewhere with her. Working on securing her trust in him.

"Principal Wallace?" He walked over to her. "If you can sign my report, we'll get out of your hair so you can restore order and get the students back to learning."

"Thank you." She scribbled her signature on the bottom of the paper where Ridge had done a write-up of the call. "I hope Ernie is all right."

"So do I." Ridge tucked the clipboard under his arm. "Have a good day."

He followed Della out to the truck, carrying the things they'd brought in. Like Amelia's axe and jacket. Amelia closed the cabinet on the side of the truck, and when Della tossed over Amelia's turnout coat, she caught it and put it back on.

"Ready to go?" he asked all of them.

Amelia shot him a polite smile and climbed in. Ridge's phone rang on the dash, so he climbed up and answered the call from his mom's number. "Foster."

He used his last name so she'd know he was at work.

"It ain't your mom, boy. It's me." His stepfather.

"What's up, Gary? I'm on shift right now, so I might have to hang up in a hurry."

Della pulled out of the school parking lot.

Ridge tucked the phone between his ear and shoulder and put his seatbelt on, then held the handle at the top of the door.

"Heard you're hangin' with that firefighter girl."

"Excuse me?" Ridge frowned. "What do you mean you 'heard'?"

Had the twins said something to their mom? It had only been a couple of days since he'd been there for the evening rather than at home. Since then, only Kane and Maria had been over at Amelia's house, squatting in the mansion to ensure no one else broke in and damaged the place. They had the training and the skills to fight off an attack—more than most people—and they'd call the police the moment anyone showed up so that the criminals could be arrested.

It was a win-win.

So who was talking?

"I've got friends in Last Chance still. Word gets around, you know? You were at the old chief's house. Everyone knows he hid money there, like, in the walls or somethin'. That's why you were there, right? To find the money. Good for you, getting close to that woman so you can find it."

What Ridge wanted to say, he couldn't. With a truck full of female firefighters, one of whom was Amelia herself, it wasn't like he could point out the parts of what Gary had said that didn't make sense. "Who told you any of that? Because I'd like a word with them."

Gary chuckled. "Keep it close to the vest. That's how you do it. I'm almost proud of you."

Ridge pressed his lips into a thin line.

"Don't suppose you'd give your momma a cut of the money when you find it."

"Who says I'm looking for it?" Ridge wanted to know how, suddenly, someone knew Amelia was the one living at the house. All Gary had said was "firefighter girl," so they knew that the woman who lived at the mansion—or behind it, in her case—was a female firefighter. Was it common knowledge around town that it was Amelia?

Surely people didn't know she was the daughter of the former chief.

No one at the firehouse knew except him. There was no way it was public knowledge. It wasn't like she even spoke about it, let alone flaunted her personal connection to a dead criminal.

And yet Gary, or one of his friends in Last Chance County, had discovered her secret.

It couldn't be because Ridge had been there or because Kane and Maria had told the wrong person. No way.

More like Gary was connected to whoever had been breaking into the house to look for the money.

Gary chuckled again.

"I'll be asking again later who told you about all this. Because you shouldn't know, and you just tipped your hand that you do. Which puts *you* in the middle of it."

Gary blustered. "I'm in New Mexico. I ain't in the middle of nothin' but your mama's attempt to photograph every sunrise and sunset and every horse in the whole ever-loving state."

"If you aren't nice to her, we're gonna have a problem."

"Like we already didn't." Gary hung up.

Ridge leaned his head back against the headrest and groaned.

Della glanced over. "That sounded like fun."

"My stepdad is a piece of work." Ridge sighed. "It's a good thing he doesn't live nearby, or we'd probably get into fights."

The radio on the strap that ran from one hip to the opposite shoulder crackled to life. "Truck 14, vehicle fire. Multiple-vehicle collision. Multiple victims."

The dispatcher reeled off the address, an intersection in the middle of town over by the hospital.

Ridge grabbed the radio. "Truck 14 responding."

"I guess it's gonna be a busy day." Della flipped on the lights and sirens and changed lanes.

Ridge felt a hand pat his shoulder. He twisted around to Amelia, who frowned and lifted her chin. She said, "Your stepdad?"

"I'll fill you in later." Ridge wanted to tell her but wasn't going to air what he'd thought was private information in front of the others.

Unless Amelia hadn't kept it from anyone outside the firehouse. Perhaps there were plenty of people in town who knew she was the daughter of the former chief. But he was pretty sure no one in Eastside Firehouse had known. So did that make them the losers who hadn't figured it out? He didn't like the idea of coming across as dense. Not when they needed the cooperation of the general public to do their jobs.

Della turned the last corner, and he spotted the vehicle wreck. One compact wedged under the hood of a full-size RAM truck, which was now two feet off the ground and sitting on the front end of the car. Flames curled around the sides of the truck hood, wafting dark smoke into the air.

"We need water on that now."

Izan said, "I'll get the hose."

"I'll help," Amelia offered.

Della pulled up. "Is that a person in there?"

Ridge shoved his door open. "Let's find out." He jumped from the front seat, leaving his phone behind. He put his helmet on, then gloves, went to the front window of the car and peered in. "I've got a victim in the front seat." He moved to the rear and did the same, spotting a crying face in a car seat. "Tender-age child in the back!"

Della grabbed the rear door handle on the other side. "Locked." She went to the front. "Same here."

Ridge tried his side. A man came over, ash and sweat on his red face. No hair on his head, and a distended belly under a polo shirt with an emblem on the chest. Jeans and work boots. The RAM driver?

"I didn't see the car. Not until it was too late."

"Stay back, sir." He waved the guy off. "Let us work." He twisted around to Amelia. "We need the Jaws of Life!"

She handed something to Izan and raced to the truck, hauling the big tool from its cabinet and running over with it. The two ends of the jaws would open like scissors and get the door separated from the frame so they could get the victims out.

Amelia eased the jaws into position to get to the kid first. Izan came over with the hose, and Della—back over by the hydrant now—got the water going. No one wanted to see the fire catch on something and get out of control.

As it was, they were all standing in fluid that had leaked from the vehicles.

"Get that door open." Ridge ran around to the other side and used a glass-breaking tool on the back window. He pushed it in so that it didn't land on the screaming child, and reached in to unlock the door.

The Jaws of Life whirred into action.

And promptly stopped.

Amelia yelped and he heard a crash before she muttered, "What on earth?"

Ridge looked over the roof. "What's going on?"

"It overheated. It's dead—and sparking."

"Lewis, get water on it and douse that fire." He looked at Amelia. "Get in this way and get the kid. Where's my ambulance?"

A faulty piece of equipment might slow them down, but it wasn't going to stop them from doing their jobs.

The problem?

It never should've happened.

Della grabbed the Jaws of Life.

"Hey, kiddo." Amelia crouched on the rear seat.

Ridge smashed the front windshield with the glass-breaking tool. It shattered, and he hooked his axe in the corner to get it to fall toward him, not onto the victim. She had blood on her face and was slumped over the airbag. "Ma'am, can you hear me?"

Della screamed and dropped the Jaws of Life. "The battery just exploded!"

Ridge heard a telltale popping from under the car. "Everyone out!"

He reached in and unclipped the driver, not willing to move without at least trying to save her. Arms under her, around her body. Thank the Lord she was slight. He pulled her out the window, backing up as fast as he could. Amelia scrambled out of the back door, holding the kid.

Another two pops and the car whooshed into a fireball that dislodged the truck and flipped the front end into the air a foot.

Ridge fell back onto the ground, clutching the driver.

Amelia landed beside him, holding the screaming child.

Pain slammed through his head, and he cried out, rolling to protect the victim from the searing heat.

THIRTEEN

AMELIA LAY BACK, AWARE SHE NEEDED TO HANG on to the child. Dazed and shaken, she fought to focus on what had just happened. *The car exploded.* Not an unusual circumstance in a traffic collision call with flammable liquids leaking out and the fire still not quite extinguished.

The Jaws of Life overheating? Not so much.

And had Della said they blew up?

Then the car did.

Amelia heard the child start to cry again. Poor guy was a three- or four-year-old, and he might not have any injuries, but he was certainly shaken up. Confused. Terrified.

"Okay." She ran a gloved hand down his back. "We should get up and get you seen by an EMT, huh." She tried to keep a warm, even tone in her voice so his alarm didn't continue to rise.

Amelia sat up, looking around at the chaos. Izan and Della were putting the fire out. The truck driver was yelling from behind them and waving his arms around. People had gathered. Other cars had pulled over for people to watch or see if they could help.

Above them, the sun fought to be seen behind a heavy bank of clouds, the day mild in temperature. Hot days with a fire to fight were the worst.

To her left, Ridge lay back on the ground, the injured woman on his other side, where Amelia couldn't see her.

She twisted around and spotted rescue squad's truck parked between spectators and the traffic trying to pass the scene on the road. Amelia covered the kid's ears with her gloves and screamed, "Medic!"

Fastest way to explain, given there was more than one victim here and the ambulance hadn't arrived yet.

Were Kianna and Trace done at the hospital yet, or had another bus been dispatched to their location?

Bryce crouched in front of her, assessing the kid.

"Ridge is hurt. He has the driver." Over the back end of the car, she saw Eddie telling the truck driver to calm down. Zack helped Della and Izan, while Zoe ran to Ridge.

"This kid will be okay." Bryce grabbed his radio and asked how long the ambulance was going to be. The response came back as mere minutes.

Amelia blew out a breath. "The Jaws of Life malfunctioned and the car blew."

Bryce frowned. "Equipment failure?"

She nodded. "Ridge got us in the car by breaking the glass. Otherwise these two would be gone up in flames."

The harsh realities of her chosen career were painful on occasion. More often than she would like, considering any loss was one too many. But it happened. The hard truth was that they couldn't save everyone they tried to rescue. Fire consumed far too much.

And to think, she'd been rattled that Ridge might've been talking to someone about her on the phone. It hardly seemed relevant right now, when innocent lives were at stake.

She turned back to see Ridge sitting up. "You okay?"

He nodded, shaking off what had happened. He rolled his shoulders. "I'm good."

"And the woman?"

He looked at her, and Amelia didn't like the despair in his expression at all. For some reason, she felt it more than she usually would, seeing his reaction to the state of the victim.

A siren cut the air around them.

Bryce said, "Give me the child," and scooped the kid into his arms. Amelia didn't have time to object. All she could do was sit and think about finding some energy to get up. She looked around at the crowd, thinking of all the things she'd have done now if she were still lieutenant.

With rescue squad here to assist them in getting this situation taken care of, Ridge had help. She didn't need to overstep the bounds of what she was authorized to do.

Faces in the crowd stared at the scene, a little bit in awe of what the firefighters were doing. She didn't hang out with anyone really, outside of Meg, so she never saw anyone she knew.

Until she did.

Amelia frowned. That wasn't . . . it couldn't be . . .

He stood between two others, behind them and barely visible. Long blond hair hung over his ears and down past his shoulders. A scar bisected his eyebrow, and he had a tattoo on the side of his neck above the collar of his jacket. She couldn't even see the rest of what he wore.

Her brother.

No, it couldn't be. Elam was locked up in prison and had been for more than ten years, convicted as an adult so that at barely eighteen, he'd had to serve his time in prison with hardened criminals decades older than he was.

The idea was terrifying, because she knew he'd be learning from them the whole time, and when he got out, he'd be so much worse.

But that shouldn't be for several more years.

"Amelia." A heavy hand grasped the shoulder of her turnout coat.

"Huh?" She turned to find Ridge's frustrated expression staring down at her.

"I was calling your name. You good?"

"I'm okay." She grabbed his wrist, and he helped her up. Unlike when he'd lowered her from the ceiling, there was no sweet close moment. Just more of that frustration.

"This callout is a disaster. We need to get things under control." Ridge turned away and stomped off.

Amelia looked back at the spot where she could have sworn she'd seen her brother.

Nothing.

Probably it hadn't been him, but given the week she was having, there was no way she wouldn't make a call and find out for sure whether he was still in prison or had been released. If he had, he'd be the one in their father's mansion, tearing the place down to studs and looking for a payout. And if anyone got in his way, it would be the last thing they ever did.

She knew some people saw the light in prison, so to speak. Her brother was the last person she'd consider that might happen to. Even the best preacher in the world wouldn't be able to get through to a guy who'd been cut from the same cloth as their father. Who took after him in every way and terrorized everyone around them.

When her mom had left her father, she'd taken Amelia and left Elam with his dad. Like that was some kind of reasonable compromise.

Sometimes it seemed as if Amelia had been in self-preservation mode her entire life.

"Patterson!" Ridge yelled her name across the top of the car. "Let's go!"

Amelia swallowed, not super impressed with that tone. She wanted to give him the benefit of the doubt, but she hadn't had the best day either. Instead of rushing to him at his command, she went to the truck and got the sand compound they put on chemicals and other fluids that spilled. The cars would be dragged away by tow truck, but that didn't mean the scene would be cleaned up.

She slung the bag over her shoulder and went to Della. "You good?" Amelia dumped the bag on the ground by her foot.

Izan came over as well. "That was crazy, right? Normally that many things don't go wrong at once."

Della took off her gloves and stretched out her hand, which was a little red on one side. "I'm good. Feels a bit singed, but don't tell the EMTs, because I don't need a doctor."

"I'm glad you didn't get hurt." Amelia squeezed her shoulder.

Zack slid out from under the car. Beside it, the truck had been secured by airbags so it didn't suddenly shift and crush anyone. "We're good to move the truck."

Eddie hit the button to deflate the bag and lower the truck back to the ground. Beside him, the RAM driver talked emphatically in his ear. The cops should have been here taking his statement, but Amelia didn't see any.

"We need officers."

Izan patted the outside of Amelia's arm and pointed to two uniformed cops coming their way, Officer Anthony Thomas and Officer Olivia Tazwell.

Exhaustion from back-to-back calls hit her like a wave. Amelia walked away and left her colleagues to the job of coordinating with the police. From his rescue squad huddle, Ridge frowned at her. Displeased.

She went to the back of the ambulance, where the kid and mom had been loaded up. EMT Nathan Welch, who she'd worked with a bit on calls like this, had the child on his lap while he assessed the mother on the bed. Securing her for transport. Amelia gave him a hand, and when they were done he said, "Close the doors. We need to get her in."

"Got it." Amelia climbed out and shut the doors, slamming her palm down on the window twice.

The ambulance pulled out into the traffic crawling past, and a lane emerged as people eased to one side or the other so the bus could drive up the middle with the lights and sirens going.

She turned back to the scene and took off her glove to run a hand over her hair, pushing the loose strands back from her face. Chaos to calm happened nearly as fast as the situation had deteriorated, but the cleanup usually took the most time out of everything. Unless something serious happened and there was no one else, they would be on scene until it was all squared away and restored to order.

A tow truck pulled onto the street where the ambulance had gone and made its way in this direction, coming to bring the wrecked cars to the junkyard.

Amelia grabbed a bottled water from the cabinet in the truck, drank half, and then poured the other half over her head. It chilled in the cool air. Helped to clear her head as much as it lowered her temperature.

She grabbed a broom and got to work.

It couldn't have been her brother that she'd seen earlier in the crowd. She must've been mistaken. Family stuff seemed close to the surface right now, with all the talking about them she had done the past couple of days. At most, she'd seen someone who resembled him.

"Hey, you good?"

She turned to see Bryce beside her. "Why?"

He frowned. "Because you're you. That's why."

Well, what did that mean? Amelia didn't know how to ask about her being "her" and that being a reason she might not be all right. "I'm doing my job."

Bryce studied her for a second. "Let me know if you need anything. Like help."

He really wanted to offer? Fine. She folded her arms. "So make a call. Get me a lieutenant's test scheduled. Seems like I have to do it again."

"Okay, I will."

"Good."

The corners of his lips curled up. "Fine."

Amelia rolled her eyes, then realized she'd decided not to do that anymore today. Good thing it was Bryce, not Ridge.

He said, "Let me know if you need anything else. Anything at all."

This was what opening herself up to Ridge had achieved. They all thought she needed *sympathy* or *help*. "My life sucks."

Bryce walked away laughing.

Amelia had to smile, even if there was nothing funny about it. The fact was, she lived with a whole lot of good people, even if she'd never told them the truth about who she was or let them into her life.

Apparently, they thought she was worth caring about—worth helping out.

And if they thought that?

Maybe it was true.

FOURTEEN

FOR A LITTLE WHILE, RIDGE HAD MANAGED TO
set aside the conversation with his stepdad. How the old man had
figured out who Amelia was and where she lived was anyone's
guess. None of it made sense, and with back-to-back calls, it was easier
to push it away and worry about it later.

All of it had added up, and in the heat of the moment, after
he and Amelia had almost died—that had been a seriously close
one—he'd found himself frustrated with her distraction. She
seemed to be more than a little shaken about everything that was
going on, making him wonder if she needed to take a break from
work for a couple of days. They could get a floater to take her place
on the truck, but the last thing he was going to do was make the
suggestion.

If she thought he was looking to bench her, even for good reason, she would hit the roof.

"Lieutenant Foster."

He turned from the sink, where he'd been rinsing dishes, and
spotted the receptionist in the doorway of the open-plan kitchen.

She said, "There are two cops here to see you."

He grabbed a towel and dried his hands. "Thanks."

Officer Thomas and Officer Tazwell stood waiting in the entryway, looking around at the space.

"I'm pretty sure this firehouse is bigger than your whole precinct, am I right?" Ridge grinned.

Thomas stuck his hand out, and Ridge shook it. "Because we don't sleep in our house. We're out on the streets arresting criminals, not at the station all shift. Or out spraying water on people's stuff."

Ridge laughed. "What brings the two of you here?"

"Just a follow-up about everything that's been happening in the last few days." Tazwell looked around. "Is Patterson here?"

The receptionist behind the desk called over, "I looked around for her but didn't see where she was. I'm trying her phone now."

Ridge shook his head. To the cops, he said, "There's a conference room just down there. Give me a couple of minutes." To their receptionist, he said, "I'll go grab her."

He rounded the halls to a set of stairs that went up to the roof and took them two at a time. The door to the roof had been left ajar, a triangular-shaped piece of wood wedged in the opening.

He left it where it was so the door didn't lock itself and stepped onto the open—and empty—gravel expanse.

Amelia sat on the edge of the roof on the side of the building where trees blocked the view from the street. Staring at the mountains, she had her hands planted behind her, bracing her weight so she could lean back and watch birds and planes fly overhead.

"Hey." He approached cautiously, not wanting to scare her into flinching and see her slip over the edge to the ground. "Thomas and Tazwell are here to talk to us."

Amelia let out a long sigh.

"Do I need to apologize?" He hadn't done anything the average lieutenant wouldn't do on any given Tuesday. Especially one who was new to the job and facing the stress of back-to-back calls.

But right now, they were something more than firefighter and lieutenant.

Given the time they had spent in her house talking about personal things, they were a whole lot more than that now. But still something far from where he had wanted them to be for a long time.

Where he still wanted them to be.

If Amelia gave him any kind of green light, then the twins would get their wish. Ridge wouldn't be leaving Last Chance County anytime soon.

At least, not without Amelia.

She didn't look at him. She kept her gaze on the mountains in the distance. "Do *you* think you need to apologize?"

Danger. Danger.

This was absolutely a trick question.

"I can give you a bunch of reasons why it wasn't anything abnormal for the job we do. I can also give you a bunch of reasons why I shouldn't have yelled at you."

She looked at him then. "I don't need you to apologize." Amelia held out one hand and bent her knees, planting her feet on the edge of the roof.

He grabbed her elbow and hauled her to her feet.

"I'm not a delicate wallflower, Lieutenant. I actually thought you might have been making up for all the times I yelled at you." She gave him a tentative smile.

"Because you think I'm a delicate wallflower or someone who needs to get their own back? I don't do revenge. It's usually not worth the effort."

Her expression shifted. "Revenge. That's something I hadn't thought of. But you're right. It isn't usually worth the effort. Unless you've convinced yourself it's the only way to get satisfaction. Or if something changed in your situation . . . Hmm."

Ridge frowned. "You're saying you think someone might be

trying to get revenge against you? That seems like something the police would want to know about."

He took a step back.

Amelia hesitated.

"You can trust them. You know these cops, and you know they're going to do everything they can to fix what's happening."

Amelia said, "Trust doesn't come easily. I'm guessing that's true for you as well, considering I knew you had sisters but didn't know they lived with you until the other day."

"True." Ridge couldn't argue with that. "These cops are people we've worked with before. Not the kind who don't care about good people. Or don't care about anything but their aim. These aren't the kind of cops who have such a narrow focus that they don't notice when innocent people get caught in the crossfire."

"I'm counting on it." Amelia followed him to the door.

It almost sounded like she wasn't certain they would believe she was one of the good guys.

Downstairs in the conference room, the two uniformed cops studied the whiteboard. They turned when Amelia and Ridge came in.

Amelia greeted both, but far more professional rather than personal, the way he had. "How can we help you?"

Anthony Thomas sat on the edge of the first row of tables.

Olivia Tazwell, also a blonde like Amelia but a few years younger, said, "We have been looking into the reports from the two fires where you spotted a possible suspect, and the attack that happened here."

Amelia stiffened at that.

Tazwell said, "It's nothing to be ashamed about, Amelia. Being overpowered doesn't mean you're weak."

Ridge wondered if she knew that was true from personal experience or from what she'd seen as a police officer.

She continued, "Is there anything else you can tell us about the fires or what happened here?"

Ridge had always seen Amelia as impervious to anything. This impenetrable wall. He'd broken through a tiny bit in the couple of dates they'd gone on, but she'd shored up when she'd cut him off personally. Now it was like he could see through the cracks.

Problem was, beneath the surface, she was overwhelmed. Scared. Maybe he was projecting a lot of what he thought she should be feeling because she wasn't giving him much. But he was certain he could see fear in her eyes.

Amelia held her arms straight, her hands in her pockets and her body tense. "One of them said 'Where is it?'"

Tazwell shifted her weight, and the heavy belt cops wore creaked. "Do you know what he was referring to?"

Ridge figured it was the same thing his stepdad had asked about. While he was thinking about it, he sent his mom a text asking how Gary knew that Amelia was Chief Hilden's daughter. If the information was public knowledge, how come he hadn't heard it?

Amelia seemed hesitant to answer Tazwell's question.

"Could it be connected to the repeated break-ins at Amelia's home?" Those were public record—even if her real name wasn't. "Are the police aware that she's potentially in danger with the frequent threats and property damage?"

The cops shared a glance. Thomas said, "What calls?"

Amelia spun around to glare at Ridge.

"You think you're safe at home?" He figured she would know he meant back in her cabin, but Ridge wasn't going to share that with anyone, not even cops. He knew what she considered sacrosanct. "It could all be connected."

She pulled her hands from her pockets to set them on her hips. "Or none of it is. Firefighters meet disgruntled civilians all the time."

Tazwell shook her head. "What's your address, Amelia? I'll look it up."

Amelia gave her the number and street.

The cop frowned. "I thought that place was abandoned."

Ridge said, "Does that make it okay for people to smash it up or tear holes in the walls?" Not to mention it wasn't abandoned right now, with Kane and Maria occupying rooms there. Anyone who broke in was in for a nasty surprise. "It's someone's property."

Officer Thomas looked up from making notes on his phone. "I'll pull the reports and find out who has been responding to calls. Okay?" Before either of them could answer, he said, "It gives us more to look into, which increases our odds of finding a lead—and a suspect."

Amelia pressed her lips together and nodded.

Officer Tazwell said, "If you're the target of people looking for the money the old chief hid—"

"Assuming there's even anything to find," Amelia pointed out.

Tazwell nodded. "The allure of wealth is enough for some people, even if the chance of finding it is slim. But that's at the house. Now we have incidents at fires and here at the station. So why now? What has changed that means all this is happening *now*?"

"Good question." Ridge settled on the edge of a table. At least the back-to-back calls of this shift had settled into a quiet so they could have this conversation in the first place. They needed to work out what might be going on.

Amelia gasped. "I haven't done anything, if that's what you're thinking."

Tazwell said, "No one is saying you have. We aren't here to accuse you."

"You didn't bring this on yourself," Ridge tried to reassure her. "And you aren't to blame, Amelia. We all want to help you. No one wants you, or anyone here at the firehouse, to be in danger."

"I know you want the firefighters to be safe." She sniffed. "This is about the department for you, but it's also *my* life."

The door opened before he could respond to that.

He didn't like that she wasn't a hundred percent convinced he was in this to make sure she was protected. Why did it seem like she didn't know she could trust him?

Their receptionist said, "Lieut—Patterson? There's a woman at the front desk asking for you."

"Thanks." Amelia took the out and practically ran from the room.

"I've never seen her like that." Tazwell bit her lip.

"Me either," Ridge said. "But we don't talk without her." He glanced between the two cops. "You're gonna look into this?"

Both of them nodded.

"Thanks." He walked them to the entryway, where Amelia was sitting on one of the waiting-area chairs with a visibly pregnant woman who had to be mid-twenties. The same blonde hair as Amelia, but not many more similarities.

He saw the cops out, his mind spinning with all that had been happening. Right now, it seemed like a bunch of random pieces to a puzzle he couldn't discern yet. Eventually it would become clear, but until then, they had to fight blind and try to get through it unscathed.

Amelia gasped. Whatever the woman had just said to her, she was terrified by it.

Ridge wanted to intervene, but Amelia glanced over at him then, and the look on her face said she didn't need his help.

After that conversation with the police, she had every right to be frustrated. They had no answers to any of this.

But she also had to know that he wasn't going to quit helping her.

He was in this for the long haul.

FIFTEEN

YOU AND I, WE'RE THE SAME, AREN'T WE?

Amelia couldn't get those words out of her head for the remainder of her shift.

The fact no more calls came in had allowed her time to absorb it all. Hooded men, assailants, and their tools being sabotaged. Now this? A destitute girl who wanted her help.

She opened the passenger door for the young woman who had asked for her. "Thank you for waiting, Cherise."

"You can call me Cherry. We're friends now, right?" The younger woman set her hand on her rounded abdomen. She'd told Amelia she was sixteen weeks pregnant.

Amelia had never been pregnant, but from what Zack had been telling the crew—updating them on Naya's progress all through her pregnancy—she knew that sixteen was a few weeks before the ultrasound where she could learn the baby's gender.

"Okay, Cherry." Amelia nodded. "I'm happy to take you anywhere you need to go."

Cherry slid into the seat, shifting on the cushion before she drew her feet in. She seemed slender—maybe more so than she should be—making Amelia want to ask if she'd eaten. But then, she also seemed like the kind of woman who expected others to care for her or provide for her. But Amelia didn't know her all that well, so it wasn't like she could assume.

She moved around the hood of the car. At least with this woman here now, she didn't have to think about herself being the victim of something dangerous. She could focus on Cherry and what this lost-seeming young woman needed from her.

Amelia had listened for a few moments before asking Cherry to go down to the Bridgewater Café and get something to eat while Amelia finished her shift. Since Cherry had no money, Amelia had given her a twenty. Having money gave a person a little confidence, even if it was just to get a muffin and a drink.

Now they had to figure out what to do.

The idea stalled Amelia so she didn't start the car. She didn't even put her seatbelt on. She shifted in the seat, holding the keys in her hand, and faced Cherry a little bit. She didn't know where to begin.

"It's almost like we're sisters."

Amelia could see how she might feel that was true. "How long did it last?"

"Two years." Cherry winced. "I'm not proud of it. I did a lot of things I realize now I shouldn't have gone along with. Nicholas . . . he just twisted everything so that I didn't know what was me and what was his idea." She shook her head. "Now that I'm out of the relationship, I can see more clearly. There was a lady at the crisis pregnancy shelter in Seattle who talked me through a lot of it. She helped me see that he manipulated me into believing him and going along with everything."

"I'm glad you got out safely." Amelia couldn't imagine if she'd discovered she was pregnant in the midst of everything that'd happened in Benson. The fact Nicholas hadn't changed and was still victimizing women he was in relationships with made her sick.

Amelia had saved herself. But in keeping quiet, she hadn't saved anyone else from going through the same thing.

"What made you come here to Last Chance County? It's a long way."

Cherry said, "The bus goes through Boise and Salt Lake City and comes here. I suppose I was thinking I'd head somewhere warm for the winter, but I ran out of money."

"How did you know to look for me?" Amelia had been targeted too much recently to not worry about this. A person she very much wanted to keep her location from . . . had discovered exactly that. Not Cherry, necessarily. But it wasn't a stretch that Nicholas might come here looking for her.

Cherry picked at a loose thread on the hem of her oversized sweater. "He talked about you. Mostly to rub it in my face when I didn't measure up. You're a firefighter, and he always told me how strong you were. How I should be stronger, stand up for myself. Then he'd drag me back down. I think he got a sick kind of satisfaction from watching me build myself up just so he could destroy me."

Amelia knew exactly how that went. She'd lived it, and in the middle of all of that, Nicholas had been lacing her coffee with small amounts of a stimulant that caused her to act erratically, with paranoia and hallucinations.

It had taken weeks and a long process of elimination for her to figure out what was wrong with her—and what had caused it.

Or, *who.*

She spotted Ridge coming out of the firehouse. Nearly everyone else had dispersed after the next shift showed up to relieve them. He saw her in the driver's seat of her car, and who she was with, and motioned making a phone call, mouthing, *Call me later.*

Amelia nodded.

"I don't know where to go. I guess I was thinking about finding a church or something. Seeing if they can help me out with some money." Cherry bit her lip. "Or I could stay with you for tonight? Just until I figure out what to do."

"I don't have room in my place."

Cherry seemed almost surprised by that. Why, when they didn't know each other? Unless Nicholas had bragged that Amelia lived in a huge mansion, just to make Cherry feel poor. It wasn't like this woman could sleep there in her condition. With no furniture or heat.

"I'll take you to a nice motel. Don't worry about the cost." Amelia turned the car on. "I can pay for a couple of nights so you have somewhere warm." She didn't mind giving this woman some money for food, even if it was only enough for a cheap fast-food meal.

Even though Cherry thought they were sisters in a way, the only thing that bonded them together was the worst time in both of their lives. Who wanted a connection like that? She'd spent the last few years trying to escape that time. Now it would be brought to mind every time she saw this woman.

"Thank you so much, Amelia. I don't know what I'd do if you weren't able to help me."

Amelia pulled out of her parking space and drove to the freeway interchange, where there were a couple of motels on either side of the road. They always seemed to cluster together. She was more of the solitary type, but not because it was her choice. She'd lost the father she loved, and thanks to the family court, she'd had to return periodically to her father. Eventually she'd lost her mother as well. Meg was the closest thing to family she had left. Except for the other firefighters at Eastside Firehouse.

She had a feeling that if she told them she considered them to be family, they'd be surprised she felt that way.

Which was why she didn't plan to tell them.

As she drove, she couldn't help thinking about her brother and if she'd really seen him at that fire scene. What a crazy day. She needed more than twenty-four hours off to process it all and get some rest. Never mind reaching the point where she actually figured out how to resolve the situation.

Now Cherry had shown up?

There was no way a pregnant woman had come here looking for an ally—or a friend—with an ulterior motive. She wasn't going to suspect this woman, because what could Cherry do to her anyway? She was going to give the woman a little money and send her on her way. Neither Cherry nor the child was Amelia's responsibility past basic concern from one person to another.

Not in the middle of whatever was going on.

After all, the last thing Amelia wanted to do was put this woman and her precious unborn child in danger simply because Cherry had chosen to find Amelia and ask for help.

She got the young woman all checked in to a room, then hung back in the lobby. Amelia wasn't going to walk her to the room, and Cherry didn't need Amelia to carry that saggy duffel for her when it didn't seem so heavy. "Take care of yourself, Cherry."

Cherry's expression shifted. "What if he comes here? What if he tracks me down?"

Now she was scared? She'd seemed relieved before, but not fearful. "Do you think he'll look for you?"

"I'm carrying his child." Cherry's eyes filled with tears. "I really should stay with you."

"I really don't have the space, sorry." Her cabin was barely big enough for one person. Having Ridge in there eating pizza with her had only reinforced how small it was.

He hadn't seemed to think less of her for having a tiny place, so she figured it was her insecurity.

"The police in this town are good people. They do their jobs well." Amelia wanted to believe that was true, anyway. Even if they had no idea what had been going on at her house. "If you have a problem, call them. They'll get here faster than I will."

"He'll take me before they get here." Cherry gasped. "I might not be able to call 911 in time."

Amelia said, "You have to do what it takes to protect your child from him. But I'll call an officer friend of mine and ask them to come by later and check on you. Is that all right?"

Cherry sniffed. "If you think that's enough to keep me safe from him."

Amelia might seem like she didn't care, but there was something about this situation that told her not to get involved. She wasn't part of Nicholas's life. She wasn't required to help Cherry beyond this. A needy woman who seemed just a little too unable to stand on her own two feet . . . Amelia wasn't like that, and people who were tended to rub her the wrong way.

She was either trying to run as far away as she could from the person she had been with Nicholas. To the point where she rejected anything that seemed even close to it.

Or she'd been burned by lies far too many times, and it had made her a horrible person.

"You have my number," Amelia said. "But you need to call 911 if you even glimpse him out the window. Or if he calls you. Okay?"

Cherry nodded. "Okay." The word sounded small.

"Get some rest."

Before she could draw Amelia in more, Amelia turned and headed for the door. She'd walked away from Nicholas and rebuilt her life. This woman was going to have to do the same thing. There were programs she could draw from and people whose nonprofits or organizations were there to offer help.

The idea this might be another one of Nicholas's manipulations didn't sit right, not with a pregnant woman. But the tiny chance it could be? She wanted to run away.

On the way out, she called Ridge from her phone.

He'd told her to.

She walked to her car, listening to it ring. Not even thinking about why she'd reached out to him.

"Hey." His strong, steady voice filled her ear.

"I don't have to turn myself in knots to help her. I don't have room. That isn't my life. It's hers. I got out of it." She had to pause and take a breath.

"Okay, so there was a lot there. Want to come over for dinner? We can talk about who that woman is and what she told you."

Amelia got in her car and closed the door fast, almost like someone was chasing her. But there was no one there.

It's not happening again. She wasn't going to let it.

"Amelia?"

"Okay," she said. "I'll come over. Give me your address."

SIXTEEN

RIDGE STOOD AT HIS FRONT DOOR. HE'D TOLD Amelia where to find the guest parking space and watched her walk from her car to the town house. She'd changed at the end of shift like he always did and wore jeans, a pair of white Converse, and a T-shirt that Maddie would approve of. Over the shirt, she had pulled on a thin gray hoodie and a black leather jacket.

Her hair hung loose around her shoulders, but like she'd run her hand through it.

On the phone, she'd sounded flustered in a way he'd never heard from her before—even with all the shocking situations they'd seen at work. Gruesome injuries. Bodies they'd recovered, burned beyond recognition because they'd been unable to rescue the person.

But it was the arrival of a pregnant woman that had shaken Amelia to her core.

He was beginning to wonder if being a firefighter was like a safe haven for her. A situation she could control—especially as a lieutenant. It made him want to give up the spot to her. If he could, and if it would help her get a handle on everything.

God, let this be the right thing. For both of us.

"Hey." She approached the porch step, a three-foot square of concrete. One of the twins had set a yellow plant pot there, but whatever had been growing died a while back from teenage neglect.

"Hey." He stepped back, holding the door open.

She came into his quiet house, the TV on low. The lighting down so it didn't have that harsh glare. He much preferred dimmer switches to the usual on-off wall plates. "I thought your sisters lived with you?" She turned in the entryway, almost nervous.

He'd never seen this side of Amelia, and he found he liked it.

Ridge shut the front door. "They both have work, so they'll be back later." Thankfully there was enough of this chicken and rice dish for a few days, something he liked to do so the twins had a good meal in the freezer if he was at work. They always made enough for more than one meal when they cooked. "Do you want some dinner?"

She looked like she needed a hug, but she might be hungry as well. "Am I a horrible person?"

"I don't know." He spoke carefully. "Are you?"

"You're supposed to tell me I'm great!" She shoved his shoulder, nowhere near full strength. "You aren't supposed to agree with me."

She was genuinely worried.

Ridge snagged her hand before it went back to her side and held it between them. "You aren't a horrible person. But I have no context, so tell me who that woman was and the whole deal. Then after, I'll tell you what I think."

Amelia said, "It's a long story."

"Then you're right on time, because dinner is ready." He squeezed her hand and let go, moving to the kitchen, where he dished up two portions and leaned over the sink to set the bowls on the breakfast bar. "The girls turned the dining room, or what should be that, into an office so they have somewhere to study other than the couch and their bedroom."

She slid onto a stool, and he handed her a fork.

"Soda? Water?"

"Water." She stared at the bowl. "Did you make this?"

"Smells okay, right?"

She set the fork down.

"We could say grace?" Was that her hangup right now?

"Not being the first to eat, it's part of the story. I don't want to jump ahead."

Ridge twisted around on the seat and faced her. "Tell me what it is. Because I've seen you wait for others to eat first, and I've wondered, but I never asked why you do that." In fact, he'd thought she might not notice she did it. But she clearly did.

"It could be poisoned." She turned to him, her attention snapping around. Almost as if she was watching for him to disagree or disparage her for thinking that. "So I wait for someone else to eat first. Just in case."

Ridge grabbed his fork and took a big bite of the chicken and rice. He blew out a breath around the food in his mouth. "It's hot."

She smiled and took a small bite.

"If you're worried something is poisoned, caution is a good idea." He wanted to ask a hundred questions about why she had that particular fear, but he needed her to feel safe enough to talk without his barrage of demands for answers.

"This is really good."

"I promise, if I gave it to you, then it's safe."

"Thanks, Ridge." She had a couple more bites, then said, "It's actually connected to Cherry. That's what she said her name was."

He'd left them to their conversation, not wanting to intrude, but was eager to hear about it now. "Is she a friend of yours?"

"Actually we've never met until today. She sought me out because . . . the father of her baby is my ex."

Amelia had dated someone?

"Calm down, it was back in Benson."

"What?" Had he reacted in some way?

She rolled her eyes. "Me dating. It was years ago, okay? And it wasn't good. That's putting it mildly, because it was a disaster that nearly cost me my job and my sanity, and it still might, since I got demoted."

Ridge finished the last bite of his meal and turned to her again, his knees either side of her stool. He wanted to touch her in a way that would be reassuring. Problem was, she held herself stiff on the stool. As if with the slightest pressure, she might shatter.

"I'd like to hear about it."

Amelia left her fork in the bowl and drank some of her water. "His name is Nicholas Danielson. He was my captain in Benson, at the fire department. He doesn't work there anymore. I haven't seen him since I left, but someone told me they did an investigation into his conduct about other things and he was dismissed."

"Your boss?"

She nodded. "My truck lieutenant's superior. Then he transferred out, and I got the spot after I passed the test." She said that emphatically, as if she needed him to believe she spoke the truth. "But Nicholas destroyed the paperwork, or he never even filed it. Everything was about earning favors from him. His entire existence is about making everyone do what he wants them to do."

"How long were you . . . together?"

"Too long." She took another sip of her drink. "Eight months. I started to push back against his demands, and he retaliated by putting something in my coffee until others I worked with told me to get checked out by a psychologist. I didn't know I was acting erratic and paranoid. I was convinced I was fine and everyone else was crazy. Until my chief sat me down, and I dissolved into tears about the entire relationship and what was going on, and he told me to leave town. Clean slate. Try something else. He didn't think I was cut out to be a firefighter."

"Because this Nicholas guy used his superior to undermine you, it sounds like. I'm guessing he's the kind of guy who told everyone what a terrible job you were doing and that everything that went wrong was your fault." Ridge wanted to find the guy and pummel him. Kane would probably help.

She nodded. "So I came back to Last Chance County. I had nothing, but I'd qualified as a firefighter here, so I got a job and convinced the chief over our house at the time to make me lieutenant." She winced. "Maybe it wasn't right, but I earned that spot fair and square. Now I have to do it again."

He leaned his elbow on the counter. "How does Cherry tie in?"

"Nicholas is the father of her baby. She left him like I did, and she was going south."

"She looked you up?"

Amelia nodded. "Apparently he told her about me, but only to undermine her. I guess he hasn't changed at all. He's still only interested in women who are subservient because he's stripped away their self-worth and self-respect until they're so twisted around in knots they just do what he tells them to do."

Ridge eased his fingers under her tight fist and took the now-squashed napkin. "I'm sorry you went through something like that."

"The worst part is that the people I worked with saw me lose my cool, acting crazy, too many times. It's why I can't let anyone at the firehouse lose respect for me. I need to get back my rank."

"I'll help you," he said. "Whatever you need."

Now that he knew what drove her, Ridge was more determined than ever to help her.

He took their bowls to the sink and removed an old yellowed photo from the fridge. He set it on the counter by her. The old man in the picture was flanked by two boys, six and eight. Ridge and Kane. "I always think what Grandpa would say about what I'm doing. It's kept me out of trouble."

Ridge rinsed the bowls and opened the dishwasher as he

continued talking. "I think about what choices he would make. And I work so he'd have been proud of me."

"How did he pass away?"

Ridge closed the dishwasher. "It was raining. The road was slick, and his heart was bad. We went off the road and lodged in the dirt in a ditch." He touched his shoulder. "I broke my collarbone, but Kane broke his leg. It took time for rescue to come, both of us sitting there in the dark."

His grandpa, dead in the front seat.

The windshield shattered.

Rain coming into the car.

"Then all of a sudden there were bright lights everywhere. We were loaded onto a helicopter, but neither of us could enjoy it with the pain and Grandpa just lying there. I was twelve, and Kane was fourteen. But even back then, I knew that was what I wanted to do. Help people on the worst day of their lives."

He looked at her then.

Tears streamed down her face. Amelia gasped and swiped at her cheeks. He grabbed two tissues from the twins' box on the end table by the couch and brought them to her. Close enough that he'd be available if she wanted a hug.

"It's okay to cry. I know that because I live with teenage girls." Ridge laid a hand on her shoulder. "What I told you is a sad story. I cry about it sometimes, when I really miss him."

Kane had told Ridge he did the same thing.

"Rest of my family aren't worth two nickels. Except the twins." Not even his mom. But he didn't often want to admit that to himself. "Grandpa was the best. There was no one better."

"I think you're living up to his memory just fine, Ridge Foster. You're a good man."

His chest tightened.

Amelia wound her arms around his middle, and he hugged her. She said, "Thank you for telling me that story."

"Thank you for trusting me with yours."

She leaned back, and Ridge found himself closer to Amelia than he'd ever been. Not because they were still touching each other, half in a hug. They were closer than they'd ever been because they'd shared those parts of their histories. They'd opened up to each other.

It made him wonder what he'd been afraid of.

"Whatever is going on, I'm going to be here through it." Even if she only ever let him be her friend, he wanted to be right here with her. Not in his house, but supporting her. "Making sure you're okay."

She stared up at him. "I don't trust easily, but I want to trust you."

"You can."

"I'm starting to believe it." She bit her lip.

Ridge tossed out all ideas of just being her friend. He couldn't resist her. In that moment, there was nothing else he could do but lean down and touch his lips to hers. Softly. Just a slight touch, so gentle. It shifted into a hug, and he let it happen, trying to keep things easy.

Her arms tightened around his waist, and he heard her intake of breath. Ridge turned his head to the side, and since she hadn't shoved him away, he eased his lips against hers again. Taking his time now. Soaking in the moment and experiencing what he'd wanted for so long.

From a distance, he heard the door lock.

Then a teenage squeal.

Ridge pulled back from Amelia's inviting mouth and looked over, only to find his twin sisters in the doorway. "Uh . . ." How was he going to explain this?

Maddie's brows rose. "Busted." She grinned and started laughing.

Ella just stared at him.

SEVENTEEN

A MELIA DIDN'T EVEN WANT TO TURN AROUND. That would mean the moment was over, which might be for the best, but she wasn't ready to let go of it just yet. The feel of his lips against hers. The closeness of his warmth surrounding her. She'd never felt safe like that—not once in her life.

It was like a dream.

And she didn't want it to be over.

She lifted her gaze to Ridge's face, which was red and flustered. He hesitated in a way she'd never seen before, and it was seriously adorable. This self-assured man had turned into a puddle.

"Maddie. Ella."

One of the girls giggled.

Amelia turned to see two slender girls, each a mirror image of the other with their long dark-blonde hair, almost brown at the center part, light on the ends. They had Ridge's height and teenage metabolism. One of them grinned, sliding off a jacket. The other looked far more shell-shocked and stared at her brother.

"Hi." Amelia sounded choked, but she waved like this might be close to normal. Which it wasn't for her. She had no idea if their finding Ridge kissing a woman in his kitchen was a run-of-the-mill occurrence.

She looked at him.

Ridge still had pink cheeks. "Um, guys, this is Amelia." He cleared his throat and indicated one twin, then the other. "This is Maddie. And that's Ella."

Maddie swept over, her hand out, and shook Amelia's. "Nice to meet you, *Amelia.*" As if her name meant something to them. Which meant he'd talked to them about her.

"Ella?" Ridge said. "Wanna come say hi?"

She didn't look happy. Amelia had no idea why that could be. The list of possible reasons was way too long, and she didn't know this girl.

She tried to smile and look approachable while her cheeks flamed.

Ella said, "I have a lot of homework." She walked through the living area and disappeared down a hallway.

"So . . ." Maddie drew the word out. "You're . . . *her.*"

"What does that mean?" Amelia glanced between Ridge and the teen. "Her?"

The girl gasped. "Did you make chicken and rice? Yes!" She whirled around and did a circuit of the breakfast bar to the pan, drawing down two bowls from a cupboard.

Ridge said, "Don't worry about what it means." He squeezed Amelia's shoulder, looking like he wanted to explain more. "Teenage girls have wild imaginations."

"And homework!" Maddie's eyes were wide and full of something that looked like excitement mixed with embarrassment. "We'll be upstairs, and we *won't* bother you guys."

What on earth did that mean?

Amelia had no idea what to say. It wasn't like she hung out with teens . . . at all. Or ever.

Maddie took two bowls down the hall in the same direction her sister had gone.

"I should leave you to . . . deal with that, or whatever you need to do." Amelia slid off the stool, which brought her closer to Ridge, who hadn't moved.

"They have homework." He didn't step back. "That wasn't so bad. Now you've met them, and no one is in tears. It could even be called successful."

"Tears? Is it me who is supposed to be crying, or one of them? And why would they cry, unless there's something to the fact that I'm *her*?"

Ridge reached for her, but she stepped out of the way. "Amelia—"

"I'm not leaving because I'm mad at you, but I would like to know what you've told them about me. Unless that was about someone else." She didn't like either option.

"It wasn't . . ." He ran a hand through his hair. "They know you broke it off with me before."

"So it isn't about some other woman?"

Ridge shook his head. "There hasn't been anyone else."

That was something, at least. But with her being so settled on never getting into a relationship, it was also a little sad. He'd resigned himself to . . . what? Waiting for her? She didn't know what that said about them. If she didn't let this continue to see where it would go, she was consigning him to being alone.

Lonely.

Until he gave up on her and moved on.

The man was so stubborn, who knew how long that would take?

But saving Ridge from being alone wasn't a good reason to get into a relationship with him. Which, technically, they weren't supposed to do right now anyway. There was nothing about him that constituted a red flag, but that wasn't the way others would see it. Or the higher-ups at the fire department.

Right now he was a lieutenant—and her superior.

"I need to go." Amelia eased toward the door. "It's late."

"We could talk about what just happened."

She shrugged, sliding her hands in her pockets. "I'm not saying I regret it, but it isn't like it can happen again. That was the problem I had last time. Sneaking around, thinking it was exciting breaking the rules."

"I'm not him."

Amelia hadn't even thought that. "That might be the *only* thing I'm certain of right now."

Relief washed over his face. "I'll see you tomorrow?"

Their shift wasn't until six in the morning the day after. "If you wanna do something, text me. Or call. We could meet up." She needed to do laundry and clean up in the big house. He had twin teenage girls to deal with. "Hopefully everything goes all right with the girls."

"They'll be fine."

If they weren't, he seemed not to want her to worry about it. Which Amelia didn't have time for anyway, with everything else swirling around, so that was fine.

She went to the door, but he opened it for her and held it, standing near her while she stepped out. Amelia vacillated on the doorstep. Maybe she should have told him that the kiss had been a mistake.

"Let's just talk tomorrow."

She nodded.

Ridge leaned down and touched his lips to hers, just a quick press and it was over. "Good night."

Yeah, that was going to get her in trouble. "Good night."

She turned away, her cheeks warm as she walked to her car. No looking back. She was going to take tonight for what it was and not wonder what was next. Or if things were a good idea. He'd kissed her, and it had been nice. More than nice.

A long time coming.

About time.

In fact, she didn't think a kiss had ever been like that for her. It was just . . . *Ridge.*

Amelia called Meg from her car. It rang a couple of times, then connected, and she heard Meg say a breathy, "Hello?"

"I woke you up." Amelia winced, pulling out of the town-house complex. "Sorry, I didn't think what time it was." Or the fact Meg ran a coffee shop that opened early, so she got up at four on a workday. "I'll call back later."

"Tell me what you're calling about first, or I'll lie awake wondering." Meg let out a moan, stretching and shifting in the covers, creating a rustle across the line.

Amelia would make it quick so her friend could go back to bed. "I went to Ridge's house. Wait, that's not what happened first. Nicholas's pregnant girlfriend showed up. She left him and found me on her way south. Also, she's out of money. I put her up in a hotel for a couple of nights and gave her some cash so she's not destitute."

"Whoa." More shuffling over the line. "That's big."

"Yeah."

"Considering . . ."

Amelia gripped the wheel. "I've been trying not to think about that."

"And you went to Ridge?"

"I just . . . she's me. But she's wrong, we aren't connected. I don't owe her anything. We're not sisters in any way. She's a stranger, and I don't want anything to do with anything about Nicholas."

"Isn't there a women's shelter across town?"

Amelia said, "Right. I heard about that, but I don't know where it is."

"I'll text you the info tomorrow. Then if she needs it, she can go stay there," Meg said. "You're right that you don't owe her anything. She doesn't need to be part of your life unless you want her to be."

"Thanks." Implementing a healthy boundary was one thing, but being reassured by your friend that it was the right thing to do meant a lot as well. "Sorry I woke you."

"I'm not. You're going through a lot right now." Meg paused. "Have you thought about . . . praying about it?"

Amelia said, "I thought we agreed you weren't going to push your beliefs on me."

"Am I being pushy? It was only a question."

She knew how Meg felt and that she saw sharing with Amelia as an imperative. That the outcome was life or death—Amelia's.

Amelia stopped at a red light with barely any cars around her. "I don't even know where to start praying. What on earth would I say?"

"It's just a conversation. Talk to Him. Because the only peace you're going to feel that actually lasts or sustains you through what's happening is the peace that comes from God."

"So it's like a survival thing?" It sounded like a way to get through the bad stuff.

"It's that when you need it," Meg said. "But when you don't need help through something hard, He is still there, and God wants a relationship with you in the good and the bad. He's the one in control of everything."

"And everything I've been through is my fault."

Meg said, "Amelia, you made some bad choices. But you also made some good ones. God is the one you can rely on to guide you, and He brought you back to Last Chance County for a reason. So He could put people in your life who care. Who want to help. You can't do this alone. You need the people around you, and you need Him."

Amelia was used to pushing back when people talked about

faith. There was so much of it swirling around her in the firehouse that she'd tried to tune it out.

But she had to admit Meg's explanations made sense.

Her friend said, "God wants to give you more than you can imagine. He wants you to have the best, because we all know how bad things can get. He wants to be a safe place for you to go and the source of peace you're looking for."

Amelia drove to her neighborhood, trying not to dismiss Meg's words, because that was what she always did.

"God wants to give you the things you've only dreamed of."

No one knew those, because Amelia had never shared them with anyone. Even Meg didn't know the things Amelia had wondered if she could have.

"All you have to do is start talking to Him."

"I guess then I wouldn't have called you and woken you up. I'd be praying, and you'd have two things you wanted." Amelia chuckled, bringing a lightness to the conversation. There was something about what Meg had said that didn't weigh heavy the way some things did.

"You can call me anytime, girl. You know that."

"Thanks, Meg." Amelia pulled into the long drive that ran down the side of this monstrosity of a house and drove slowly toward her cabin. "I'll let you sleep now."

Amelia passed the big house and didn't see any sign that Kane and Maria were staying inside. No lights on. But that was by intention since they didn't want intruders to know anyone was waiting there.

She'd never had family worth anything after her stepdad died.

Ridge had lost his grandpa, a man who'd shaped who Ridge was even after the older man's tragic death. His family were the kind of people who showed up to help each other out, and it said a lot about the kind of man he was. The man she already knew him to be.

If she were going to pray, she'd pray she measured up to the woman he thought she could be.

EIGHTEEN

RIDGE PUT THE LAST DISH IN THE DISHWASHER and turned it on. He wiped down the kitchen counters, because it was much nicer to wake up to a clean kitchen than stuff everywhere and food dried on the Formica.

This was the first house he'd owned, and he'd discovered he liked it a lot better than renting apartments. Maybe because he didn't have to be here alone. Until they grew up a little more and left home for college, or got a place of their own, he'd have the twins here.

Ridge went down the hall and knocked on their door.

He could hear soft music playing. Not the kind he'd ever listen to, but it wasn't terrible. The soft sound of conversation halted.

"Come in."

He couldn't tell which one of them said that, but it wasn't unusual. From the day they'd been born, he had made sure he was the big brother they came to and their friend. Ridge didn't know his dad because he hadn't stuck around, and the twins' father hadn't lasted all that long either.

At fourteen, he'd known he would never be the kind of man

who left his kids. The twins were his sisters, and he'd have to be dead before he abandoned them.

No way would he be the kind of guy either of their fathers had been.

Or the kind of parent who would sign their rights away, like Mom had so they could stay with Ridge.

He eased the door open. The girls had twin beds pushed to either side, end tables between them. They sat sideways on their beds, backs to the wall. Books on their laps. They had a rug on the floor and an armchair in the corner that they'd picked up from a yard sale and made him load into his truck so they could bring it home. The room looked like a college dorm.

"Did you guys get your homework done?" He didn't want to launch into a conversation about Amelia right away, but that was what he wanted to talk about before he left them to it.

Maddie shot him a look. "It's never done."

Ridge smiled. "And your chores?"

Ella said, "I did mine."

Maddie made a face. "Fine. I need a break anyway, and the dryer is probably done."

"Pretty sure that load has been in there since yesterday," Ridge said. "Not that I'm better about that."

"Better at hiding things though."

Ridge glanced at Ella. "Maybe you should just share with us what you're thinking rather than making comments under your breath." He felt like a father rather than a brother, and less like a friend the longer they lived with him. The friend part could come later, when they were adults. "Whatever you have to say, I want to listen."

"That was *her*, right?"

Ridge nodded. "Yes, Amelia is the one I dated a few times."

"Before she broke it off."

Maddie said, "You were pretty torn up about it."

There wasn't much point in arguing with that. "We only went out a couple of times."

"Then you shouldn't be kissing her now!" Ella pushed her books aside and got up off her bed, looking upset in a way he didn't see much. She was so quiet it was often hard to tell how she felt, let alone whether she was sad or having a hard time. "She didn't see how you felt about her before. Now she's back?"

Ridge wasn't sure he entirely grasped what the issue was.

Maddie slid her books off her lap and bent her legs, wrapping her arms around her knees. "You don't see it because you like her, but Ella thinks she's just using you."

Her sister shot her a look, a twin thing. The silent communication they understood but which no one else was privy to.

"She isn't using me." Ridge wasn't going to share all that Amelia had been through. "She had good reason to break it off, given the awful relationship she was in before."

Ella didn't say anything.

"She was in a bad relationship?" Maddie asked, concern in her tone.

"The kind I'm going to pray neither of you ever get in." They'd know that meant he wasn't about to explain more than that. "She has reason to be wary, but relationships are about trust. We've worked together for a long time, but neither of us shares much that's personal."

"Because you don't want people to know we live here?" Ella's voice sounded so small.

Ridge shook his head. "I keep my personal and my professional lives separate. Not because I'm ashamed of you or don't want anyone to know I'm your guardian. It's the kind of person I am that I want to live a quiet life. Uncle Kane wants to save the world, and Maria was in the CIA. But I'm just a small-town guy living a simple life."

Maddie said, "But you don't tell people we live here."

He could tell they'd been worrying about this, which meant they'd been talking about it with each other. Enough he had to explain and put their fears to rest. "The kind of things I see at work, the kind of calls I go on . . . I get nightmares. I wake up in a cold sweat. I don't want you guys to know those things because they're mine to live with. Keeping that dividing line between home and work helps me leave work at work, so that when I'm home, it's just you guys and the town house and our peaceful lives."

Ella's expression turned thoughtful.

"Does that make sense?"

Maddie nodded.

"I'm not ashamed of you. Either of you. I want you guys here, and not just because I'd be worried if you were anywhere else."

"Because Mom is a loser."

Ridge's eyes widened. "I don't want you to talk disparagingly about her."

Ella chimed in. "Even if it's true?"

He moved into the room and opened his arms. The girls hugged him from either side. "Maybe one day she'll explain it to us and we'll understand, but it won't make it hurt less. Right now we have to make sure her actions don't make us bitter toward relationships. Or scared to trust people who are worth it because they are good people."

Maddie said, "Amelia should know you're good."

Their heads reached his chin, which meant he couldn't see the look he was sure they shared. He said, "I think she's figuring it out. I at least made progress today."

"Gross." The twins started laughing.

Ella said, "I don't want to know about you kissing anyone."

Ridge smiled, holding them tight in the hug. "Whatever happens, I'll keep you guys apprised."

"Maybe we don't need *all* the details."

"I'm not going anywhere."

"Because of Amelia." Maddie lifted her chin, smiling at him. "Guess we aren't moving to Benson."

"We're still talking about colleges," he said. "I'm not budging on this."

A slight flicker in Maddie's expression caught his eye.

"Mads?"

"I just . . . had an idea about summer. That's all. Ella doesn't want to do it, so she'll still be here."

"It's not about college?"

They stepped out of the hug, and Ella sat back on the bed. Ridge sat on the armchair and waited for Maddie to explain.

She sat on the edge of the bed, her back straight. Like she was nervous about the outcome—which meant she cared about his opinion of the choices she made. She took a breath and said, "I've heard about this camp. It's in Ember, Montana. They have, like, a summer thing for people my age, where they teach them how to be wildland firefighters." She looked at him, a mix of hope and earnestness in her gaze.

"Is that what you want to do?" he said carefully. "Be a hotshot?"

Had Kane and Maria been telling stories about the couple of years they'd just spent as wildland firefighters? If they had persuaded Maddie to do this, then his cousin was going to get a right hook to the chin.

His Maddie? Fighting wildfires?

Maddie shrugged her slender shoulders. "I don't know. It's just for the summer, and I'll be safe there. It's called Wildlands Academy."

Ridge said, "I've heard of it. I know the people who run it." Did he want to let Maddie go to that place when Charlie had told him some hair-raising stories? "How did you find out about it?"

"Alexis."

"Charlie's daughter?"

Maddie frowned. "I don't know. She was on the cheerleading

team when I was a freshman, and we still talk. She's an EMT now, but she spent the summer in Montana last year. She said it was amazing."

Ridge turned to her sister. "Ella, how do you feel about Maddie going to learn how to fight wildfires?"

Ella hadn't completely snapped out of her funk, but she seemed a little more animated now. And a little less irritated at finding Ridge in the kitchen kissing Amelia. Then again, he'd been as surprised as anyone else that his evening had turned out like that.

She brushed hair back from her face. "We need to know what we're capable of. That we can be strong and do something that means we've gotta be tough. Or smarter than someone else."

"You don't have to prove anything to anyone."

Ella said, "But if we don't see what we're made of, then we never know what we can do."

Ridge frowned at her. "When did you get to be so wise?"

Ella's eyes smiled and her cheeks pinked.

"It's not for months yet," Maddie said. "I can't even apply until spring. But if I don't know what I want to do, maybe I can try some different things. See what I like. Do I have to go to college?"

Ridge wanted to say yes, unequivocally. But this wasn't about what he wanted. "Not right away. There isn't a rush."

Maddie said, "Uncle Kane told me to pray about it. To ask God what He wanted me to do."

"I guess we're all getting wiser and wiser."

Maddie smiled.

Ridge blew out a breath. "And old people get tired." They thought he was ancient because he was older than thirty—and sometimes he felt it. Especially after a long shift followed by a long evening.

Ella said, "And they have to do their chores."

He laughed on his way to the door. "Touché."

Ridge glanced back before he shut it, pretty sure he was going to get Ella a kitten this Christmas. Maddie probably needed a new phone. Ridge knew what he wanted, but only Amelia could give him a chance to prove to her that a relationship could work.

He headed to his room and flopped on the bed. Deep down he was a little boy with a flighty mom and no father, a boy who'd lost his anchor after Grandpa had died. Kane had been his brother and best friend, because Kane's mom wasn't so different from her sister.

Ridge had always avoided risk so he could do what he knew he'd succeed at. Even firefighting, and with rescue squad. He'd taken far longer than anyone had expected to finally go for lieutenant. He'd only gone after it once it was a sure thing.

The first time he and Amelia had dated, he'd played it safe. This time there was nothing for him to prove to himself. What he needed to do was show her that he was worth taking a risk.

Not just because being together made sense every way he looked at it—at least, it would once he wasn't her boss anymore. But also because he wanted, with everything in him, to make her life as happy as it could be.

Because it was what she deserved.

NINETEEN

GO." BRYCE CLICKED THE BUTTON ON THE STOP-watch.

Amelia grabbed her gear, piece by piece, and pulled it on. Rain drizzled from the sky, dampening everything. She was soaked from standing out here for so long in the afternoon precipitation.

Turnout coat.

Air tank.

Thankfully it wasn't also freezing, or this would be miserable. But she had to be able to do her job in any weather, and if the department needed her to prove she could be who she knew she was . . .

Well, as far as she was concerned, they were going to give her that paper whether they liked it or not.

She raced to the bottom of the wooden stairs of the training house and grabbed the rail. It swayed with the force of her grasp, but she ignored how precarious this might be and raced up the stairs.

Total focus.

"Go, Patterson! Go!" Izan shouted from over by the display monitors under the white awning. He even had a cup of coffee.

She entered the training house, which was considerably warmer than outside and thick with smoke so heavy it obscured everything. But she knew this place inside out and backward—unless Bryce and Izan had moved a wall again. That had been a fun day. She was pretty sure she still had that dent in her forehead.

Get the rescue dummy and get out. Efficiency.

No thinking about Ridge and the fact she'd blown him off yesterday. It was far better to get this lieutenant paperwork because she had passed the test. Again. Then they'd be on even footing, and she wouldn't feel so off-kilter around him.

"Fire department! Make some noise if you can hear me!" Amelia searched the first room, sweeping through so she didn't miss a corner. Or come up on a wall too fast. Nice and steady.

No surprises.

No thinking about kissing Ridge. Or wondering what his sisters thought about her. He'd obviously told them something, because they'd seemed to know who she was. *Focus.* She'd fought this battle all day yesterday, going for a punishing trail run just to get her head clear.

Blasting music.

Pounding out miles until she was too exhausted to worry about any of it. A couple of times, she thought someone might have been following her, but it had turned out to be Maria. Because apparently she needed an ex-CIA agent as a bodyguard.

No complaints on that count.

If Ridge wanted to make sure she was safe, that was his business. She slept a whole lot better now than she had only a week ago, thanks to him.

Amelia entered the next room, and someone tall brushed past her. "Hello?"

This had to be part of the exercise. Bryce was throwing her off her game.

"Fire department!"

Izan wouldn't be able to see anything on the cameras, and it was too hot for heat sensing. The whole room would be a blurry mess. He was on comms though.

"Guys," Amelia said into her radio. "Is there someone else in here with me? This wasn't supposed to be a rescue."

Her air tank yanked backward, pulling her with it. As if it had snagged on something and she was hung up with no way to get free without unhooking herself. Amelia spun around. "Who's there?"

No one answered on the radio.

"Collins!" Why wasn't Izan responding to her?

Amelia needed to get out of this house.

She backtracked out of the room she was in and turned right, down the hall. Two doors. She found the end and shoved it open, breathing hard like she had been chased all the way out. Ran down the stairs. Over to where Bryce stood.

He clicked the stopwatch. "You'll have to be quicker than that, Patterson."

She tore off her helmet and mask. "What was that? There was someone in there."

Bryce flinched. "Izan!" He headed for the awning.

Amelia followed him.

"Did anyone go inside?"

Izan's dark features drew together. "Only person in there was you, Patterson."

"Someone brushed past me." She folded her arms, the bulky turnout coat making her bigger. "I wasn't the only person in there."

"I can show you the footage."

"Show me where I got on comms talking to you and you never responded."

Izan looked at the headphones next to him on the desk. "Uh . . . oops?"

She stared at him.

Bryce said, "Okay, okay. Maybe there was a rescue dummy we

missed hanging somewhere. Or you snagged an obstruction. You need to run it again, Amelia."

She pressed her lips together. He was her superior right now, not a firefighter who was the same rank as her. But unlike Ridge, this wasn't about feelings. Bryce was a professional, and so was she—which was how it had always been and how it would stay.

If he wanted to, he could make things hard for her.

He could even block her ability to take the lieutenant's test. Which meant that, right now, her success would depend on her ability to keep her mouth shut and not mouth off because she was annoyed.

"The test is in a few days, and you need to complete the course like you've been training for months, not like you only found out about it three days before."

Amelia wanted to let out a grunt of frustration, which was why she didn't.

She turned around and stomped back to her starting position, using all the frustration and anger she felt about this entire situation to fuel her movements with the strength and energy she needed. But it wasn't about proving to the department that they were right to have faith in her as a lieutenant.

That should've been what it was about.

But no.

It was about gaining the same rank as Ridge. Which was the same reason he'd become a lieutenant—to put them on equal footing.

So they could date.

Did she want a relationship with Ridge? If the past few days were anything to go by, the answer to that was yes.

Was she terrified of the idea? Also yes.

Though she figured that was normal.

". . . even listening?"

She glanced at Bryce, who had rain running down his face. Wet hair, wet clothes. She nearly said no but caught herself. "Just tell me when to go and I'll do this."

Amelia eased into a slight crouch. Soft knees. Ready to move as fast as she could.

"Are you good?"

"Of course." He just needed to hit the stopwatch and say the word.

Soon enough, the others were going to show up. She didn't want to do this with an audience. Who wanted to fail in front of people when they could fail in private?

He turned his head to the side. "Izan, got the headphones on?"

"Yep!" he called out over the space. Then in her comms earbud, she heard, "Copy me, Lieut—uh, Patterson?"

"Yeah." She wanted to sigh. "I read you loud and clear, Collins."

Bryce called out, "Ready?"

She yelled back, "Ready!"

"Go!"

Amelia got her gear on and raced up the stairs. She wanted to kick the door open, but that would cost her crucial seconds. Who knew what surprises they had in store for her? Not walls in different places or rescue dummies to trip over, but there were some tricks they could implement.

She kept her head and scanned the space.

"Fire department! Call out if you can hear me!"

The thick smoke in the air had a blue-gray tint to it now, which could be part of the new problem they were likely cooking up for her. Literally. That color smoke usually meant burning oil, and they generally only saw it in old houses, car accident fires, or in a garage.

Another thing she didn't need to be distracted by.

Search the house, every room, and get out the far side. If she came across anyone, she would "rescue" them along the way.

She moved quickly but as steady as she could and didn't waste time in the room where she thought she'd spotted someone.

There was no one there.

Just as she'd—

Grasping hands tore the radio from the front of her turnout coat. She swung out at whoever had grabbed it, but no one was there.

Her mask was torn off, dragging her forward with it. She bent, but he didn't let up. She gasped and inhaled the thick gray air. *Can't breathe.*

He shoved her back against the wall. At least, she assumed it was a guy. She couldn't see him but got the sense that he was taller and more powerful than her, and she was quickly overwhelmed.

A split second later, strong hands grabbed her around the neck. With all the gear she had on, it was her only vulnerable spot. The break in the collar at her throat, bare skin. The neck of her jacket and the bottom of her helmet, which had gone flying. She was exposed, and he knew exactly how to target her.

When. Where.

He'd ensured no one knew she was in danger in the training house. So close to the rest of the fire crew, showing up for their shift.

She grabbed her attacker's arms and called for help the only way she could—by yelling. "Izan!"

Her attacker squeezed her throat.

The radio was too far, torn off her. Probably broken. There was no way Izan could even hear her right now. No one was going to come and help her. She had to get out of this situation herself.

Amelia tried to get air. She couldn't peel his arms off her throat. His grip was too tight.

She couldn't see his face, not clearly. It looked like he had a mask on—something to protect his lungs from the choking air in here. The smoke had thickened until she could barely see her hand in front of her face. Or his face in front of hers.

His fingers tightened on her throat.

I'm going to die.

Amelia slammed her gloved hands against him and fought for her life. When he didn't let go, she tightened her grip on his arms, shifted her weight, and brought her knee up. She wasn't going to hit any planned target, but kneeing him anywhere at all was going to hurt. She was pretty sure she managed to catch him in the stomach.

He backed up his hips, hopefully surprised and injured. Trying to get out of reach of the next swing of her knee. But he didn't let go of her neck, so she didn't let go of his arms. There was no way she would go down without a fight.

His grip on her neck started to loosen. She didn't have much time before he rallied, maybe a second at most. Enough time to kick him again, twice in quick succession. She put all of her strength into the double swing of her knee. Hard as she could.

Finally his hands fell away. She shoved at him, ramming him back, and ran for where she thought the door was. *Turnabout's fair play, buddy.* He slammed against the wall.

But she wasn't sticking around, breathing in this toxic air, just to finish him off.

Amelia hit a wall, traced it to the end, and found a door. Her head swam. Each inhale was a desperate gasp for air. She nearly collapsed, the hallway beyond it long and clouded to obscurity. "Help." The word was barely audible.

She had to get out of here before she succumbed, because they had no idea she was down.

Izan should've been on the radio.

Why wasn't the overhead speaker system echoing with his voice?

They should've shut the whole exercise down by now.

What was he seeing on the cameras?

Or not—as the case might be.

Amelia collapsed onto her hands and knees, choking. She had to get up, or she wasn't going to make it out of here. Whatever was tinting the smoke in the air right now seemed to be something entirely different from simulated smoke.

And it was going to kill her if she didn't get out of here.

TWENTY

RIDGE SHOWED UP EARLY FOR HIS RECKONING with Amelia. He knew she would be here well before their shift started, and not just because he'd had Kane text when she left the house. She'd been here at least an hour, and he'd forced himself not to jump on the time.

Turned out to be a good thing, given the activity over at the training house.

A light drizzle dampened everything. Not even enough rain to run the wipers in his truck, but enough to put him in a bad mood. She had responded to him yesterday. She hadn't completely ghosted him, but she'd also told him she was too busy studying for the lieutenant's test to get together on their day off. The first chance at a date in years—not officially, since they weren't supposed to—and she'd turned him down.

Ridge slammed the truck door.

Della looked over from her white compact. "Uh-oh."

He slung his duffel over his shoulder and strode toward her. "Don't worry about it. How are you?"

Della shot him an inquisitive look before rounding her car to the sidewalk.

Part of him wanted to sit on the three-foot-tall brick wall at the edge of the firehouse property and not even go in or face Amelia. "No, I'm serious. How are you?"

Della said, "O-kay, assuming you're not having some kind of medical emergency that's making you want to get personal . . . I'm fine, thank you, how are you?"

Ridge squeezed the bridge of his nose. "We're not the personal types. I know. But it's just small talk." He was going to have to start somewhere if he wanted to be a better leader and a better team-mate. That meant letting in more than just Amelia. "For example, I tried that new chicken place at lunch. The spicy chicken bacon sandwich was really good, but the fries were only mediocre."

Zoe walked over with her backpack on both shoulders and her hair in two braids that started at the top of her head. "What are we talking about?"

Della said, "Lunch."

Zoe frowned. "What?"

"We're trying small talk." Ridge tried not to act like this was completely awkward, but of course it was.

Della frowned. "Fine. My grandmother was making aloo gobi because I'm going to be gone, and I don't like it. She'll probably eat it for breakfast, lunch, and dinner while I'm on shift. And she thinks I'll never keep a man unless I learn how to make saag paneer better than I do right now." She lifted her chin. "Is that good enough?"

"It's not about *good enough*," Ridge said. "It's about getting to know each other."

"We need to get inside." Della wandered off toward the door.

"Can we do this in the kitchen, not in the rain? My hair is gonna frizz." Zoe followed Della, jogging to catch up so the two women could walk together.

Ridge heard Bryce shout something, so he headed for the training house to the side of the main firehouse building. They still had fifteen minutes before the briefing started. When Bryce ran over to Izan, his body language signaled that there was a problem.

Ridge jogged over. "What's going on?"

Izan set his phone down, a game open on the screen. He motioned to the screens in front of him. "There's nothing wrong. She's right there." He pointed, but Ridge couldn't see the monitor.

"She hasn't come out yet." Bryce sounded worried. "She should be done by now."

"So she met up with one of our surprises, that's all." Izan shrugged. "It's Amelia in there, not a rookie."

Bryce turned to Ridge.

"She asked you guys for help with lieutenant training?" Ridge didn't know what to think about that. She hadn't asked *him* for help, and why not?

"We need to make sure there's nothing wrong in the training house." Bryce grabbed his radio on the strap across his body and squeezed the sides. "Patterson, do you copy?"

No answer.

"Patterson, report in."

Ridge dropped his duffel under the table to keep it out of the rain coming under the pop-up awning. "How long has she been in there?"

Izan lifted his phone to look at the screen. "Nine minutes."

Ridge started off walking but quickly broke into a jog over to the exit door of the training house. In there for that long, she had to have made progress through the course. That meant she'd be closer to the end than the beginning.

Right?

He hoped so.

Ridge pounded up the stairs on the far side of the squat two-story structure. Underneath was mostly storage, but the upper level was a fabricated residence they used to put rookies through their paces. He was three steps from the top when the door swung out and Amelia fell through the opening.

She stumbled against the rail, tipped over, and fell to the ground level.

"Amelia!" Ridge jumped back down the stairs and rounded the bottom, moving to where she lay on the asphalt in her gear.

Face flushed. No mask or helmet. She still had her air tank on. Her radio was missing, her turnout coat open at the front.

"Amelia." He landed on the ground on his knees, ignoring how much that hurt.

Ridge turned his head, about to yell for help, when he saw Bryce race over, followed by Izan. "She needs medical attention." He took Amelia's head in his hands and lifted her eyelids. Her pupils were dilated and didn't react—maybe that was due to the dim light outside. The clouds were blocking sunlight. He checked her pulse even though he didn't want to.

Thank You, Lord.

"She's breathing."

Bryce squeezed his shoulder, but the move did nothing to re-assure Ridge.

He pulled the tabs on her coat, opening it so he could check for injuries. The red marks on her neck didn't look good. "What . . ."

"She didn't have those marks when she went inside."

"They're from someone's hands." A person in the training house, who had tried to strangle her to death while she was running the exercise. His gut burned. *She could've died.* "Who went in there?" Ridge held Amelia's hand because he needed the warm reassurance to keep him from totally flipping out.

"No one," Izan said, worry in his tone. "She was the only one in there. I was watching the monitors."

"Go get the chief," Bryce ordered. "Tell him I'm calling 911." Bryce got up, his cell phone in his hand.

Kianna and Trace ran around the corner of the training house, carrying some of their gear. "What happened?"

Ridge sat back on his heels, still holding Amelia's hand. "I have no idea."

They crouched around her, listening to her breathing. Talking to each other in phrases that meant something to them and should mean something to him, but right now he couldn't process any of it. His mind was a firestorm of fear he couldn't control. Like the second when lightning flashed across the sky and everything paused for a moment, as if the world held its breath.

A sound cut through the haze, and he realized the HVAC unit under the training house had kicked on to vent the smoke inside. Ridge wanted to get in there and look for whoever had attacked Amelia, but he also didn't want to leave her side.

"I'll bring the ambulance over." Kianna touched his arm. "She's going to the hospital."

Amelia had an oxygen mask over her face now. Kianna jumped up and raced away.

"Is she going to be okay?" He glanced at Trace and knew he'd see how Ridge felt about Amelia. And not just because he hadn't let go of her hand.

"She inhaled something nasty." Trace looked up at the house. "Find out what it is and the doctors will be better able to treat her."

"And the strangle marks on her neck?"

"They aren't helping things," Trace said. "Figure this out before it gets worse."

Kianna drove the ambulance around the corner and parked it close. They loaded Amelia on a gurney, and as soon as the doors were shut, Ridge jogged back around the house. Izan and Bryce stood with Chief James and a few of the other firefighters.

Ridge said, "Truck 14 is out of service until you can get floaters to cover me and Amelia." Now he was going to check that house. "Is it clear?" He pointed at the structure.

"It will be in a second." Chief James lifted one brow. "I'll call headquarters and put the request in to get your shift covered."

A cop car pulled into the driveway and stopped over by the training house so they weren't in the way of an engine going out in a hurry.

The setup with the monitors let out a long buzz.

"It's clear." Izan leaned down. "I backed up the footage, and she moves through rooms, but I don't see anyone else. And she doesn't look like she's in trouble. Unless . . ."

"What?" Chief James rounded the table to stand beside Izan and look at the screens. Something similar had happened to the chief's wife, Natalie, when she'd been getting to know the firefighters over a year ago. Was Macon reminded of that right now?

"I think this is footage from the first time she went through. It's just been repeated so we had no idea what was happening." Izan shook his head. "No wonder it seemed boring. I'd watched it once already."

Ridge motioned to Bryce. "Let's go."

They moved to the stairs that led up to the entrance door. Bryce said, "You don't think whoever attacked her is still in there, do you?"

"A little gun-shy since you tangled with a cartel and dirty politicians?"

"My fighting days are over. I'm getting married. There will be no more kidnapping, car chases, bad guys, or fighting for my life. Thank you very much."

Ridge chuckled, but the humor didn't last long. Officer Thomas hurried up the stairs behind them and said, "Want the guy with the gun to go first?"

Bryce shrugged. "I doubt there's anyone in here."

"Still." Anthony eased by them and checked it out. He disappeared into another room in the house and called out, "There's an open window over here."

Ridge and Bryce found him.

"And a ladder." Anthony stuck his upper body out the window. "Only goes down a few rungs, then they jumped. There are shoe prints in the dirt."

"So we know someone was in here." Ridge folded his arms. "We just have no idea who."

Bryce said, "Maybe Patterson saw something."

"Or someone across the street." Anthony thumbed over his shoulder. "I'll go knock on doors. Maybe someone has a camera that saw something."

"I'm going to the hospital to check on Amelia." Ridge clenched his jaw. "She could've died in here."

Bryce didn't look much happier than Ridge felt. "I'll find out what was in the air. And how the computers were messed with. We'll figure it out."

Ridge nodded. They walked through the house but didn't see anything else. He picked up Amelia's helmet and mask and the broken radio. "What about pulling prints from this?"

Officer Thomas said, "Running prints takes weeks, and you just picked it up."

Meaning he'd smudged any that had been there. "So we have no way to find this person unless Amelia saw them."

"Detective Cartwright is working something right now. I'll keep you posted if Jess manages to ID any of the guys you've all seen so far."

"Great." He tried to sound like he had confidence in them, but there was far too much at stake to sit back and do nothing.

Ridge was going to employ some investigators of his own. This situation was getting out of control. Someone was targeting Amelia, and aside from the mysterious hidden money, they had no idea who was behind it. Or how far they intended to go.

She needed someone to watch her back.

TWENTY-ONE

AMELIA SWIPED THE SCREEN OF THE TABLET through another set of images. Mug shots. Detective Jessica Cartwright and Officer Olivia Tazwell sat drinking their coffees, nonchalantly waiting for her to go through the series of images, as if they had nothing better to do than be here.

On the other side of the closed door, the bustle of the hospital kept to a low level, but she could hear nurses talking. A phone ringing. The overhead intercom system.

Her doctor had thoroughly checked her out, told her to not remove the clean-air mask until he said she could, and sent off vials of her blood so they could run whatever tests. But being out of the training house and breathing clear air had brought her back to the land of conscious people.

Amelia didn't like the idea she'd been vulnerable. Not one bit. She was a firefighter, not the victim in any scenario.

Even sitting up in a hospital bed, wearing one of their terrible gowns and all tucked in with blankets like a little kid, made her feel weak in a way she didn't like. It was far too close to the kid she'd been after her stepdad died, subjected to whatever her father ordered her to do when he had visitation. Quit basketball. Give up piano. Mow the lawn at the big house while her brother threw rocks at her.

As an adult, she'd become the kind of woman who didn't see the signs until it was too late. Who accepted things with a man as normal because he said the right things. Or apologized after. Only when she'd begun to push back had Nicholas kicked up his narcissism another notch. Tearing her down by convincing everyone else—and her—that she had lost her grip on reality.

"You okay?"

Amelia looked over at Jess. "My mind is wandering."

The detective smiled. She was about the same age as Amelia but not someone she'd hung out with. Amelia did know that her husband was a tech genius who worked online and made tons of money creating amazing tech programs Amelia would never understand. Her husband's brother was Dean, who ran the Ridgeman Center up in the mountains. Their paths had crossed because Dean worked with Kelsey and Natalie—Trace's and Macon's wives.

In a town like this, she knew plenty of people's business. It was why she'd determined to keep to herself. No one needed to know she was Steven Hilden's daughter. Except, now it seemed like everyone knew. So all that trying to keep things private hadn't worked at all. The truth was out.

Jessica wore black slacks and a white shirt, a cargo jacket over it that had a tie for around her waist. A gun holstered on her hip and the police shield on her belt both displayed who she was. She was blonde, like Olivia and Amelia, making Amelia wonder if they'd planned this. Sending these two women to reassure her because neither was a guy officer she didn't know.

"We can take a break if you want." Jessica got up and tossed her empty paper cup in the tiny trash can in the corner.

"It won't make a difference." Amelia let the tablet fall flat on her lap. "He had a mask on, so I never saw his face. Like I didn't see the guy's face at the fires. I have no idea who is doing this."

"It was worth a try just looking." Jessica took the tablet from her.

Olivia said, "It's always worth a try." Officer Tazwell had her uniform on, comforting Amelia by her presence in a different way than Jess's gun and badge did.

"I appreciate your coming here and trying."

Both of them seemed surprised. Jess said, "Of course."

Amelia had realized, in that moment in the training house when she'd thought she was dying alone, that she had friends close by. There were people in her life who cared about her.

Cared if she lived or died.

And they had come to her aid. She knew that, because Ridge had been here when she'd woken up. He'd gone down to the cafeteria to get them both something to eat and would be back soon enough. The worry on his face when she'd opened her eyes had been enough to let her know how he felt about her.

She wasn't alone.

"Anything else?" Jess asked. "Or we'll get out of your hair."

Amelia bit her lip. "Have you had a chance to look up my brother?" After she thought she'd seen him in that crowd, she'd contacted Jessica, but now she wasn't sure what to think. Since she'd never been mentally unstable—despite what her ex had done to her—there had to be an explanation.

Jess eased back onto the chair, sitting on the edge of the seat with her hands clasped between her knees. "We ran his name." She indicated Olivia with a chin lift.

Officer Tazwell said, "Nasty rap sheet."

"He's been in prison for more than ten years." Amelia hadn't seen him and didn't want to.

Jess frowned. "He was released a month ago. Didn't anyone inform you?"

"Like, as a courtesy?" When they indicated yes, Amelia said, "I'm not listed as his family. I have a different name. No one is supposed to know we're related."

"I'll call his parole officer. Make sure he's squared away, following the rules. There will be conditions on his release, and if you believe he means you harm, then I'd recommend filing a restraining order."

Amelia wanted to point out that a paper wouldn't deter her brother from doing whatever he wanted. But the reality was, it would enable the police to lock him back up if he violated it. He had to follow the law, or he couldn't be free.

"Are you worried he might come after you?" Olivia asked her.

Amelia blew out a breath. "I have no idea. I thought I saw him, and now that I know he's been released from prison, I guess that makes sense."

Jess picked up the line of thinking when Amelia stopped, saying, "Whether or not that makes him part of what's happening to you is something we'll need to find out. I'll track him down through his parole officer and get an alibi for the times you were accosted. Does that sound good?"

Olivia stood. "At least it would rule out his involvement if he can prove he had nothing to do with these attacks." She went to the door and opened it, revealing Ridge holding a tray. "We'll leave you to your dinner."

Jess took the tablet and handed Amelia her card. "Call me direct with any questions, or if you have a problem. Any problem."

"Thanks." Amelia held on to the card, watching them leave.

Ridge eased the door shut with his foot. "Did it go okay?"

"I didn't recognize any of the pictures, but I think I gained two friends."

He smiled, set the tray on the rolling table that would go over the bed, and wheeled it to her. "That's good, right?"

"It's different." She was different.

At least, that's how it felt. Given everything that'd happened over the past week or so, who wouldn't be shaken or off-kilter?

Before he could ask her about it, she said, "Are you really missing a shift just because I'm here? You should be running Truck 14 so that I know it's in good hands while I'm working on getting my rank back." She shot him a look. "One tiny issue and you've abandoned your post."

His brows rose. Ridge sat by her feet on the end of the bed. "You want me to leave?"

"No."

He stared a little longer. "Good, because I'm right where I want to be."

Now what was she supposed to do with that?

Amelia grabbed the bowl that turned out to have grains, beans, and pieces of chicken in it. And it smelled amazing. "Who knew hospital food would actually be good?"

She swallowed a big bite so she didn't have to talk and say things she wasn't ready to say.

Ridge grabbed a couple of fries from beside his burger and folded them into his mouth. Once he was done chewing, he said, "How are you feeling?"

She held the bowl with one hand, her fork with the other. Pausing before the next bite, she said, "Like someone tried to kill me."

She knew what the marks on her throat looked like.

As if someone had tried to strangle her.

His gaze lowered to her neck. "You got out of there. If you hadn't, you might've . . ." He cleared his throat.

"I'm glad it worked out."

"The trick will be making sure nothing like that happens again. Not to you or anyone else." Ridge grabbed his burger and took a bite. He'd never even changed into his uniform for the shift. She needed her bag of street clothes from the firehouse if she was going to have something to wear when she left—which would be a good idea. Hospital gowns were breezy.

They ate in companionable silence for a few minutes. She was eyeing the pudding cups, wondering what flavor they were, when he said, "Can we talk about yesterday?"

Amelia didn't want to. At least, the Amelia she'd been the past few years anyway. The person she seemed to be now, the woman she wanted to be—who was open and relied on her friends—might be willing to share.

"I really did have things to do," she said. "I had to do three loads of laundry to catch up on everything, and I cleaned my whole cabin. Plus I went for a run."

The edge of a smile pulled at his lips. "Maria said she had a hard time keeping up at a couple of points."

"I need to stay in shape if I'm going to pass the lieutenant's qualifier. The written test is one thing, but the training exercise as well? Bryce told me I have to show up like someone who's been training for months."

Ridge had to concede that, right? He'd just taken it.

"How long did you prep for?"

He smiled. "Months. The girls helped me study, getting me on this app that has flashcards."

"Because heaven forbid we use paper for anything these days." She rolled her eyes. "Why is there an app for everything?"

He chuckled. "I do better writing it out on paper. But they wanted to help me, so they showed me all their tricks."

"That's really nice."

He patted her knee.

"I'm glad you made it." Amelia really was happy for him.

"You'll make it back there as well. Of course you will."

"And then we'll be allowed to date officially." She froze.

His brows rose again. But was it really so surprising?

Amelia said, "If I pass the test, we'll be the same rank. Truck 14 or rescue squad, we'll be back on equal footing." She shrugged like it was no big deal, when actually it was *everything* right now.

"It's why I . . . blew you off yesterday. So I could focus and get there faster."

"So we can date."

Amelia shrugged, but the answer was yes.

Ridge said, "Why don't I help you study?"

"Too distracting." She shook her head. "I'll have a couple of days off after this—"

"More like a whole week."

"I can lie in bed and study. Then get back to the gym."

"Stay at the town house." He seemed to have surprised himself saying that.

"I don't need to."

"You'll be alone at the cabin. I'll worry." Ridge cleared his throat. "Stay at the town house, and I'll sleep on the couch. The girls can take care of you on evenings I'm on shift. Kane and Maria can watch your place and the town house since there's two of them. Or we can all move to the mansion."

"That monstrosity." She made a face. "We should, just to stick it to my father. I hope he rolls over in his grave with all the trouble he's causing me. We should throw a party in the house and invite a bunch of church people to come by and do their thing. Cleanse it from evil or something."

He grinned. "Or something."

"I thought it was a good idea."

He stood up and came over, hands on either side of her on the bed. He lowered down in a kind of push-up until his face was close to hers. "It was an adorable idea."

"I'm not normally adorable."

"I like it." Ridge touched his lips to hers.

The woman she wanted to be now kissed him back. That was when she knew there was no turning back.

Ridge was what she wanted.

TWENTY-TWO

RIDGE WEDGED THE LAST PIZZA BOX INTO THE trash, finally done cleaning up the town house. He eased over to the couch, slumped down on what would be his bed for the night, and let out a long sigh.

The doorbell rang.

He groaned and got up again. Given the state of things lately, he checked the app on his phone and saw it was Kane and Maria at the door. They'd missed pizza, but they were here now? Who was watching the house?

"Hey." He stepped back, opening the door all the way so they could come in. As usual, the twins had upped the temperature in the house because it was chilly outside. They didn't know he set it to lower dramatically overnight and then kick back on and warm the town house an hour before they woke up.

Maria came in first, then Kane. "Hey."

"I thought you guys were supposed to be watching the house."

Kane offered him a fist bump. When Ridge tapped it, Kane said, "Cameras are set. We'll get alerts if anyone tries again, but we searched the place top to bottom. There's no money to find."

Ridge said, "And the other night?"

"We scared them off. If we're elsewhere, we'll get more information. The cops can use the camera feeds as evidence to make arrests."

Ridge knew how to put out fire, save lives, and protect property. He didn't know how police investigations worked or even have a clue what skills Kane and Maria had between them.

"Maria is gonna stay here." Kane stood in his entryway. "We're going out."

"I'm so tired I'm about ready to fall asleep," Ridge said. "Where are we going?"

"Out. Get changed." Kane waved at him. "You need to look . . . rough. Being tired will help. You'll look like you've been on a three-day bender."

"Great." Ridge probably had something older at the back of his closet—a checkered shirt he should've thrown out years ago and jeans he wore when he worked on his truck. "I'll be back in a sec."

He trailed down the hall and eased open the door to his room. The center of his bed had a lump, a form smaller than his, covered in enough blankets that there was only a small section of blonde hair visible.

She'd gone to bed shortly after they'd arrived, after just enough time to eat half a slice of pizza and tell the twins she would have more for breakfast. Apparently "everyone" knew pizza tasted better cold the next day? Ridge wasn't sure he believed that. She was exhausted from everything though, and rest would help her recover better than anything.

Ridge padded to his closet, through the bathroom. He changed quickly into a couple of things from the back, behind what he normally wore, and retrieved a pair of boots he'd had for years that he used when the weather was bad. He carried those back to the hall where he quietly shut the door.

Having Amelia in his bed like this wasn't something he'd contemplated much before. Thoughts like that just got a red-blooded male into trouble he didn't need to get into. Especially when he was living God's way right now.

It wasn't the scenario he'd ever envisioned, and she wouldn't be here long. No matter what happened, he'd be on the couch until there was a wedding band on her finger.

Right now, his focus needed to be on making sure she wasn't in any more danger, not thinking too much about kissing her again.

He knocked on the twins' door.

"Yeah."

Ridge stuck his head in. "I'm going out with Kane. Maria is here."

Maddie's expression lit up. "Sweet!" Both girls got up and came out with him.

Kane drove, which was fine by Ridge. The guy had a nice car. But Ridge still didn't know what they were doing. "Where are we going?"

This wasn't just about hanging out. There was something else his cousin had in mind.

"The cops have suspects, but they can't move on them until there's enough probable cause to get an arrest warrant." Kane headed for the highway, a couple of miles over from Ridge's neighborhood. "So we're gonna see if we can't get them some intel to run on."

"You're friends with cops now?" Ridge glanced over at his cousin, a notoriously solitary guy. Kane was the kind of person who had a small number of super-deep friendships. Once a person was "in," they were there for life, and that connection was soul deep.

Ridge was the same way because it was who they were. It was also who Grandpa had been.

Kane chuckled. "I commiserated with them over the red tape they're under. Kind of like military rules. Suggested I might be able to provide some assistance."

"You're a confidential informant now?" Ridge shook his head. "I thought you were gonna be a firefighter?"

Kane drummed his hands against the steering wheel. "I'm waiting for God to show us what we're supposed to be doing. We have options, but what's the answer?"

"Maybe it's not so much what you're doing but who you are. Could be there are plenty of paths, and there might not be one that's the most perfect life you could live."

Kane shrugged. "So focus on who I am, not who I'm supposed to be? At least that gives me something to do while I'm waiting."

"That could be the entire point of waiting."

"Even though we don't like it."

Ridge chuckled. "I'm glad it's not just me."

"You seem like you're making headway. I mean, she's staying at your house and not in that shed she lives in."

Ridge had to admit that was true. "I hope it sticks. It feels . . . fragile. And there's nothing about Amelia that's fragile. But I'm just hoping I don't do anything to mess it up."

"Making sure she's safe is going to help. So that's what we're gonna do. Plus, it'll make you feel better." Kane pulled into the parking lot of a roadhouse with a line of motorcycles in front. More motorcycles than Ridge had seen in the dealership the one time he'd gone to look.

With the twins in his life, he didn't want to take that risk. But one day he was going to get one.

Now he wanted to know what Amelia thought of bikes.

"Coming here will make me feel better?"

Kane said, "Let's go. Quit being terrified that something is going to happen to her. She's protected right now. We need to see if her brother is in there and ask a few of his friends where to find him if he isn't."

Ridge got out of the car without telling Kane he was right. Fact was, he'd hit the nail on the head with that one. Despite being exhausted, Ridge would likely have lain on the couch, worrying what was going to happen to Amelia next instead of sleeping. Either way, he'd wind up more exhausted. So they may as well do something.

A couple spilled out of the front door of the roadhouse, their boots clicking on the worn wood beams. The stumbling pair both wore jeans and button-down shirts. The woman had tucked her fitted shirt into tight jeans. She giggled, hanging on to the man, whose shirt remained untucked. He grinned, barely noticing Ridge and Kane coming in.

After sidestepping the two, who continued on down the porch steps, Ridge and Kane went inside. Music blared from speakers set high on the walls, an old classic rock song no one could argue with. The place was packed, an ocean of denim and leather. The sound of clinking glasses rang around him, and patches of floor were sticky when he stepped on them.

Kane headed for the bar, and Ridge followed him. He knew they looked similar enough to be mistaken for brothers, and that was fine by him. Kane ordered two beers, and they grabbed stools at the bar.

Kane turned slightly toward Ridge. "If I sit like this, I can see all the way from the front door to the pool tables."

"I can see the hallway to the restroom and who is coming and going. Who are we watching for?"

Kane unlocked his phone and showed Ridge a photo. "This is the prison-system image the police have. Truth is, they don't know what he looks like now. He could have a beard, and different clothes can be a disguise of their own."

"Elam Hilden."

Long blond hair about the same length as Amelia's fell over the man's shoulders, but that was where their similarities ended. Amelia's eyes had life in them. She knew how to hope and that dreams could be rescued from where they were buried and brought back to life. He kept praying she would one day understand that it was the power of God that resurrected things, but she hadn't embraced it yet.

"He could've cut his hair easily enough, but he's kept it this long." Ridge studied the image and the man's dead eyes. The set of his jaw and what looked like the corner of a tattoo at his collar. "Why do you think he'll be here?"

"It would take too long to explain. He might be. It's not a sure thing until it is." Kane took a sip of his drink.

Ridge did the same because they'd stick out if they didn't actually drink what they'd bought.

An hour later, a group of guys came in the front door. Friends all chatting and joking around, each of them the kind of kid who'd be found behind the sports storage sheds at school, smoking weed and trying to convince girls to skip class.

Four or five of them, and Elam was in the center. Like a man recently released from prison with a new lease on life.

One of Elam's friends collided with a guy on the way to the pool table. The guy spun around, about to give him what for. He spotted who it was in the center of the group and changed his mind.

Kane muttered, "Now, isn't that interesting."

"Maybe he's hiring and you can get in the group. Go undercover."

Kane said, "Why don't you?"

"Because I'm not the superhero."

Kane's attention shifted from the men across the room back to Ridge.

Ridge could see them in the mirrors behind the bar, shoving people off a pool table and taking over the game.

His cousin said, "What's that?"

"I'm not ex-military." Ridge shrugged. "I'm not some bigshot, trained, kill-you-with-my-thumb guy. Even your fiancée is scarier than I am."

Kane's lips twitched around the top of the bottle as he drank.

"I need to keep the twins safe so they can make poor choices and never replace the toilet roll in the bathroom because they know they're loved no matter what. No conditions."

"You're doing an amazing job."

"I'm not the undercover guy or the save-the-world guy like you are."

"That isn't a bad thing. Knowing who you aren't can be as powerful as knowing who you are." Kane tapped the top of his bottle against Ridge's. "You're a humble guy living life, making his community a better place. People are alive because of you."

He could say the same about Kane, but that happened on a much larger scale. Or it had, until he'd been cut loose into retirement. Kane needed a job in civilian life now. At least until next year's fire season started.

"You don't need to be something you aren't. That's not the guy Amelia is into."

Ridge took a drink, one eye on the glass mirror. "They're settling into their game."

"Then it's time to make our approach." Kane slid off the stool, taking his drink with him.

Ridge left cash on the bar and followed his cousin, hanging back while Kane approached the crew that included Amelia's brother.

Elam had his head down, his concentration on his shot.

Right before he hit the ball Kane said, "You probably didn't play much pool in prison."

Elam broke off from the shot and strode over, holding the pool cue by his shoulder. All of his guys shifted. He waved them back and stopped in front of Kane. "You think you can beat me? Otherwise, why mouth off when it only ends in a world of hurt for you?"

"We could put a wager on a game."

Elam's lips curled up in a sneer. "I'm gonna enjoy taking your money."

"I don't want money if I win," Kane said. "I want information."

Ridge kept part of his attention on Elam's friends, just in case this went sideways. Who knew if the guy would actually go through with what he'd said. Ridge didn't trust any of these guys. One of them could be the person who'd entered the training house and nearly killed Amelia.

"Let me guess." Elam lifted his chin. "You wanna know about my sister."

TWENTY-THREE

A CAR PULLED INTO THE DRIVE. AMELIA WATCHED as it rolled slowly down the gravel toward where she stood in front of the house. Kane and Maria were close by. The twins had gone to school hours ago, and Ridge had to be on shift later, but right now he was beside her.

The light breeze making everything feel colder than it should be ruffled her hair. At least it wasn't raining.

"Tell me again why we agreed to this?" She glanced at Ridge, who had been in the kitchen this morning making pancakes. Sweats and a tight T-shirt, his feet bare.

That little peek into his personal life had been like being launched away on a rollercoaster. They'd gone from easing into personal conversations to sleeping in the same house in just a week. She felt like she'd been spun around too fast and was still trying to get her balance at the sudden change.

"Flam offered information freely, but this was the price." He didn't look any happier about this situation than she was, which counted for something. But not enough to void the fact that he'd gone out with Kane last night and not woken her to tell her.

Though, the way he'd told it, Kane hadn't even told him they were going after Elam. Just that they were following a lead.

"He could have knocked on the door when he got out of prison." For her father, this would've been about leverage. And when had Elam been so different from him? "Now I have to let him walk through the house and do whatever he wants? There's nothing I can do about it. He could take anything . . . or burn the place down."

All that had been her fear every night she'd stayed in the cabin out back.

That something terrible would happen during the night.

But last night, she'd slept great and woken up in Ridge's bedroom—which had been a little unnerving, if she were honest. Her cabin had become a sanctuary, not just a home. His place was different from her style, but knowing she was safe in a way she might never have been before counted for a lot.

Ridge said, "It sounded like he just wanted to retrieve something."

Even though she didn't think there was a huge payout hidden somewhere by Steven Hilden, her brother might be aware of something in the house. A secret compartment where the old man had left . . . whatever he would leave. Amelia tried not to think about it.

"I hope so. This could go so many different ways, and most of them are nasty." She glanced at him. "Did I tell you what kind of kid he was?"

"Sorry, but it's a means to an end."

"I'm just scared." She had to admit that to someone. "Not that I think he's going to make my life a nightmare. It's that he *could*, but I have no idea if he intends to or not."

Ridge's expression softened. "I'm not going to let anything happen to you."

The car stopped on the gravel in front of them.

She felt Ridge's hand a second before he slid his fingers between hers. Her brother climbed out of the passenger side, which meant he had someone in his life he trusted to drive him around . . . or he was honoring the fact his license had no doubt expired while he was in prison.

He still had that long hair he'd grown in high school. Their father had hated it long and threatened to shave his head clean while he slept, but the elder Hilden had never followed through on it.

He'd much preferred the mental game of fear.

Elam's hair was tied back behind his head. He wore a T-shirt over jeans, with a denim jacket over the shirt. Black boots. Chains around his neck, and a few days' worth of stubble on his jaw. He was more slender than he'd been before prison, but at the same time he seemed more solid. As if he was tight-packed muscle under those clothes.

"Elam." She had no idea what to say. It wasn't really nice to see him, but she did live in his childhood home.

Did he want it back?

"If you want the house, you should just ask." Amelia tried to sound strong but not obstinate. With the weight of fatigue on her shoulders, she had to fight to be who she wanted him to see her as. "It's been on the market for a long time. No one else wants it, so there wouldn't be any competition."

Elam's expression shifted. "No kidding."

Not what he'd expected her to say, she supposed. She wasn't going to be who he thought she was, because he'd never bothered to get to know her. And wouldn't now—hopefully. As far as she was concerned, he could have the house and *she* would leave. He'd never have to see her again.

Elam gave the house an assessing look.

Ridge said, "Not a bad place to house a criminal empire. You and all your buddies. There's plenty of room."

"It would be a little on the nose, considering the house's history," Elam said. "Don't you think?"

Amelia didn't know whether to laugh or not. "Well, I don't want the place. And no one else will buy it. Maybe you should take it off my hands."

Elam scratched his jaw.

Probably trying to figure out how to get the down payment.

"How about five thousand dollars?" Amelia said. "You can have it all free and clear." He'd get a shock when the first tax bill showed up, but by then it would be firmly his problem.

"I'll think about it," Elam said. "For now, I just need five minutes inside."

They didn't need to follow him because of Kane's security cameras. Elam wouldn't even know they were there, but she would be able to see exactly where he went and what he got later. After he left.

"Go ahead." She and Ridge moved out of the way, staying outside. Even though she owned the place, Amelia tried not to go inside unless she had to. Sometimes it seemed like the house had a . . . darkness to it that seeped into her skin. Almost like it would poison her with its history.

"You okay?"

She looked over at Ridge. "I don't like the house. It scares me. More than just what it represents. I want to get rid of it."

"Maybe he will buy it. Or we can figure out something else to do—like donating it to an organization. Someone could turn the place into a small charter school or a church annex."

"It just feels like . . ." She looked at the exterior. "Oil. The way it sits on water and doesn't mix. The way it coats your fingers and takes forever to wash off." In her nightmares, the house was a living thing. She could run and run but never quite escaped it.

"Or the way sin stains a person's soul."

Amelia needed to let him share his faith. "How do you get rid of it?"

"We don't. The death of Christ paid the penalty to wash our sins away. Forever. To cleanse us from all unrighteousness. No matter who we are, we've done wrong."

"We all need that?" It didn't sound complicated. She could easily admit she didn't know everything and often wanted advice. Getting it from the Being who had created the universe meant it would probably be good advice.

He said, "It's the only way to have hope and peace."

She loved that look on his face so much. The softness of his expression and the way he so clearly believed what he was saying. Before she could respond to it, her brother stepped out of the house.

She wanted to talk more with Ridge about what he believed, but that would have to happen later now. This afternoon, maybe. He had a twelve-hour shift tonight, so it would be breakfast before she saw him—unless she hung out at the firehouse.

"I'm done." Her brother wasn't carrying anything, and none of his pockets were bulging.

"You didn't find it?"

Elam sniffed. "Don't worry about me, Amelia. I don't deserve it." He started to walk away.

"That's always been true enough."

He stiffened and slowed a little.

She continued, "But that was before. It's been a long time. I'm guessing we're both a lot different than who we used to be."

He opened the door and looked back at her. "Not that different. Stay away from me."

She bit her lip. Elam's driver pulled out. She said, "It would be easier to believe he's still a jerk."

Ridge watched the car head down the drive. "If he cares about you, but in the circles he runs with you'd be in danger through association, it makes sense to push you away."

"That would mean he's had a total personality transplant." She rolled her eyes. "Prison might've changed him, but making him empathetic? I'm not so sure. He never cared about me then, and he doesn't care about me now. I want him to take the house so I can walk away."

Ridge shrugged. "At least we'll be able to see what he took from here. He might get back to you about the house."

"What he took or what he did. Given we don't know which it was yet." She glanced at the house. "I really hope he agrees to take the monstrosity off my hands. Then the police will know whose door to knock on when there's a crime in town." She let out a sigh.

Ridge grinned. "It'll be okay. Really." He tugged her into a walk. "You can rest today, take a nap. Hang out with the girls a bit and do some studying for the lieutenant's exam. You'll be back to work in no time."

They circled the house and met Kane and Maria on the back patio, which now had weeds growing in the cracks of the concrete. From back here, the place looked like a deserted psychiatric facility—the kind featured on scary TV shows she couldn't watch.

"What did he take?" Amelia said.

Kane looked up from the tablet. "He went downstairs, into the cellar. There's a panel that opens, and he took a pouch from some kind of compartment."

"Small enough it fit in his jacket?" When Kane nodded, she said, "What did he give you guys? Because I can't help wondering if you got double-crossed in this trade."

"Who knows what's in that pouch? But we can look at the compartment." Kane studied the screen of his tablet. "He didn't do anything else but look around while he walked. He went right to what he was looking for and then straight back. No detours."

"And the trade?" She looked at Ridge.

"Kane took it to the police."

His cousin said, "I met with Sergeant Donaldson this morning and passed him what Elam gave me, which was security footage from a gas station down the street from one of the fires. It shows your hoodie guy running from the scene. He goes into the gas station and pulls his hood down, so they'll be able to ID him."

"Which means they can interview him and find out who he's working with and why he did that to us." Amelia felt better than she had in days. A little more rest and she'd be back to work. Then things would feel normal once more.

Once she passed the lieutenant's exam, she'd have her life back. No one would be able to take it from her ever again.

TWENTY-FOUR

WHAT DID HE TAKE?" EDDIE LEANED ACROSS the table in the firehouse kitchen.

Ridge had caught them all up on the entire story so far. All the firefighters—including the floater, Warren Kaminsky, who was here to cover Amelia's absence—were drinking coffee and listening intently. "We don't know. Aside from the fact it was a pouch."

He showed them the screen of his phone, where he'd taken a picture of Kane's tablet screen on the surveillance of Elam Hilden. Was it really after eight in the evening already? They'd fried up burgers for dinner and cleaned up, opting for coffee for dessert. Because coffee.

Zack said, "Money? Couldn't be much. That's the size of a checkbook."

Eddie nodded. "Paperwork, like the home's title or bank bonds. So he can cash in. Maybe that's the stash everyone has actually been looking for."

Zoe gripped her mug, sitting beside Eddie across the table. She seemed to have fit in well enough on rescue squad while Ridge worked Truck. She said, "I still can't believe people break into her house all the time. That's crazy."

Bryce, at the end of the table, shook his head. "She never said."

They all would've helped her, and maybe that was precisely the reason she'd never said anything. Not just refusing to let her coworkers into her personal life but also using the separation to keep herself safe. Given how she'd been raised and the disastrous way her personal and professional lives had collided in Benson, he couldn't really blame her.

"Anything on that Nicholas guy?"

Bryce gave him a slight nod. "I'll tell you later."

Which Ridge took to mean when there wasn't a room full of people.

Eddie said, "What's this?"

The whole crew would be all up in Amelia's business if they told them all about her former boss and ex-boyfriend. Ridge had no intention of explaining to Eddie what they weren't talking about.

He was just about to change the subject when Bryce said, "All the talk of rank tests has got me thinking. I might go for captain."

Zack grinned.

Della said, "That's a great idea, Lieutenant."

Ridge set his mug down and stared at Bryce over at the head of the table. "Captain?"

"Means an open lieutenant spot." Bryce took a sip from his chipped Midnight Sun Smokejumpers mug. "In case anyone was interested."

Amelia back on Truck 14 in the lieutenant's spot with him working alongside her as the LT of rescue squad? "I'm definitely interested."

Bryce grinned.

"How is Logan doing?"

Bryce's twin had recently suffered a health scare after being knocked out one too many times. He was grounded from smoke-jumping until he could recover or chose a new position to work in at the Midnight Sun base in Alaska, where the wildland fire-fighters lived.

"Andi and Jude just got back from a quick visit before she gets so late in her pregnancy she can't fly." He took a sip of his coffee. "Logan isn't happy about what happened, but he's all right. I think he'll take a ground position at the base, and he and Jamie will live there for a while after they get married. Which I don't think will take too long." Bryce smiled.

"It's good he's okay."

Bryce nodded. "Concussions are nothing to mess around with."

"It's a good thing for all of you to remember," Trace said. The EMT sat down at the opposite end of the table, reading from a novel.

Ridge hadn't even known he'd been listening.

Trace said, "Head injuries aren't something you ignore. Or walk off."

Eddie made a dismissive noise. Zack chuckled.

Trace shot them both a look.

Zack lifted his hands. "We know. We know."

Ridge drank the last of his coffee. By end of shift this might be over, with the police already moving on intel Kane had passed to them from Elam. They could arrest the guy who'd targeted fire-fighters, and put this whole thing to bed. Amelia would be pro-tected, and knowing Elam held no ill will toward her meant she could have a little bit of peace.

Standing beside her while she faced her brother had been one of the best moments of his life. He was so proud of her. The whole thing made his affection for her grow. And he was already mostly in love with her. Did she know?

She might not be aware of how far his heart was wrapped up in this thing. But with quiet ahead of them, they'd have time to spend together, and he could show her. Tell her. Prove she was worth it and at the same time that she had *nothing* to prove to him.

High on the wall, the speaker blared to life. "Rescue 5. Truck 14. Ambulance 21. Structure fire. Possible victims."

Chairs scraped back on the floor, and cups of coffee were left abandoned as the crew jogged down the hall, dispersing to their vehicles.

Ridge got his turnout pants and coat on and climbed into the passenger seat. Della took her spot as the driver, Izan and the floater, Warren Kaminsky, in the back.

Ridge pulled up the information on the dashboard computer. "Looks like it's the company SparkTech. Don't they make circuit boards and such?" He was pretty sure they were hardware, not software.

Kaminsky said, "They don't make that stuff here. It's transported down from Idaho, where they manufacture it."

"Three stories, two hundred employees," Ridge said.

Izan chimed in. "Most of them probably went home at five."

Ridge scanned the information he had. "Whoever called 911 said there were up to thirty employees inside. They were having a dinner meeting."

Kaminsky muttered, then said, "That's a lot of people."

"Makes sense both us and Rescue are responding," Izan said.

Ridge kept reading. "And Westside. They're sending their truck. We'll have multiple teams on site for this."

Della swung the truck around a corner.

Ridge spotted the glow above the buildings when they were within a mile. When Della turned the truck into the business complex, he scanned the structure. "Looks like the upper two floors are engulfed. We probably need to vent the roof."

Izan patted the back of Ridge's seat. "Let me go up the ladder. Please, please."

Della laughed.

"Kaminsky too," Ridge said. "Both of you go up on the roof."

Making holes in the roof allowed smoke and heat buildup inside the building to exit, clearing the air inside and releasing some of the heat. That would make it easier for the firefighters entering from below to see their way through the structure.

"Chief James is behind us." Della pulled up.

They all climbed out. "Get the ladder going," Ridge said. "I'll check in. He'll have a plan already."

Each of them said, "Copy that."

Ridge jogged to Macon. Bryce and the Westside lieutenant met him there. The chief studied the fire for a few seconds, his eyes intense under the brim of his helmet. "Okay, we go floor by floor from the ground, but I want two pairs to get to the third-floor conference room first while the others start a search. That's where the victims should be. And I want water on the west wall. Foster?"

"Vent the roof?" Ridge asked.

Chief James nodded. "Exactly. Get to it, people. And be safe."

They dispersed to their individual crews. Ridge ran to the truck, where Della had the controls for the ladder. Ridge got his pole and climbed up behind Izan and Kaminsky.

"Spread out." Ridge took the left side, opting to use the building's own ventilation system to help him. He could also break some windows in the upper floors by leaning over the edge and hammering the glass with this pole.

Izan hammered his spiked pole into the asphalt of the roof.

Kaminsky had the same idea as Ridge and pulled back a vent. He knocked it free and hammered into the hole with his pole, creating greater airflow than there had been before.

"Whoa!"

Ridge turned to Izan in time to see flames whip up through the hole he had made.

"Things are nasty down there!"

"Let's get this done and get back downstairs," Ridge ordered. He went to a spot a few feet from Izan's fiery hole and slammed down through the roof. The spike got hung up on the layers between him and the floor below, or the drop ceiling like that school.

Amelia was going to be upset she'd missed a fire like this. Such a large-scale callout didn't happen often.

From the radio between the open lapels of his jacket, he heard the other crews report in as they entered.

Ridge pulled the pole out and backed up fast. Flames burst out the opening, spraying sparks. "Chief," he radioed in. "Lot of activity up here on the roof." Conditions inside had to be bad for there to be flames and sparks like this. "We're about done here."

"Copy that, Foster," the chief responded. "Take the ladder down to three and get in through a window. We need to get those people out."

"Got it, Chief." If whoever was funneling those people out of the conference room down the hall on three heard that, they could find the window and he could retrieve the people with his ladder. Get them out that way so the victims didn't have to go down flights of stairs to safety.

Back on the ladder, they climbed down far enough for Della to lower them to the third floor. "We need to break that window."

Kaminsky moved fast to the end of the ladder and used his pole to break the glass. Hot air, smoke, and flames flashed out the window. The floater ducked down on the ladder, crying out. The flames came out so fast they seemed to wrap around him, disguising him from view before they billowed up into the sky.

"Kaminsky!" Ridge rushed up the ladder, Izan right behind him.

He gently rolled the firefighter over and spotted some light burns on the man's cheeks, giving him a flushed appearance. "We need to get him down."

Izan said, "I'll get the basket." He moved down the ladder faster than Ridge had seen anyone else do it. Trying to make up for what had happened in the training house with Amelia?

He had zero problem with the guy going above and beyond for a while.

Ridge shot an assessing glance at the fire raging high through the open window. They'd need to get water on it before they could evacuate people. He passed that information to the chief, who told him to get Kaminsky down, then take the hose back up.

Izan returned with the basket, and they slid the stunned but awake firefighter onto the backboard with its high sides. They strapped him so he didn't fall out and brought him down so the EMTs could take care of him.

Ridge raced back up the ladder. He pushed his arms and legs to do the work, enjoying the burn of exertion. Doing it to save lives gave the whole exercise thing a different spin. Later, when the situation was over and the adrenaline had dissipated, each of the firefighters would crash hard. For now, he kept his focus on the task at hand—making a safe path for the others down that hall to the window.

He half listened to the radio and tracked their progress to the victims, spraying water on the fire. Missing Amelia, but knowing she'd be here if she could. They'd never work on the same crew again, but even side by side on callouts like this, he'd be around if something ever happened to her. Like Kaminsky being caught off guard by that rush of fire—or anything worse. Ridge would be right there. By her side.

No matter what.

Firefighting had always been about the kind of men Grandpa had raised him and Kane to be. Now it was more. It was about life with Amelia.

Finally, he saw the first teammate appear. The firefighter handed off a civilian, a round woman in a skirt suit. Flustered and crying. Ridge said, "I'm right here with you. We're going down together. All right?"

She nodded, sobbing.

"I've got you."

He lifted two fingers to indicate to the firefighter he was good—he had the woman. Through the face mask, he couldn't tell who it was, but it didn't matter. They were all a team. He'd give his life for any one of them.

But for Amelia?

For her, he wanted to live.

TWENTY-FIVE

"YOU KNOW WHAT I'M THINKING?"

Amelia looked over at Maddie, on the other side of the huge picnic blanket the twins had brought over from the town house. All because they hadn't wanted Amelia to be alone and hadn't wanted the group split between two houses, with both needing Kane's and Maria's protection. "I'm going to regret saying yes, aren't I?"

Maddie looked at Ella, and they both smiled as if they knew what each other was thinking. Which, of course, they didn't because they weren't telepathic. But given they seemed to be on the same wavelength and shared moods as if their emotions mirrored each other, they probably got the gist. It made Amelia wonder what that would be like.

The girls had insisted they order pizza but have it delivered to the monstrosity, coming over here like it was a field trip. Now the five of them sat on the blanket with two pizza boxes in the center, only one slice remaining. Kane had finished at least four while Maria ate three small slices. Amelia had done the math on the rest and concluded three each for her and the twins, which meant one of them hadn't finished their third. Which wasn't surprising, since Backdraft cut their slices huge. But they did make great pizza.

Sitting here thinking about something so . . . normal meant this was one of the best dinners Amelia had enjoyed in months. Hanging out with Ridge's family, even if he wasn't here, chatting about anything and nothing in the light of all the candles Maria had brought in.

The girls had been curious about the house as soon as they'd found out where she lived and that Kane and Maria were staying here.

Hence the field trip.

A thick pad and sleeping bag, and a pillow and backpack had been slid over to the corner, out of sight of the window. Either Kane's or Maria's.

The kind of people who roughed it because someone was in danger. Who put their plans on hold to help out. Amelia had enjoyed getting to know them a little.

Maddie leaned back on one hand, her legs crossed in front of her. "Laser tag. Or those dart gun battles."

Amelia laughed. "That's what you're thinking?"

"We set the place up for rent—like parties and stuff like that. Put in some obstacles, blind corners and obstructions. People could pay to run around the house for a couple of hours. Play capture the flag."

Maria said, "We could set up some black lights and put some paint on the walls. Make people who wear certain colors show up bright in the dark."

"Smoke machine." Kane nodded. "Definitely a smoke machine."

Amelia shook her head. "It's October. Do you know how many people have stopped by to find out if I would rent the place for a Halloween party or haunted house? It happens at least twice a week. I usually just clear the place out, leave the doors unlocked, and go hunker down in my cabin for Halloween if I'm not working. People do whatever they want, and I clean up in the morning."

"You could make some serious money renting it out," Maddie said.

Amelia shrugged. "That's not really my goal."

"It's Maddie's goal." Ella grinned. "She never has enough cash." The quiet twin swept some napkins together and dropped them in the empty box, closing the lid. She grabbed her fizzy water can and finished the last few drops.

Maria lifted the pizza box, but Kane intercepted it and stood.

"I'll go throw this out." He headed for the door.

Amelia eyed the twins. "College is expensive these days, and saving for something you really want is a good thing." Sure, it was generic advice that not many people would argue with. But that was why she was comfortable saying it.

Amelia assumed that was what Ridge had been steering them toward, and she didn't want to contradict his wishes for the twins. He was every bit their father as well as their much older brother, and she loved seeing the side of him that showed paternal care.

She had learned more about what a father should be in those moments than she'd ever learned from her own father.

And it made her fall for him a little bit more. As if she needed another reason to know he was an amazing guy. She wondered if he had any flaws she would discover the more they got to know each other.

Amelia had spent so long pushing to get people to believe her, respect her, or value her. It wasn't so surprising she felt as if she didn't measure up to a great guy like Ridge. He'd told her to take herself to God and ask for forgiveness—as if the past could be washed away. Gone.

Sure, it was tempting to believe it. But was it true?

Maddie turned the screen of her cell phone to show Amelia.

"A pair of jeans?"

Ella giggled.

"I tried them on at the store." Maddie sighed. "They're two hundred dollars, but when you put them on . . . they feel like butter. They're *so* soft."

"Two-hundred-dollar jeans?" Amelia hadn't been aware such things existed.

Ella laughed aloud. "That's what Ridge said."

Amelia smiled, the teen's laughter infectious.

Maddie pouted, lifting her phone to take a picture of herself and her sister. Did she want to capture the light in her twin's eyes when she laughed? Amelia figured the picture turned out amazingly.

She was about to ask to see it when the doorbell rang through the house.

Kane came back in, his phone out. "It's the cops. I got the motion alert while I was in the kitchen."

"The cops?" Amelia stood, brushing her hands on the legs of her non-buttery jeans.

Kane lifted his chin. "Let's go see what they want."

Because he was the kind of guy who had nothing to fear from local cops. Even when they could have called to ask any question they might have rather than driving all the way out here.

He opened the front door, and Amelia introduced PD Lieutenant Alex Basuto and Detective Jessica Cartwright to Ridge's cousin, who shook both of their hands.

See? He had no fear of the police.

She knew better than to assume she would be considered innocent. Amelia didn't invite them in. "What can we help you with?"

Jessica deferred to her superior even though she was likely the investigating detective. Basuto was only a little taller than Amelia, with dark, handsome features and a stocky build. His wife was scary—but less so these days when she had a brood of kids running around her.

Kind of like Jessica, whose husband had been a troubled teen hacker but, after working for the police department for years, now worked for a private agency.

People who had come through difficult circumstances and suffered hard times and now got to live out their happily ever after. But things like that didn't happen to people like Amelia. They happened to folks like Ridge and his family. Bryce and Penny. Kane and Maria.

Lieutenant Basuto said, "Amelia Patterson? Or is it Amelia Hilden?"

Her stomach clenched. "It's always been Patterson. I don't know why you'd think I go by Hilden."

"Seems like a wise choice. If you're looking to create distance between you and a man who terrorized this town."

"Yeah? Just the town?" Amelia wasn't going to roll over and get stepped on just because her biological father had been an evil tyrant. These people didn't know her, and they might *think* they knew her father, but they only knew what he'd done. Not who he'd been when no one else was around.

They didn't know about the mind games.

Basuto frowned. "We need you to come to the police station for questioning. Understand, you aren't under arrest, but your cooperation in answering the questions we have will go a long way to establishing some goodwill with the department."

Kane shifted a fraction closer to her. "Questions about what?"

"Voluntarily accompanying us to the police station isn't an admission of guilt. On the contrary, it's a way for you to state your case and your innocence in this matter."

He wasn't going to answer the question.

Amelia folded her arms. "What matter?"

Jessica's expression shifted, her lips thinned, but she kept the rest of her features steady. Even if she didn't like this and how it was going down, there wasn't much she could do. Defying her superior wouldn't go well.

Amelia figured Basuto thought Jessica might actually consider Amelia the victim, and that would make her unable to be impartial. Which meant they had reason to wonder if she was guilty.

But guilty of what?

Basuto said, "It's regarding the incidents at fire scenes."

That was all the two of them were willing to tell Amelia. She had to ride in the back of the police car, and they didn't answer even one of her questions. Even Jessica said nothing but, "We'll be there soon, and then we'll get all this figured out."

It took forever to actually get to the interview room, a tiny box probably designed to look like a prison cell. One table, four chairs. A huge one-way glass window so whoever was next door could listen in without her knowing they were there.

When Basuto finally said, "Please have a seat," Amelia slumped into it, completely exhausted. Not good. She needed her wits about her if she was going to survive this guy and his questions.

Jessica sat beside Basuto, across the table from Amelia. "Coffee? Water? Anything else?"

"No, thank you." Even in a police station, she wasn't going to accept a drink she hadn't witnessed being made. Too many times she'd allowed even a tiny risk, and it had backfired in her face.

Jessica set a manila file on the table in front of her. "I understand you're aware that information was provided to us regarding the identity of whoever ran from the fire scenes recently."

"Thankfully, no one was hurt." Amelia sat back in the chair. "Then I was nearly killed in the training house, which is why I'm not at work right now." She looked at her watch, but the time wasn't really a factor. She didn't want to think about how long this would take, but considering it was after nine already, it would be a late night.

By design?—so they could catch her in a slip of the tongue because she was tired?

"We aren't sure those events are connected." Basuto shifted in his seat. "But the first two are the ones we're here to talk to you about."

Amelia glanced between them. Elam was the one who'd turned information over to Kane, who'd given it to these cops. They might not even know that she had been part of that, letting her brother enter the house to retrieve something from a tiny hidey-hole lockbox or safe or whatever had been in the wainscoting that she'd never noticed. But he had what he wanted now, so what did it matter?

Jessica flipped open the file and slid a page across, a printout of an image. The security video that Elam had passed on. "Have you ever seen this man? Do you know who he is?"

Amelia slid the photo across the table so she could see it more clearly. "I've never seen that guy before. I don't know who he is." She was pretty sure this wasn't him, even if she had been too far to get a good look.

"And this?" Jessica slid over a bank statement.

"Amelia Hilden?" That was the name on the account. "With the mansion's address? That's the first clue something is wrong here."

"How's that?" Basuto asked.

But Amelia's attention skimmed down the transactions. "This isn't mine." Cash in. Cash deposits. "Nine thousand nine hundred seventy-four? Why not just find twenty-six dollars and make it an even ten thousand?" She shook her head.

She'd never seen that much cash in her life.

Basuto said, "Because ten thousand is the threshold where your deposit has to be reported to the IRS."

"So this person is staying under the radar?"

Basuto said, "Looks to me like that person is you."

Amelia shook her head. "I don't use the house address on anything. I have an address from the PO Box company that looks like a residential address. I have nothing to do with that house, apart from the fact that, technically, I own it."

"You live on the property."

"I don't use this name." Amelia tapped the paper with her index finger. "I don't claim that address. I don't need anyone finding out my personal business, and I've been trying to sell the house for years. No one will buy it."

Basuto stared at her, and crow's feet flexed around his eyes in his dark skin. "And the money?"

"What money?" She looked at the paper. "Whose account is this? Because I could use the cash to pay the outrageous taxes on the house I don't want. Maybe they can help me out."

It couldn't be her brother.

Who would fake a bank account to look like she had tons of cash coming and going? And why would they even need to do that?

It was absolutely something Nicholas would have done, but she hadn't seen him in years. Tried not to think about him at all. If it hadn't been for Cherry showing up in town, she'd have maintained her streak another while. Each day with him out of her life was one closer to being completely free of him and the hold he'd had on her.

"This man"—Jessica tapped the surveillance photo—"confessed to causing the explosion at the apartment fire and the fire at Wiltern Road."

Her childhood home.

Making her wonder if she was a target—putting her on edge so that she saw things Nicholas would've done in the actions of everyone around her.

Basuto continued. "He says you paid him to be there and told him exactly what to do."

"Paid him." She shifted the bank statement paper toward him. "With this, I suppose?"

"You tell me."

Amelia sat back in the chair. "Guess the case is closed, then."

"You're admitting you hired this man to endanger firefighters?"

"As soon as you answer one thing for me." Amelia glanced between them.

"What's that?" Jessica asked. Animated now—as if she'd been looking for an explanation.

She pointed to a particular transaction. "See that deposit? Cash, in person?"

Both cops nodded.

"I worked a twenty-four-hour shift that day to cover for the B-shift lieutenant, Albert Morris. Started at six the night before, ended at six that day—after banks close. Ask my coworkers on that shift, but that day, I can tell you we worked back-to-back calls, and I never had the truck detour to the bank. We don't do that. We run errands on our days off."

"You weren't supposed to be working that day?" Jessica asked.

Amelia nodded. "I covered for him as a favor at the last minute. So it wasn't me who deposited that money. Which has to make you wonder if I deposited any of that money. Do you know who did? Banks have surveillance cameras, don't they?"

Jessica pulled another image out of the file. A woman, definitely. Blonde hair hung down her back, but her head was covered with an oversized straw hat so there was no shot of her face.

"Clever."

Basuto huffed. "You expect us to believe someone is setting you up?"

Amelia leaned forward in the chair, her forearms on the table. "I expect you to do your jobs. As in, follow the evidence and find the person responsible for the crime. *Beyond a reasonable doubt.* Isn't that how it goes in court?"

She slid her chair back and stood. "You said I was free to go at any time."

Jessica nodded, a slight smile on her face.

"Then bye."

Amelia walked out of the interview room.

TWENTY-SIX

RIDGE OPENED THE OVEN AND PULLED OUT THE tray of cookies, which he set on the wire rack on the counter. He'd give it a matter of minutes before one of the firefighters swung by to—

Zack strode by the counter, on the other side where the coffee carafe was now empty, and tried to grab one of the cookies. From the hot tray. With his fingers.

The cookie bent in his grasp and started to fall apart.

Ridge rolled his eyes, looking for a spatula so he could transfer the cookies to the wire rack. "You need to let it cool."

"Sorry, Mom."

Ridge snorted. He couldn't find the spatula, so he just lifted the tray and used the parchment to slide the whole sheet onto the rack. "Ten minutes. No sooner."

Someone over on the couch groaned.

Zoe sat up, looking over the back of the couch. "Is there coffee at least?" She had a kids' cartoon movie on the TV, and after the callout they'd just had, he didn't blame her. And no one had asked her to put on something else.

"Coffee is Eddie's job."

The rescue squad firefighter jumped up from his seat, where he'd been playing a card game with Bryce and Della.

"I'm on it. Tell me when it's my turn again." Eddie jogged over to the container where they kept the coffee grounds, stealing a cookie on the way past. "Ah. Hot. Haha." He chewed. "Okay, those are good."

A distinctly teenage voice called out, "What did you make, Ridgey? Chocolate chip or the banana ones?" Maddie, of all people, stepped into the room at the far end, by the entrance. Followed by her sister.

Then Amelia.

Then Kane and Maria.

Ridge stared at them. "You guys are here."

Way to state the obvious. But Kane had messaged him about Amelia getting taken in for questioning, so he figured he knew why they were here.

Everyone in the room, which was most everyone except the EMTs who weren't back yet, stared at them.

"Of course we're here." Maddie widened her eyes, wordlessly telling him something was up. She came around the counter and wound her arms around his middle, giving him a side hug. "Banana?"

Ridge shook his head. "Just chocolate chips."

"Sweet!" She eyed the coffeepot.

"No caffeine after dinner."

Maddie rolled her eyes. Eddie looked over from his spot across from them and said, "Okay, she looked a lot like you when she did that." Eddie glanced at Ella, then back at Maddie. "Your sisters . . . or?"

Yeah. They were young enough to be his kids—though only barely.

"Everyone," Ridge started, keeping an eye on Amelia, who had gone to the kettle and hadn't said a word. Something heavy on her mind. The real reason they were here—not just so the twins could break his separation rule. "This is Maddie and Ella. They're my sisters."

The firefighters gathered around, shaking the girls' hands. Kane introduced them to Maria. Bryce told Maddie and Ella that he had a twin brother but that they weren't identical.

Zoe beamed at them. "So great to meet you. Ridge doesn't talk much about his family."

Maddie said, "That's cause they're all losers except us."

Ella snickered. "What she means is . . ."

Maddie finished, "It's nice to meet you."

Both the girls grabbed a cookie at the same time. Maddie said, "Ridgey's cookies are the best."

Zack snickered, as did Izan, who had appeared out of nowhere.

Ridge folded his arms. "Not that I'm not happy to see you guys."

"Sure," Maddie interjected.

"It's a school night, and it's late."

"We had pizza at Amelia's house," Ella said, as if that explained things. Which it sort of did. Maddie always got restless when she had a heavy meal for dinner. Add dessert and she was going to be bouncing off the walls.

Ridge leaned over and said, "One cookie."

"Fine." Maddie pouted.

"I'm glad you came so everyone could meet you." Even if it was because there had been some kind of problem that meant they needed to bring Amelia here.

Maddie leaned close to him and whispered, "The police took her in for questioning, but she only said she's being set up."

Ella continued from where her sister left off. "She proved to them it wasn't her, but we didn't think she should go home."

They'd brought her to see Ridge.

He kissed one twin on the forehead, then the other. "Don't get comfortable. This is a one-time thing."

Maddie gasped, her attention in the direction of the TV. "I love this movie!"

Ella followed her to the couch, where they sat with Zoe.

The others had gathered around Maria and Kane, all talking but too low for him to hear what they were saying.

Ridge took the opportunity to go over to Amelia, still by the kettle. Staring intently while it boiled, shaking slightly with white steam coming out of the spout. He moved beside her so she knew it was him, faced her left shoulder and ran a hand between her shoulder blades. "I won't bother asking if you're all right."

"I will be."

He gently squeezed the back of her neck, under the fall of blonde hair. "Come to the LT office and talk about it with me?"

"What's to talk about?" She grabbed the kettle and poured water over the tea bag. "They know it wasn't me. They're wrong."

"It shook you."

"It made me think of—" She stopped suddenly, glanced around to see where everyone else was, then said, "Nicholas." Keeping her voice low so the information stayed between them.

"Are we a hundred percent certain he isn't here in town?" Ridge said. "I had Bryce ask Penny to run his name and see if she could find out where he is, but he hasn't mentioned her having any results yet."

Amelia shuddered. "I don't want to see him. But it would explain a lot."

He wanted to pull her close, but it couldn't be here and now. "You'll get through this. I know you will."

No matter what, he wasn't going to let anything else happen to her. He'd been praying all shift for her to cry out to the Lord for salvation. She needed Jesus in her life so that He could give her peace. Ridge wanted to make her happy, but God was the only one who could fully satisfy her.

She leaned over and he heard her inhale. "Cookies? On a shift where you smell like smoke? That can't be good."

"You should try one."

She smiled for a second, then said, "It was bad."

"Seventeen rescues, half a dozen with minor injuries. One fatality."

Amelia winced. "Sorry. I should've called before the twins showed up. I had no idea what kind of atmosphere they'd be walking into."

A rough call would produce a bunch of grouchy firefighters who needed to blow off some frustration. He'd done what he could, not even knowing his sisters would show up with Amelia and his cousin and cousin's fiancée, and it needed to be enough.

"How do you deal with it, as lieutenant?"

Amelia shrugged. "Give people space to process. Everyone deals in their own way. Della is probably bench-pressing right now, and Izan will check on her."

Ridge walked over to see their Hispanic firefighter walk out of the room toward the gym. When he turned back, Amelia had a cookie in her mouth. Her eyes widened.

He waited while she finished, pleased that she was clearly enjoying it. When she was done, he said, "We can find somewhere quiet to talk about your evening if you want."

She studied him, her tea on the counter forgotten. "What do you want?"

"A cookie, some more coffee, and for the twins to go to bed at a reasonable hour since this is a school night."

"I meant from me."

Whoa, there was a loaded question. "Amelia—"

"I'm serious. What do you want?"

She was serious. Ridge wanted to back up and wipe the counters down, but that would only delay the inevitable. And it would make it look like he didn't know or hadn't decided. When the reality was that he'd never been surer of anything, with the exception of having the twins come and live with him.

"I want you to become a lieutenant again so I can kiss you in the firehouse."

Her eyes flared.

"I'm also serious." Seriously in love with her. "And I'd like to be around to help you with whatever is happening. Anytime, anywhere."

One eyebrow lifted. "You're on shift."

"Then hang out here. Kane and Maria can make sure the twins are safe at the town house."

She bit her lip. "If anything happens to them . . ."

"I know." He touched her shoulder. "That's why it's good that they're here, because now we have the best of the best, elite-trained operators to protect Maddie and Ella." He glanced over and saw the twins were both looking at them over the back of the couch.

Watching Ridge with Amelia.

He was counting on his cousin and Maria a whole lot to see that there was a satisfying outcome to this. One second to the next, anything could happen, and Ridge would lose everything. What if that happened? Tangling in this business with Amelia put the twins at risk.

Was he really willing to do that?

The answer was yes, provided Kane and Maria—and anyone they called—helped. He couldn't do much when he was on shift, as Amelia had pointed out. But no one would object to her being here.

Amelia said, "Kane and Maria have been amazing. They're running down the information I gave them on the bank account that's supposed to be mine. Trying to figure out who opened it." She took a breath. "Who is setting me up."

"That's good, isn't it?"

"They believed me." She lifted her chin and looked at him. "No questions. No qualifiers. They just believed me that it's a setup and said they'd do anything they could to help."

"Isn't that a good thing?"

She seemed unsure. "It's never happened before. They just took my word for it."

"Because you're telling the truth."

"I wish I knew who it was. The woman with the hat."

Ridge frowned. "What woman?"

"In the bank. She had a hat on so no one could see her face," Amelia said. "The cops said they were going to talk to the teller tomorrow, but I won't be holding my breath for what they come up with."

Ridge touched her cheek. "It's going to work out. You didn't do anything wrong." He had an odd thought that might distract her. "I saw a hat tonight as well. At the callout. Must've been fifteen people we took down the ladder out of that blaze. Every time I went back up, I saw it on the hallway floor. This huge straw thing with a black band around it." He shook his head. "That was random, but I saw it so many times."

Amelia frowned. "That sounds like the hat in the bank surveillance video."

"Okay, but it's just coincidence, right? It isn't like it's the same hat."

Amelia took her mug from the counter. "I have no idea what it is, but with my history, it's more likely that this turns out to be the thing that proves I'm the one who set the fire you fought tonight. So it isn't like I'm going to ignore something like that."

"Forget I mentioned it." Ridge lifted his hands. "Let Kane and the police work the case. Just focus on getting better, okay?"

"When someone is most likely going to show up tomorrow and tell everyone that I'm so stressed out by being injured that I set that fire because I'm an arsonist? Sure, that'll help me rest easy." She blew out a breath.

His phone ringing cut off anything either one was about to say next. She didn't know what she'd have said anyway.

Ridge frowned at the screen of his phone. "Hey, Mom—"

He was cut off by the caller, who had a deep voice. So loud that Amelia could probably hear it. *Did you get her to tell you where that money is yet?*

Amelia flinched. She stared at Ridge.

His cheeks heated. "Don't call me unless it's because you've decided to set up a college fund for the twins." He hung up.

The girls looked over from the couch.

He set his phone on the counter beside him. "That was my stepdad. He doesn't—"

"You think I'd believe you're actually after the money and nothing else?"

"Maybe not, but—"

"Listen, I'm glad we came. It's just that nothing in my life ever goes smoothly. I'm glad you think it will all work out fine. But why would I believe that when it never has for me?"

"Amelia—"

"Thanks for talking to me. It means a lot." She squeezed his arm. "But I'm going to drink this and then go with the girls. Right now I want to be at your house, where I can pretend none of this exists and I'm just a normal person no one is targeting with an elaborate plan to destroy my entire life." She lifted up on her tiptoes and kissed his cheek, then wandered off.

Leaving Ridge standing there wondering what had just happened.

TWENTY-SEVEN

AMELIA CLIMBED OUT OF HER CAR JUST AFTER nine, when the bank would be open. She had a few hours until she was supposed to meet Meg at the Bridgewater Café for lunch. The twins were safely at school. Ridge's shift lasted until six tonight, and she didn't know where Maria and Kane were. It didn't matter. She had business to take care of.

She was still off-kilter from hearing his stepdad on the phone the night before. Plus not wanting to help the cops with anything if they weren't going to trust that she wasn't a criminal.

It was like her last few years being a firefighter meant nothing.

Dark clouds hung in the sky, giving the busy street an ominous feeling—which was of course ridiculous, since the weather didn't have feelings. Just an association that came with the dim light, the cool temperature, and the breeze that sent strands of her hair across her face.

She slid her wallet into her jacket pocket and her phone into the back pocket of her jeans. For a second, her mind flashed back to the night before. Ridge had walked her to her car. Even after she'd made her point about people never believing her, he'd walked her to her car.

The twins had gone with Kane and Maria, so Amelia had used the drive to think in private. Kane didn't leave until she did, following her the whole way. Which meant the twins saw Ridge kiss her.

She knew he'd done it on purpose and because he wanted to. Staking his claim in front of anyone watching, making it clear they were . . . together? She wasn't sure about that, since they hadn't officially even been on a date.

Did she want Ridge to show up at her house, freshly showered? Ironed shirt and slacks? Gel in his hair?

Never mind. Of course she did.

Amelia might even consent to wearing a dress and heels for the occasion, even though that meant going shopping. The twins would probably love to go with her and pick something out for Amelia's first official date with Ridge.

She sighed, pushing out the thoughts. The last thing she needed was to stand here with a faraway look on her face, thinking about Ridge and his kisses.

What she should do was march into that bank so she could prove she wasn't the Amelia Hilden listed on that account. *Should've changed my first name as well.* She'd become "Patterson" after her mother had remarried Matt Patterson and he'd adopted her. Best decision of her life so far.

She crossed the street. No matter what, the staff at this bank, where she wasn't even a customer, were going to tell her something. The building looked ancient, with red-brick exterior walls and white columns either side of the front door. It had been here since the town's founding in the mid-twentieth century, which, in a place like Last Chance County, didn't bode well.

The town had been started by a group of men who had served together in Vietnam and wanted their own kingdom back in the US. A place they could rule, taking prominent positions in the local government, police department, fire department, and medical services. Her father had been the last of that group to be stopped, thanks to the current police chief and his friends. Good people who'd known the town should never have allowed evil to infuse it like that.

So they'd rooted it out.

The bank doors slid open in front of her, and she strode inside. There were about ten people in the lobby, with customers lined up for the teller counter on the left where two staff members worked their way through the line of people. To the right were three cubicles along the wall, blinds over the windows. Spots to meet with a business account rep or a mortgage rep.

Amelia turned back to the door and spotted a security guard sitting at a small round table, drinking coffee from a paper cup. The rotund man had a full head of curly red hair and managed to bite the powdered donut without getting a speck of sugar on him, which was pretty impressive.

"Can I bother you?"

He set the donut on the plate. "Dunno, can you?" He gave her a toothy grin and shifted, revealing a tattoo on the inside of his forearm. A military unit.

"How long have you worked here?"

He brushed his hands off with a napkin. "Coupla years. Got out of the Corps just before that."

Perfect. "I wonder if you can help me." She didn't know how to convince him to help her by lying, so she told him about the account in her name and how the police believed she'd paid someone to endanger firefighters.

His eyes narrowed on that.

Amelia said, "I'm a lieutenant with Eastside Firehouse, but my commanding officer at my previous department never put in the paperwork for my rank."

He didn't like that either.

"So now I've been bumped down in rank because of an oversight," she said. "The idea that anyone would think I'd put firefighters in danger . . ." Amelia shook her head. "It's insane. I'm being framed."

"So what do you need from the bank?"

Amelia sighed. "I don't want to ask for anything you can't provide."

Like a look at their surveillance.

"Maybe I could speak with a teller who has seen the account holder, or whoever set the account up. They might recognize her—and it would be helpful for them to confirm that it isn't me." Sure, it was a long shot. But if she didn't try, then she couldn't say she'd done everything to fix this. Amelia wasn't going to just roll over and play dead, allowing the police to make all the accusations they wanted.

He scrunched up his face, rising to his feet. "Let's see who's free that you can talk to."

"Thanks. I'm Amelia, by the way."

"Daryl Merton. Good to meet you." He went to a cubicle and looked around. "Cynthia, you got a sec for a customer? She's a firefighter. Amelia."

Over the cubicle divider, with its felt surface, she saw a woman pop up and look at her. The wide-eyed expression shuttered for a second. "Oh, uh."

"You thought I was someone else?" Amelia asked. "Because that's a great place to start."

"Well, you said a *firefighter*, and your name is Amelia."

"And that means something to you?"

The woman eased around Daryl and said, "Thanks."

"No problem." He wandered back toward his donut.

"What's your name?" Amelia asked.

"Oh, I'm Cynthia." She held out her hand for Amelia to shake. "Nice to meet you."

"How many firefighters do you know that are named Amelia?" She wanted to interrogate this woman but needed her to be forthcoming and not shut down, because Amelia wasn't going to back off until she had the whole story.

"Of course, I can't give out private information about our customers."

"She's probably from another county or some town close by. Because there aren't any Amelias who are firefighters in Last Chance County." Except her.

Cynthia frowned. "No, I'm sure this one is. She works out of . . . Eastside Firehouse."

"I'd love to meet this woman. She sounds impressive." Amelia, on the other hand, was terrible at this. She'd never have made it as an undercover agent. "How long has it been since she came in?"

"Only a few days, but it isn't like you can stay here until she shows up." Cynthia looked her up and down. "Are you some kind of stalker?"

Only when I have a point to make. "Of course not. I'm no threat to this woman."

The police, on the other hand . . .

Amelia continued. "I just have one more question."

Cynthia didn't object out loud.

"If the police were to ask you to ID the person who holds the account with that woman's name on it, would you be willing to make a statement confirming that person *isn't* me?"

Cynthia frowned, but her eyes flared. "Why are the police involved?"

Now that she'd had a whiff of intrigue, she was interested. "It's a lot of money, and it might have been used to target first responders. The cops aren't sure who is responsible, so they could probably use your help."

That puffed her up a little, because she'd be important to the investigation. Deep down, most people wanted to help, and adding in the chance to be recognized hit on more than one need inside this woman. Not that Amelia was a student of human nature, but being twisted around by a narcissistic man and finally breaking away had allowed her time to think over why she'd let herself fall for it.

Everything about Ridge was a giant green flag.

If there were any potential problems that she could see, she might be more comfortable with the whole thing. At least then she would know what was in store for her if she committed to him.

"There you are."

Amelia had been about to thank the woman and leave, because she'd done as much as she could here without overstepping boundaries.

She turned to the source of the male voice.

"Elam?"

A couple of similarly dressed guys stood behind him in jeans and denim and boots. They'd spread out around the bank lobby as if they needed to stand guard. One of the men in line turned to look at them, instinct flaring so that he tensed and kept one eye on the man closest to him.

Elam walked right up to her. "Thought you were going to wait for me." Her brother grasped her arm, just above her elbow. Hard.

Amelia stiffened.

"Well, you look like you have your hands full." Cynthia looked overlong at Elam, those eyes flaring again.

As if her brother were remotely good-looking or a ticket to excitement.

He was a ticket to something, but it was more likely going to be heartbreak.

"I was just about to leave." Amelia lifted her chin. "By myself."

"We have an appointment."

Elam's friend over by the front door swung his arm back and clocked the security guard, still on his break, in the forehead. Daryl tumbled backward on the chair, tipping it over and landing on the floor behind it. Out cold.

Amelia gasped.

Cynthia stammered and started to back up.

Elam pulled a weapon from his hip, under his jacket, and swung it up to point at the bank employee. "Like I said, we have an appointment."

The other men Elam had brought moved in. The customer in line spun around and started a fight, grappling for the man's gun. Elam fired off a shot over his head.

The fighting duo froze.

"No one moves. No one tries anything … like hitting the emergency switch." Elam swung his gun around and fired another shot over the teller's head.

She screamed and backed up, holding up her hands.

"Don't do this, Elam." Amelia had to say it, and letting them all know his name meant they could identify him.

He ignored her, but that grip on her arm didn't let up. Her fingers started to go numb. He scanned the room. "Everyone come sit in the center of the room."

Two more men came in the front door, both carrying duffels.

Elam said, "Lock it down." He waved his gun, and the customers and employees gathered in a group in the center of the room, by the island with stacks of deposit slips and brochures about savings accounts.

The men who'd come in fixed something to the front door that covered the handles, like a lockbox, wire arms that stretched to the corners. Once they were done with the front door, they continued around the room. One disappeared down a back hall—to secure the back exit?

"What are you doing?" Amelia's mind only concluded one thing. "You can't rob a bank!"

Elam said, "All we're doing is making a withdrawal."

"We?"

He turned to her, a sinister look in his eyes. "Amelia Hilden and her brother Elam Hilden are here to cash out their father's account."

Amelia gaped at him. He'd planned this entire scenario. "And if I refuse?"

She didn't want that money. It was her whole reason for being here, proving she had nothing to do with this place.

Elam stared at her with cold eyes. "I'll kill every innocent person in this room."

TWENTY-EIGHT

RIDGE GRIPPED THE HANDLE ABOVE THE DOOR while Della brought the rig to a stop outside the bank, where it seemed like an ocean of cops had gathered. There was no formal SWAT team in Last Chance County. Each of the officers on duty took on the role as needed.

"What's happening here?" Della shut off the truck. "This is chaos."

Ridge said, "The call was for police assistance, so it could be anything they need us to do." Usually that involved Rescue 5, but there were plenty of things Truck could do when someone was trapped—or hiding. Including some skills that would get a firefighter on a bomb squad in a bigger town, or on a special HAZMAT team.

"We might need tools, but let's find out the situation first." Ridge jumped out of the truck and slammed the door, trudging over to the huddle of senior officers. "Chief?"

Macon stood with Conroy Barnes, the police chief. "Good, you guys are here." Macon nodded.

Chief Barnes said, "We may need you to gain entry. Something is blocking the door, but we're not sure what. The surveillance isn't super clear on it."

Ridge nodded. "Whatever you need."

He started to turn away, but Macon snagged his arm. "One sec."

"Chief?" He faced Macon, who had black slacks and his white uniform shirt on, over which he'd pulled a waist-length rain jacket.

"Surveillance has the hostages in the center of the room."

"Anyone injured?" Ridge didn't like the idea this might turn into a tragedy.

Macon shook his head. "So far it's been peaceful. One of the tellers managed to hit the emergency button under the counter in time, so the call went out. We know there have been shots fired inside, but no one has been hurt as of yet."

It sounded like he was giving a press conference.

Ridge frowned. "Why are you—"

"Amelia is in there. With her brother. He's the one holding all those people hostage." Macon waved a hand at the building.

"Elam Hilden is the hostage taker?" Ridge looked at Chief Barnes.

He confirmed with a nod. "His sister is cooperating. From what we can see, she's part of this. An accomplice, even."

Heat built in Ridge's abdomen. "She isn't working with him. She doesn't even like him."

"Let us do our jobs." Chief Barnes turned away.

Macon said, "Your team is here to be on hand in case you need to assist the police. Make sure that's what you're doing. Prove to me right here and right now that having her in the middle of a call doesn't stop you from doing your job because you're more concerned about her than the entire situation."

"Yes, Chief."

Ridge turned away and headed back to his crew, all coming to meet him with axes in hand. Their expressions curious about what was going on. Until they spotted the look on his face.

Izan said, "What's going on?"

Kaminsky stopped between Izan and Della. "Yeah, Lieutenant. What's going on?"

Della saw something in the scene behind Ridge that she recognized as not good.

"We're on the sidelines for now. Until we either get sent back to the house or we breach the doors." He took a breath. "Amelia is inside with her brother."

"She's a hostage?" Izan flinched.

Ridge kept his voice low so no one overheard the conversation. These guys needed to know though. With the exception of Kaminsky, they considered Amelia family. The floater would as well, but only in the FD brother-sisterhood.

He said, "The police aren't sure, but she isn't with the hostages. She's with Elam. They think she might be an accomplice."

"That's loco." Izan shook his head and turned to pace away a few steps. "Isn't that Kane?"

Ridge looked where Izan pointed and saw the crowd that the police had blocked behind a barrier, a couple of uniform officers holding the spectators back. In the center, Kane was barely visible between people.

His cousin motioned him over.

"I'll be back in a second." Ridge jogged over to the cop, who turned out to be Anthony Thomas. "Hey, can you let him in?" He indicated Kane.

"He's with you?"

"Yes."

"Then he's your responsibility. I'm not getting in trouble for it." Anthony smoothed back his perfect brown hair.

Ridge's was smashed under his helmet.

Kane's—

"Focus, bro." Kane was already over the barrier. "You with me?"

Ridge took a breath. Kane squeezed the back of his neck above the collar of his coat, and Ridge said, "She's in there."

"I know."

Ridge stopped, not quite back at his crew. He bent and put his fists on his knees.

"Breathe."

He sucked in a breath. The world closed in around him, and sound became a blur he couldn't hear. Whomps instead of voices. Just a mass of sensation with nothing to pick out and anchor himself to.

Lord, You are with me. Be with her as well. I know she doesn't quite believe, but she could. Draw her to You.

Kane's hand was still on the back of his neck. The way it had been that night when Grandpa had died. Ridge focused on it, the steady presence of the man who was more like a brother to him than anything else, and his best friend. The only family who'd been worth anything while he was growing up, and even now, with the twins in his life—and his home—he still needed Kane to stand beside him.

Ridge straightened. The world quit spinning for a second.

"She'll be okay."

"You can't know that."

Kane had a look in his eye.

"What is—"

"Maria is in there too." Kane's brows rose.

"What?" He dragged Kane by the sleeve over to his crew. "What do you mean, Maria is in there?"

Kane just shrugged, like it was a completely normal coincidence. "She was keeping an eye on Amelia today. It's just that Amelia didn't know she was there." He grinned, but it didn't last long. "When she went into the bank, Maria was waiting for her to come back out. Instead, she saw Elam go inside, followed by his guys.

She went around the back and broke into the employee exit. Hid in the back when they locked it down."

"You need to tell the police chief that."

Kane nodded. "You're coming with me. You need to hear what Maria told me."

They walked together toward the two chiefs.

"Sirs?" When Macon and Conroy turned, Kane said, "My fiancée is inside the bank, and she's been communicating with me."

Conroy said, "How is she doing that?"

"She sent me a text to come here, and when I got in range, our comms worked." Kane tapped his ear.

Macon frowned. "You and Maria wear comms earbuds all the time?"

"No," Kane said. "We keep them on our person. Just in case."

"Just in case what?" Macon asked.

Kane just shrugged.

"So we have eyes in there," Conroy said. "And now we have ears too."

Kane nodded. "Maria is with the group of employees. They have been whispering when they can about the Hilden family. Speculating about an account at their bank with the old man's treasure in it. They figure the brother and sister are there to withdraw their money."

Ridge folded his arms. "Why would Elam need to create a hostage situation to do that?"

Conroy said, "And why would he secure the doors with military tech that will detonate and kill everyone inside?"

Ridge shook his head, trying to think it through. If the doors detonated, that would kill a lot of people, including Elam and his men. Amelia.

His stomach twisted, but he couldn't get hung up on the risk. Macon was right about that. He had to prove he could do his job even while Amelia's life was in danger.

"He has to have a plan to get out." Kane shrugged. "He isn't going into this with a plan to get killed, not when he just got out of prison."

Conroy looked at Kane. "And you know this how? Have you spent time with Elam Hilden?"

"Maybe ten minutes."

"This way, please." Conroy led Kane with him, away from Macon and Ridge. The huddle of cops nearby had Lieutenant Basuto—the one who'd brought Amelia to the station for questioning—and Sergeant Donaldson. Good men. Family guys. He knew because he saw them dropping off their kids in the children's ministry classrooms on Sunday morning at church rather than drinking coffee and leaving the task to their wives.

Macon cleared his throat. "I don't believe Amelia is working with her brother."

Ridge glanced over.

His boss continued, "If she's in there with her brother, it's likely coercion, even if she isn't with the other hostages."

"That isn't going to convince the police of her innocence." That's what she'd been worried about the night before. That no one ever believed she told the truth. He didn't know what it felt like to be so distrusted, to not have his integrity. "What if Elam is the one behind everything that's happened? The fires where the crew was hurt and the incident in the training house. Someone tried to kill her, but who would have done it that way? It's just odd enough that it might make her sound crazy, believing that she was nearly murdered in the training house."

"It would make anyone who heard it wonder about her credibility if it wasn't for the marks on her. No way she could have fabricated those, or the smell in the air from the toxin he released." Macon folded his arms, stretching the sleeves of his open rain jacket. "Easy enough to figure out what was wrong with the computer program and discover it was deliberately tampered with."

Ridge gaped. "She was right?"

"You doubted her?"

"Of course not, but it's nice to hear we can prove it." Ridge squeezed the bridge of his nose. "Why would Elam do all that just to get her to come here? He didn't tell her to or coerce her. Unless I missed something huge."

Had her brother been harassing her all this time and she hadn't said anything?

Ridge continued. "Just to get her to make a withdrawal? Why does he need her for that?"

Macon shrugged. "He's been in prison long enough to make a plan, and it could hinge on her being there so he can get the payout. Which was apparently in this bank branch all along." He frowned over at the red brick front of the building.

"There's more to this that we're not seeing."

Macon nodded. "Like how to get through that setup he's got on the doors so you can go in after the cops clear it and get those people out."

Ridge studied the upper floor . . . Maybe the roof. "You think we can move the truck out of sight, get it around the back or something, and take the ladder to the roof? Come down from an upper floor?"

Conroy turned and pinned him with a stare. "Can you get my SWAT team in that way?"

Macon said, "Only if you ask nicely."

Ridge folded his arms. "Amelia isn't guilty of anything. She's a victim, like the rest of the hostages."

Conroy swallowed as though choosing his words carefully. "I'll instruct my people to treat her as such." He lifted his chin. "Get your truck into position, and I'll inform my people to be ready to go."

"Copy that." Ridge nodded.

Conroy turned away. Macon slapped Ridge on the shoulder and said, "Get her back."

Ridge ran to the others. "We're clearing out!" When he got close, he said more quietly, "There's a plan to get in."

Della navigated the busy street and drove around the corner. A lane behind the buildings offered access to employee entrances and had a few spaces for cars to park. She stopped beside the neighboring building, which had been the library until they'd built the new one on Anderson Avenue, hopefully parking out of sight of anyone that might be a lookout.

Ridge shoved his door open. "Let's go."

TWENTY-NINE

"YOU REALLY THINK I'M GOING TO JUST DO WHATever you say?" Amelia stared at her brother, a sick feeling in her stomach. She'd always disliked him because he had been nothing but horrible. She tried not to hate, but the amount of pain that had been dished out in her direction by him and others . . .

She'd have every right to be bitter at the world if she allowed it.

But something told her that if she did that, if she succumbed to the justification to hate, she would turn into a shriveled-up version of herself. If it went on long enough, she would never be able to come back to the kind of person she wanted to be.

So as she stood there, staring at her brother, she tried to feel nothing. She wanted to feel sorry for him, that he'd wasted his whole life working toward this.

She wanted Ridge.

Her brother jerked toward her. "You'll *do* whatever I tell you to."

"I'll sign my half over to the women's shelter in town. The church. The foundation that saves stray cats and nurses them back to health. Anyone who wants it can have a donation from me. Anyone *except* you."

His arm swung out toward her. She tried to flinch away, but it was too fast. The butt of his gun slammed against the side of her head.

Amelia blinked and realized she was on her hands and knees. Knocked down, but not out.

How many times in her life had she been forced to get back up? She'd lost count.

Amelia stared at the industrial-style carpet on the floor of the manager's office, her head pounding with pain. Her blonde hair hanging down on either side of her face. A nail chipped. The mother of all headaches ricocheted around her skull.

She sat back on her heels and braced her hand on the edge of the desk when she swayed. There was barely enough room to turn around in here. The manager sat at the desk, and she could see his feet under it, curled back with his ankles crossed in a defensive position.

He was nervous.

She looked over the desk and saw the fear on his face. Sweat rolling down his heavy jowls.

Elam said, "Is it done?"

He nodded, his cheeks wobbling. "It's printing now."

"Good. I'll need the safe open so y'all can get me my money." Elam backed up two steps and turned around to face the bank lobby. "All right—"

A swarm of police officers in SWAT gear raced into the room, spread out so that it seemed like they filled every spare inch, and started to call out.

"Police, hands up!"

"Hands up!"

"Drop that weapon!"

"Freeze! I said, freeze!"

Amelia backed up, clapping her hands over her ears. She wouldn't have been surprised if Elam had turned his gun on the cops and ensured they killed him. But he didn't. He froze, held the gun where the cops could see it, and set it on the floor when instructed.

He wanted the money.

Even if he had to wait until he was out of jail again to get it.

Amelia lowered her hand and heard a choking sound from the manager's direction. She glanced over, spotted the telltale gasping. Clutching his chest, confused why his arm hurt. "Medic!" She screamed the word and ran to the manager. "What's your name?"

She grabbed his wrist with one hand to feel for a pulse, and with the other, tore the top couple of shirt buttons free. He gasped, but his eyes rolled back in his head. "I'm a firefighter and an EMT." Her head still pounded, but it didn't matter when a man's life hung in the balance. A man who had just passed out.

A police officer she didn't recognize stuck his head in. "We need to get the doors open, then the EMTs can come in. Hang tight."

"Get the doors open or this man doesn't make it!" She paused for a second. "His heart stopped!"

Maria appeared at the door. "I'll find an AED."

The lobby was a mess of people, all of them talking. She didn't spot any of *her* people now that Maria was off hunting for an automated external defibrillator. The one thing that could save this guy's life.

A police officer raced in a few seconds later, hauling the life-saving device. "We've got it."

She spotted the intent on his face and moved out of the way, leaving them to it. If they didn't know who she was, they'd assume she was one of the victims here. She knew that because no one had arrested her.

Amelia stepped out of the manager's office and realized she might not be getting arrested, but she wouldn't be going far.

Lieutenant Basuto, in his SWAT gear, strode over. "Are you hurt?" His gaze scanned her, snagging on the source of the pain on her temple. "Much?"

"I could use an ice pack. And an explanation."

Basuto's dark brows lifted. "Let's get control of the scene, make sure everyone gets where they're supposed to be, and then we'll talk."

"He wanted the money. Which *apparently* has been here the whole time? At the same bank where someone was trying to frame me for paying people to hurt firefighters." She wanted to shake her head over the fact this didn't add up, but that would only hurt more. "And probably even that I paid someone to nearly kill me in the training house."

"Did you?"

Amelia stared at him. "If I say no, will you believe me?"

Before he had the chance to answer, Ridge yelled, "Amelia!" He raced over.

She moved around Basuto, done with their conversation. She'd much rather see Ridge.

He looked relieved to see her and opened his arms. She burrowed in, sliding her arms inside his jacket and wrapping them around his waist. He held on to her, and she pretended she could disappear into his hug. That they weren't in the middle of a room full of people.

Amelia let out a long breath.

"Are you okay?" He whispered the question in her ear. "That knot on your forehead looks nasty."

"Looks like she got pistol-whipped." That was Izan.

"Ouch." Della.

Apparently everyone was here. "How did you guys know to be here?"

Ridge said, "They called us to breach the door, but it looks like Maria is doing it."

Amelia turned in his arms and saw Maria speak to the cop beside her. He handed her a multitool.

Maria turned to the mechanism on the door handles, and a

second later, the doors swung open. "You'll want to call the National Guard, Chief." She was speaking to Conroy Barnes, the police chief. "They're missing some of their tech."

Maria went to the nearest window and removed a little block that looked like gray modeling clay. "Remove these carefully, separate the detonator, and it's safe."

"He rigged the place to blow?" She turned back to look up at Ridge, still in his arms. "Like . . . explode?"

"Who knows what his plan was?" Izan said, like the group was having a conversation, not just Amelia and Ridge. "It's not a great way to get out."

Amelia bit her lip.

Ridge smiled, then touched his lips to hers. Short and sweet. "I'm glad you're all right."

"I will be." She squeezed his middle with her arms, not quite ready to let go. "Seriously though. How was he going to get out of this situation?"

Della shrugged, catching the eye of a cop and waving. The woman actually blushed, which was interesting. Her Indian heritage gave her gorgeous Middle Eastern features. But it was the care she showed toward victims, particularly children, that made her a great person.

Ridge said, "The explosion could have been planned not just for if the police tried to open the doors but also for him to deliberately set off so he could escape in the confusion."

"That's a risky move, but I wouldn't put it past him to kill everyone inside just so he can have all that money." She wasn't sure what route she'd have chosen if she were Elam. As if she would ever rob a bank—even if he'd called it a withdrawal. "How did you guys get in?"

Izan clapped Ridge on the back of the shoulder, jogging them both. "Your boy here got us onto the roof next door, and we shimmied over a ladder between the buildings like we're the high-wire guys in a circus."

Amelia lifted her brows.

"The cops wanted to do it first," Ridge said, a gleam of little-boy delight in his eyes. "But we had to make sure it was secure."

"All right! If you're not a cop, you need to make your way outside." Basuto waved them all toward the door. "Ms. Patterson, don't go far."

She didn't respond to him. Her head thrummed with pain, and she touched her fingers to the spot. Ridge caught her hand. "Careful. We need to get that looked at."

Amelia nodded, which made her head hurt more.

"Come on." He walked her out, heading for the front door.

"No ambulance."

He turned them around to go the other direction. "We'll go to the truck."

She liked that idea much better. Ridge held her steady all the way out the back door, and before long, he was lifting her by her hips to set her on her seat in the front—his seat. *Their* seat. Until she passed the lieutenant's test and got her spot back.

Then where would he be?

Amelia decided not to worry about that right now. Ridge took a look at her head and shone a light in her eyes. He shook an ice pack to activate it and said, "Hold this to the spot where it hurts." So she knew she wasn't bleeding and didn't have a concussion.

Ridge grabbed the handle at the top of the door, leaned in, and kissed her. "I'll tell the chief we're headed back to the house."

Amelia closed her eyes in lieu of nodding.

She watched him jog away to the back door of the building, speak with Macon, and then jog back. He closed the door for her, and she buckled her seatbelt with only a little help from Della.

Amelia tried to turn around and look at the back seat. She

twisted most of the way before it hurt, far enough to say, "Thanks, guys."

"You think we're gonna leave you to those cops?" Della snorted and put the truck in Drive, easing slowly down the lane behind the building. "They don't call the shots. We're the real heroes."

Amelia frowned. What was that about? "Are you okay, Della?"

"Sure." She cleared her throat. "Why wouldn't I be?"

Izan chuckled and leaned forward to squeeze Amelia's shoulder. "We didn't know you were in there when we showed up, but if we had, we'd have driven faster to get there." He frowned at Della. "I could take a turn driving anytime you want."

Della said, "I don't."

Ridge snorted. Even the floater laughed.

Izan said, "I took a picture of Ridge on the ladders between the roofs. I'm gonna blow it up on canvas and put it on the wall in the firehouse kitchen."

Amelia grinned. "I want a copy for my house."

The truck jerked, the engine stuttering. Della said, "What—"

A loud bang sounded behind them, and the back of the truck lifted up. Flipped them over. Amelia saw a ball of fire in the rearview and didn't even have time to gasp.

The truck slammed back down on the street.

Everything went black.

THIRTY

RIDGE'S AWARENESS CAME BACK SLOWLY. THE tang in the air smelled like smoke and something chemical and hit his throat, making him cough. His body jerked with the motion, and pain exploded in his chest. He let out a moan but only heard the roar of his own breath in his ears.

He blinked. Smoke hung in the air, but he didn't have his helmet on or his air tank. What was . . .

The truck lay on its side on the street.

Light from the afternoon sun beamed through the front windshield, illuminating the particles in the air and the smoke all around them. *Fire.*

They'd been driving along, shooting the breeze. Blowing off steam. Relieved the bank situation had been resolved without anyone getting killed. He'd been praying quietly for the manager, that his heart attack hadn't been fatal.

Then . . . *boom.*

Ridge shifted, his shoulders at an odd angle. Even inhaling made fire flash through his chest. He gritted his teeth against the pain and tried to get his bearings.

Izan's legs were under him, his buddy knocked out cold by the look of it. Between Ridge and the seat. On his other side, toward the front, the floater, Warren Kaminsky, lay at an odd angle, blood running down from an open wound on the side of his face.

Ridge jerked into motion, causing more pain to roll through his chest. He looked around for something to press against Warren's head. The medical duffel . . . It was farther back down the truck, stored in a cabinet on the exterior. Now between the engine and the ground they were lying on.

What on earth had flipped the truck onto its side?

He heard yelling voices but couldn't make them out. *Focus.* He couldn't put pressure on an open wound that big. It looked like a section of Warren's skull had been crushed. Ridge sniffed back tears that wanted to fall down his cheeks.

Izan was still out. Over the front seat, he spotted Della's dark hair, but not Amelia.

"Hey!"

He twisted around and saw an older man in the open rear door, lying so he could see into the truck cab. Ridge said, "We need help."

"We called it in. One of your people was here earlier, but I don't know where they went." The man's face reddened. "Give me your hand. I'll get you out of there."

Ridge shook his head. "I'll pass you one of these guys. Can you lift them?"

"No, but someone else up here might. One sec." He slid out of sight.

Ridge realized the guy must've climbed up there. He didn't even know what street they were on or who'd caused the back of the truck to blow. It had sounded like an explosion, and in the moment, they'd all gone airborne, as if seatbelts were a figment of the imagination.

He checked Warren's pulse, then looked at the door above. "We need a basket."

"Ridge!" Bryce's head appeared in the open door. Eddie held

the door pushed back, up in the air. It was an odd sensation to have them looking down on him. To be the victim.

He tried to process what to ask for first.

Bryce looked at his rescue squad guys and said, "Get the basket."

Ridge could've cried right then. He touched a hand to his chest and breathed through the pain.

"Did you crack ribs?"

He shook his head. "I don't know." Ridge looked up. "What happened?"

"Once we get you all in ambulances, we can figure out the answer to that question." Bryce lowered his legs into the open doorway, set his boots on the back of the seat between rows, and lowered himself to sit there. He looked in front.

"Are they . . ." Ridge was scared to ask. He pushed off the door to sit up, trying to create enough room they could get Warren out as fast as possible.

"Della is out cold." Bryce looked around. "Where's Amelia?"

"What—"

"Basket!" Zack lowered it through the door and Ridge reached up, but Bryce caught it.

The lieutenant said, "Get Izan out of the way so we can load Warren in there. He doesn't look good."

"He still has a pulse." Ridge rolled Izan so he was tucked against the seat. The guy stirred, coming around. Ridge braced Izan out of the way with the back of his shoulder, which left his hands free. "Easy, Collins."

Bryce angled his legs into the small gap, lifted Warren by his armpits, and hoisted him onto the basket. A few seconds later, he had the straps secured. "Go!"

Zack and Eddie lifted the basket up out of the truck, and Ridge spotted a flash of Zoe's dark hair. The fact it was them made Ridge feel better, if only a little. *Thank You, Lord.*

Izan came awake yelling, flailing his arms.

"Whoa, buddy." Bryce caught him, and Ridge found a space to switch places with the lieutenant.

He scrambled to the back of the front seats and hoisted his body over enough to see around the seat, his head swimming with the disorientation of everything being sideways. "Amelia—" She wasn't here.

Della blinked up at him, crumpled against the passenger door.

Bryce said, "I asked where she was. I thought she went with you guys."

"She did." Ridge reached over the seat to Della. "Let's get out of here."

She grabbed his wrists, and he pulled her up. Ridge gritted his teeth against the pain in his chest. Della let go of his hands and got herself up. "You're hurt."

Bryce looked over his shoulder at Ridge. "I'll get Izan. Della, you're with Ridge."

"Copy that, Lieutenant."

Ridge didn't like that they felt they had to take charge to get him out, managing his injury when Della had been in the same crash. But if it was going to be anyone, he was glad it was them. "What happened to Amelia? She should be in here with us."

Della said, "Feels like someone stepped on me." She waited for Bryce to haul Izan up out of the open door, where he was pulled out by Eddie and Zoe, which meant Zack had gone with Warren to make sure the guy got to the ambulance.

Ridge needed Amelia. "Where is she?"

Della and Bryce held on to him, steadying Ridge so he didn't fall over. He reached one arm up, and Eddie caught it. When his friend started to pull him out, pain flashed through Ridge's middle. He cried out. Eddie let go, and Ridge slumped back down.

Bryce wriggled Ridge's T-shirt up out of his belt and looked at his chest while Ridge just stood there and breathed through the pain.

Della let out a hiss through clenched teeth at what they saw.

Ridge said, "I don't need the basket."

"You've probably got broken ribs. No one is pulling you out."

Della said, "We'll give you a boost. Send you up."

Ridge had to nod, because the other alternative was being helpless. "Get me out of here. Someone has to have seen what happened to Amelia."

Bryce made a cradle with his hands, and Ridge stepped into it. "Meg was on the sidewalk. She saw the whole thing, since it happened right in front of the Bridgewater Café."

Eddie caught Ridge under the shoulders. Zoe pulled him onto the side of the truck until they were sitting over the insignia on the driver's door. Della climbed out, followed by Bryce. The crowd of a few people who'd gathered on the sidewalk started to applaud.

Except Meg.

Ridge got down, thanks to a little help, and led the way to where the café owner stood on the edge of the curb. Traffic had stopped. An ambulance pulled around the corner at the end of the street. Probably a second rig, deployed to the call because the first had taken Warren to the hospital already. Rescue's intact truck was parked behind Truck 14. He might need a second to get his bearings on solid ground, but there was no time.

Zack wandered to his left side, Della on the right.

Ridge said, "Where's Amelia?"

"Dude," Zack cautioned.

"Did you see her, Meg?"

The café owner sniffed, and tears rolled down her cheeks. He knew who she was but didn't think he'd ever talked to her other than to give her his coffee order. And that hadn't been for a long time, since he'd cut out expensive coffee to save some money when he bought the town house.

"He took her."

"What—" Ridge moved one arm around his ribs. He wasn't going to the hospital. He was going to find Amelia.

Della said, "What happened, Meg?"

"He was dressed like a firefighter, so everyone thought he was one of you guys. He climbed down into the truck and used this strap thing around her to pull her out."

Della shifted, rubbing her shoulder. "That's why my arm feels like it's been stepped on."

Meg bit her lip. "He said he needed to get her to the hospital fast. No one said anything because we all thought he was a firefighter. No one else had climbed up there yet. We didn't know."

Ridge set his hand on her shoulder. "Did you see his face?"

"I don't know if it was Nicholas. It wasn't her brother."

He frowned. "You know about her ex?"

"Amelia is my best friend. Our fathers died in the same fire."

"Steven Hilden didn't die in a fire." Ridge wasn't sure what she was talking about.

"Not him." Meg's expression shifted to disgust. "Matt Patterson. The firefighter her mom married."

"Right. She told me about him." Ridge wanted to squeeze the bridge of his nose, but that would mean letting go of his ribs.

"We didn't know you guys were close," Zack said.

Meg shrugged. "We were supposed to have lunch today, since it's been a few days and we haven't caught up."

Ridge said, "If I can show you a photo of Nicholas, do you think you can ID the man who took her?"

Meg nodded. "If you show me his picture, I'll tell you if it was him or not."

Ridge squeezed her shoulder. "Thanks."

"Just find her. Because I don't think he took her to the hospital."

"Would Nicholas blow up a fire truck?" It couldn't have been Elam, though he wouldn't put it past the guy to get a friend to do this. He was currently in jail, however. Ridge couldn't help wondering if there was a connection between what had happened at the bank . . . and this.

Seemed like a golden opportunity for someone with ill intentions to deal Truck 14 a serious blow. Had Nicholas used the cover of the robbery to get his hands on Amelia?

Meg's face flushed. "Nicholas has left her alone for years. Why would he come here now?"

"If it isn't him," Ridge said, "then we have no idea who took her. Or why they would."

And they'd have no idea where to find her.

If it wasn't Elam and it wasn't Nicholas, then someone else had it in for her, and Ridge had been blind to it. This wasn't about the money in that bank account. It was about Amelia herself.

And all her nightmares coming true.

Della turned to look at the truck, which was still smoldering, though the rest of rescue squad were dealing with it. "There's something seriously not right about this."

Ridge spotted Kane sprinting toward them, Maria right behind him. He nearly collapsed in relief, seeing his family rushing to help them. With their skills and the firefighters' knowledge of the area, they'd locate her. They *would*. Before it was too late.

"We'll figure it out, Della." He promised her as much as he promised himself.

He prayed it happened fast, because the longer she was missing, the greater the risk that Ridge would lose her. The woman who'd come to mean so much to him that he didn't want to live without her.

Lord, where is she?

THIRTY-ONE

MELIA'S WORLD INVERTED. HER FACE SMACKED
against his back, against the material of a T-shirt beside the
buckle of the suspenders Benson Fire Department used to hold
up turnout coats. She wriggled and tried to get off, her mind a violent
haze of lightning. Nothing but panic, sharp edges, and the bottomless
fear of knowing she was trapped and there was nothing she could do
to save herself.

The truck.

He stomped up steps and inside, which made her realize the
bone-chilling cold had been because they were outside and she
didn't have a jacket on. Her head swam, and her stomach threatened to deposit the last thing she'd eaten on the floor.

He moved down hallways, through rooms, until her mind spun
so much her eyes started to roll back in her head.

Then he bent his knees and flipped her onto her back. A clang
reverberated around her, and Amelia found herself surrounded
by bars.

A cage barely big enough for her to turn around in, or sit up.

The ceiling stretched high above her, almost like a ballroom.
Lights glared down, filling the room with a yellow glow that

should've been soothing but cut knives through her eyes. She wanted to squeeze them shut but had to know.

Amelia lifted her head off the floor of the cage and looked at him.

Nicholas stared down at her.

She heard someone whimper, and it wasn't her. A glance to her right showed her another cage with Cherry inside. Her blonde hair matted and ruffled, her face pale, and her eyes wide—bright with tears.

Amelia whipped her head back around to him. "Let her go. She has nothing to do with this." Her voice was barely audible.

Nicholas sneered down at her. "You think you have a say here? In any of this?" He waved his arm.

She followed the sweep of it. More cages to her left. Who knew how many? Amelia's breath shuddered. They might be empty right now. But who was he planning to have occupy them?

"What do you want?"

His lips curled up into a terrible grin, but he said nothing. He just walked out through an open doorway, out of sight.

Amelia let out a breath. She twisted around and spotted a thin pad under her, a mat. This had to be a cage for a big dog. She couldn't stretch out in it. She tucked her knees up to her chest and tried to sit, leaning against the back of the cage.

"Cherry?" She cleared her throat. "Cherry, look at me."

The other woman stared at the empty doorway.

"Talk to me. What's going on?"

Cherry turned to her then, an angry expression on her face. "This is all your fault."

"Tell me what's happening." She curled her fingers through the metal wire enclosing her. Nothing in her life had ever been this bad.

She had no idea what would happen next and no idea what she would be subjected to.

But Cherry was pregnant. There wasn't much she and her baby

would be able to survive unscathed. Amelia had to take the punishment he intended for Cherry, to save the mother and child from harm.

And maybe that was the point.

"We both angered him." Amelia didn't want to say it, but she had to. "This is about revenge."

"It's about *you*. Everything is always about you."

Amelia bit her lip.

"It's why I'm here, isn't it? Because of you. Now I'm going to die, and that will be because of you too." The words echoed in the huge room.

All the way to Amelia's heart.

"I'm sorry," she told Cherry. "I'm sorry you're in harm's way because of me."

"You should be sorry."

"Can you tell me if he's said anything to you?" The need to know was a desperate thing that swelled in her like a wave.

Cherry looked away, leaning against the far corner of her cage. Dejected. Out of hope or the strength to talk to Amelia.

"What is going to happen to us, Cherry?"

"He'll kill us." Cherry shifted a little. "Isn't that obvious?"

Amelia closed her eyes for a second, the pain in her head almost overwhelming. She pursed her lips and blew out a long breath. An image of Ridge crossed her mind.

The twins.

Maria and Kane.

Meg, her best friend and the closest thing to a sister Amelia would ever have.

Her coworkers, who were like family to her even though they had families of their own. Were they dead? Was Ridge gone? Amelia felt the burn of tears behind her eyelids. The twins would lose their anchor.

They would be devastated.

She sniffed. *Don't do that to them.*

She didn't know how this thing worked, but right now, it seemed so natural to talk to someone who could help. Maybe the only person—Being—who could.

I know You're listening.

Okay, so that sounded like a threat. But if her friends were right and there was a God, then He knew who He was dealing with.

Are they all correct? Because I'm kind of out of options here, and I could use some help. Cherry and her baby need You to . . . swoop down and save them. However You'd like to do that.

Yeah, she was terrible at this. But it wasn't like she'd ever prayed before.

In fact, had she ever done the right thing? Or had she simply spent years doing whatever was best for *her*, with no regard for any kind of higher power or where she fit in some grand plan.

This wasn't really the time to have existential thoughts. She needed to figure out a way to rescue herself and Cherry.

She shifted over to the door, pushing on the wire. A padlock on the latch kept it secured, but if she could bend it far enough, she might be able to climb free. Maybe not, but she couldn't lose hope. That would only lead to giving up, and then she'd never get out of here.

If she wanted to get back to her life, such as it was, she had to get free.

Amelia kept pushing on the bottom edge of the door, even though she'd never fit. Between the padlock and the hinge on the other side, she wouldn't be able to create a gap big enough to wiggle through.

She sighed aloud and quit pushing.

Amelia backed up again, her movements awkward in the cramped space. She checked her pockets and everywhere she could think but had nothing on her except jeans, a T-shirt and thin sweater, and her socks and flat canvas shoes.

It wasn't like she carried weapons on her day off, but that would have come in handy in the bank.

Elam.

He had to have been working with Nicholas, or they had some kind of arrangement. The timing of the bank incident and the truck blowing with her in the rig was a little too coincidental for her to believe otherwise.

Not that it mattered now. She was here.

Amelia turned and looked at the other woman. Cherry stared back at her, betrayal and anger in her features. There was no one else here, and she needed to blame someone. It made sense that person was Amelia.

"I don't understand why I'm here. I wanted out. I left him, and I got away."

"I did the same thing." Amelia tried to show this scared young woman empathy, when she really wanted to tell her that she should have simply kept running. That she never should have stopped.

"It's you he wants. Why am I here?" She sniffed and swiped at her cheek.

Leverage.

It was the thought that popped into Amelia's mind. Relief flooded her that she hadn't said it aloud. This woman didn't need to know that Nicholas and his mind games would likely pit the two women against each other. He knew Amelia wouldn't let an innocent mother and her child suffer, and so he would threaten Cherry and her child in order to get Amelia to comply. He would use items like those explosives Elam had in the bank—definitely supplied by Nicholas and his connections. She had no doubts about that.

But what would he want her to do?

Her stomach churned, but she forced her thoughts to focus on nothing so that she didn't think about it.

She needed to be reassuring. "Cherry, I don't think he would hurt his own baby. He wants a child that will take after him, some-one he can mold." Twist. Corrupt. Like her father had done with Elam. She knew how that worked because she'd lived it. "He's not going to risk losing that."

She caught the look on Cherry's face.

"Is the baby his?"

Cherry's head jerked around. "It doesn't matter. We're both in danger."

"How did you get involved with him?"

She looked away, a hard expression on her face.

It's why I'm here, isn't it? Because of you.

"Cherry . . ." Amelia needed her to start telling the whole truth. "How did you get involved with him?" She looked like Amelia. A strong enough resemblance that Amelia would believe he'd stuck to his type. And with the added bonus of the pregnancy, she'd be sympathetic when this woman showed up needing help. "You came here purposely to dupe me?"

"He said he'd give me five grand." Cherry sniffed.

And now she was a target. A pawn. "I'm sorry."

"You should do what he wants. Then I'll be able to go free."

Amelia wasn't so sure about that, but Cherry needed to believe in something. "I'm praying we can figure a way out of this. That someone will find us and help us."

"Praying?" Cherry scoffed.

"Maybe you should try it as well. Increase our chances." Two prayers were better than one, right? No matter how Cherry felt about religion, she knew as well as Amelia did that they needed help.

Nicholas's form darkened the doorway.

Cherry whimpered and curled into a smaller ball in the cage.

Amelia watched him wander into the room and scanned his features now that she could think more clearly. His hair was a little longer than regulation, as if he didn't care to cut it. The dark strands were nearly chin length. Mussed from where he'd run his hands through it, far too excited to be calm.

Anticipating what was going to happen next.

That same gleam in his eyes, but a little different. More reminiscent of the calls Truck 14 went on where they met drug addicts, whether on the street or squatting in a house. They helped everyone they could, passing on information about local services available to help those who wanted to change their lives. So many were stuck in a hopeless cycle.

He had that same edge in his gaze.

"What do you want?" She held herself very still.

"You'll find out." He stared at her, so still that she had to move just to break the anxiety-filled tension.

Amelia's sore muscles protested.

The knot on her head pounded through her skull.

She bit the inside of her lip. "Just tell me. You owe me that much."

His eyes flashed. "I do owe you. But not what you think. This is going to be the worst punishment you've ever received."

"Why? I've been gone for years. I have nothing to do with you—not anymore."

"You cost me everything. You ruined my life."

"I didn't do that." She had to say it. "You did that to yourself."

"You'll pay."

He turned and strode out of the room, his footsteps echoing up to the ceiling. She heard a heavy door shut, the thud practically shaking the house. A few moments later, headlights flashed across the front of the house, moving across the floor through the open front window.

Freedom, so close she could see it.

But there was no way out . . . back to Ridge. Where she could finally tell him that she was in love with him.

God, help us.

THIRTY-TWO

COME WITH ME." KANE'S STATEMENT WAS MORE of an order than a request.

Ridge watched his cousin stride to the break room at the police department. Olivia said, "Go see what he wants."

He needed answers, but if Kane wanted to pull him aside, it had to be important.

"Shut the door."

"Are you going to keep ordering me around all day? I have things to do. We need to keep pestering the cops until we have a lead on where Amelia might be. Now that we know it was Nicholas who took her—"

"Interviews take time. Elam isn't going to give up his only ticket to a deal easily." Kane dumped his backpack on the small round table, which wobbled under the weight of it. He drew out a roll of bandage. "Maria told the twins what happened. Now take off your shirt."

Meg might have confirmed that the man she'd seen was Amelia's ex, but what did that get them? They still had no idea where to find the guy. "We don't have time for this."

"You don't want to go to the hospital, you take off your shirt."

Ridge stared at him.

"I'll cut it off and give you another one." It might not have been meant as a threat, but with Kane's broody stare, Ridge wasn't sure.

The guy was mad that Ridge had been hurt, the truck had exploded and a man was in critical condition at the hospital, and Amelia had been taken. Not exactly under his nose. Kane knew he wasn't responsible for what'd happened. Him or Maria, who was currently at the town house with the twins, keeping them safe.

"I can get it off." He had ditched the turnout pants and found tennis shoes, so there were no suspenders. Ridge got one arm through the hole, ducked his head, and moved the shirt to the left, where he drew it down his arm.

"You should've gotten an X-ray."

"So they can tell me what I already know?" Ridge dropped the shirt on the table. "They're not broken. Just cracked."

Kane ducked his head to Ridge's side.

If the twins found out he'd been admitted, they'd be more freaked out than they probably already were about everything that had been going on. As freaked out as he was not knowing what had happened to Amelia.

Where is she, Lord?

Kane wrapped his ribs. Ridge gritted his teeth through the whole painful process, but when his cousin was done, he said, "That actually feels better, thanks."

"I've had the same injury a time or two." Kane grabbed Ridge's shirt and tossed it back at him, followed by a bottle of over-the-counter pain pills to take once he'd put his shirt back on. That would take the edge off.

"You could always go home to the twins. Let Maria and me find Amelia and bring her back to you."

Ridge put the pills on his tongue and ducked his head to the faucet at the small sink. Some glorious person had put a fresh pot of coffee on, and the scent of it hung in the air while the carafe popped and sizzled as the dark brew dripped into the glass container.

He turned to his cousin. "Is that what you would do? Sit back and let someone else find her?"

Ridge knew the answer already, because it had only been a matter of months since Maria had gone up against dangerous men who would have torn this country apart with a terror attack. Kane had a personal interest in justice, along with the rest of his former Delta Force team. All of them had stopped the threat and saved a whole lot of people who would never know they'd even been in danger.

"No." Kane's expression didn't lose any of its shadows. "But Maria doesn't like being cooped up any more than the rest of us."

"And she's trained but I'm not."

"But Amelia is *your* woman." Kane lifted his chin.

"I'm glad we have that figured out." He spotted Olivia in the doorway.

"You guys need anything?" She glanced between them, now in her street clothes where she'd been in her uniform just a moment ago. "I just clocked off."

Ridge said, "How do you feel about private protection detail?"

"Can you afford me?" Her eyes gleamed. "Actually, don't worry about it. The twins? I heard they came to the firehouse. They're probably worried about your people, and Amelia."

All Ridge had done when he'd shown up here twenty minutes ago was ask her about Elam. It choked him up a bit to know she cared about them. She wanted to help.

Kane said, "I'll tell Maria you're relieving her."

"Sure, but I have her number." Olivia shrugged. "I'll give her a call. See if they want any dinner on my way over."

"Thanks, Liv." Ridge swallowed against the lump in his throat.

She nodded. "Find your girl."

Ridge poured two mugs of coffee while Kane made his call and explained to Maria what was happening. He handed Kane's over, and they went back to the main PD office, pretty quiet and almost empty except for Sergeant Donaldson at his desk over in the corner.

"You guys want to listen to the interview?" Aiden got out of his seat, smoothing down his tie as he moved.

"Is that allowed?" Ridge asked.

Kane nudged him. "He offered."

Aiden tipped his head. "This way."

The back hall between the bullpen and the rear entrance had doors all down it. Holding was downstairs, and the city was working on plans to expand the whole building or even move it to a different location, considering the cops were crammed in here on a slow day.

Aiden opened a door that said VIEWING. "You were never here."

"Thanks." Ridge ducked in.

Kane turned the dial on the wall so they could hear voices, and Aiden shut the door.

In the interview room, Jessica, the detective, and Lieutenant Basuto sat across from Elam, who faced them.

"…expect us to believe that." Basuto sat back in his chair, clearly unimpressed.

Ridge didn't need to be able to see his face to register that. Not that he liked this guy much right now. Considering he'd dragged Amelia here and interrogated her, Ridge wasn't going to be best friends with the guy anytime soon.

Jessica said, "You got that equipment from a guy at the National Guard who conveniently 'loses' items and then sells them to whoever will pay the most."

"I never bought anything from him," Elam said. "I don't even know the guy. I found that stuff."

"Found it? Really?" Basuto leaned forward. "You expect us to believe you enacted that fiasco at the bank because you *found* C4 and a locking mechanism? That seems convenient."

Elam didn't say anything.

He didn't seem to have asked for a lawyer, or he'd have representation in the room with him. Which meant he thought he could handle this by himself. *So he's cocky.* Prideful enough he might easily make a mistake.

"Not such a good plan. I mean, it didn't work." Basuto shrugged. "Whose idea was it? You should probably fire that person. I think they steered you wrong."

"Ain't nobody calling the shots but me." Elam lifted his chin.

Basuto said, "So you're the big man."

Jessica tipped her head to the side. "Seems to me like you're the failure. Going back to jail, nothing to give us to score yourself a sweet deal. You'll be sixty by the time you get to use that money. Assuming, of course, that the government doesn't discover the account and seize your assets."

"What do you want?" He tried to be nonchalant. "Maybe I've got something to trade."

"Try me." Basuto shrugged. "We'll see."

"She's gone, isn't she?" Elam glanced between the two cops.

Ridge shifted, his body jerking as he realized what Elam was talking about. Pain flashed through his ribs despite the pills he'd taken. "He knows."

Amelia was missing and her brother knew.

Jessica said, "She who? Who is gone, Elam?"

He only rolled his eyes. "As if you don't know. Her crazy ex. That guy is . . ." His voice trailed off into muttering mixed with some colorful curses.

Ridge said, "Tell them where she is," to the glass.

Basuto was the one who said, "Yes, it would seem that your sister is gone. Are you confessing that her ex is the one who orchestrated your plan?"

"Set me up, didn't he?" Elam made a face that was pure displeasure. "I'm gonna kill that . . ." He quit talking.

"Good idea not stating your intention to murder someone in front of two cops who *will* testify against you," Jessica said. "Who is he?"

"Nicholas. What kind of name is that?" Elam sneered.

"And where did he take Amelia?"

Ridge held still. "It can't be that easy. He needs to bargain, he's not just going to answer the question."

Kane made a small sound of acknowledgment in his throat. His phone buzzed, and he lifted his wrist to look at the screen of his smartwatch. "Maria is here."

Elam studied his fingernails.

"Good," Ridge said. "We could use her help as well."

Finally, Elam shrugged. "My father had a lot of properties all over town."

"I'll run a search." Kane strode out, probably going to meet Maria. Whatever he had in that backpack of his, Ridge prayed it was tech that would enable them to get Amelia back.

With no one in the room, he let out a breath, braced a hand on the glass, and hung his head. The persistent ache in his ribs flared to life again as if increasing simply because he was acknowledging it rather than skillfully pretending it didn't exist.

When he drew his hand back from the glass, it flexed. Not glass, thick plastic. Basuto glanced over his shoulder, one brow raised.

He turned back to Elam. "So this stalker ex has her, and you want us to go on a wild-goose chase through every property your father owned just to find her? She'll be dead by then. Or he's already put her on a plane. He'll take her somewhere no firefighter will ever find her."

Ridge groaned.

Basuto knew he was in here.

"Find her." Elam shrugged. "Don't find her. What do I care? I'll have my money to retire with."

Ridge went to the door and let himself out. In the bullpen, Maria and Kane bent to look at the same laptop screen, Aiden standing nearby. A couple of uniformed officers sat in the break room, drinking coffee.

"Anything? Because Elam is giving them nothing." He told them what had been said.

Aiden nodded. "Basuto has a point. A wild-goose chase is a waste of resources. We need intel and probable cause so we can get a warrant and go kick a door in."

Ridge sucked in a long breath.

"We're looking at options." Kane didn't even glance over.

Ridge paced down the aisle between desks and then back over. He'd never felt so helpless in his life as he did right now. *God, how do I get her back?*

He prayed Amelia wasn't hurt or in imminent danger of being hurt.

That things didn't get worse before they got better.

And he prayed she would find peace in Jesus so that she wasn't alone. If she cried out to Him, she would find safety in His arms. No matter what the outcome would be.

That was the promise he believed in.

Aiden said, "I'll be right there."

Ridge twisted around to the sergeant's desk, where Aiden set the phone back on its cradle. "It's okay if you need to go."

"You'll want to come with me." Aiden slid his holstered weapon onto his belt and grabbed a set of keys. "A call just came in from one of your neighbors. There's a disturbance at your house."

Ridge ran for the entrance as fast as he could.

The twins.

THIRTY-THREE

AMELIA CAUGHT A GLIMPSE OF HEADLIGHTS ON the front window. The temperature in the house had descended far enough that she couldn't stop shivering.

Cherry said, "He's back."

Amelia shifted in the cage and tried to look, but twenty feet away from the window, there wasn't much to see. "He's back."

Maybe they both needed to state the obvious, grasping for the truth. Not reality so much. Just a clear handle on what was happening. He'd been gone a while, maybe an hour—possibly two. Long enough that they might be outside of town. And the PD jurisdiction. They could be in an area overseen by state police.

Cherry started to cry quietly.

Amelia was going to face him with her chin high, or she wouldn't be facing him at all. She was so different from the broken, scared woman who had left Benson and come back to Last Chance County with nothing. That woman hadn't seen the signs until it was too late. She'd wrapped her self-esteem and her confidence up in Nicholas and allowed him to dictate everything.

When she'd begun to object to his treatment of her, things had deteriorated. He'd become even more controlling and, as she'd later realized, started drugging her coffee.

She wanted coffee.

Okay, so she wanted to get out of here first. Then she was going to have a cup of coffee, finally. She refused to live in fear anymore.

He entered the room, pushing two teenage girls in front of him. The girls were wide-eyed with cloth around their mouths and their wrists secured in front of them. That man wasn't anyone she had ever loved.

"What did you do?" Amelia screamed the question at him, clutching the bars of the cage.

That's who the cages were for.

She scanned them for injuries.

Maddie screamed behind the cloth, her cheeks flaring. Desperate for Amelia to help her. Tears rolled down Ella's face.

"Let them go!" Amelia would break this cage apart and throttle him. "They have nothing to do with this."

Nicholas didn't look anything like the man she'd fallen for. He hadn't been the same when she'd left Benson years ago, and now seemed more like a stranger. Had he suffered some kind of breakdown?

He jabbed something into Ella's back, and the girl arched. She screamed behind the cloth, and Amelia saw he had a sort of cattle-prod-looking thing in one hand.

"Don't hurt them! They haven't done anything to you!" She rattled the cage.

He shoved them without pressing the button, and they stumbled forward. He swiped out with his boot and kicked her cage, laughing. "All part of the plan, sweetheart."

That word. He'd used that word when he'd needed to justify getting angry or pushing her around. Tearing her down. *Sweetheart.*

"I'm not your sweetheart. And those girls are innocent. Let

them go, they have *nothing* to do with you." Anger burned in her stomach like a fire blazing. "Don't—"

"Get in." He shoved them toward two of the cages.

The girls whimpered, finally complying with his instructions.

"Nicholas. Let them go." She stared at him, fully focused on her mission to get him to let the twins go. If she looked at them, she would shatter. "You're only here for me. Why are you involving all of them? Just take me. I'll go with you. I'll do whatever you want. Nicholas, please."

He looked at her, that cattle prod in his hand. "You know I like it when you say *please*."

She gritted her teeth. "Let them go, please."

Two long strides brought him over to her.

"Nich—"

He stuck the cattle prod into her cage and jammed it into her side. Every muscle in Amelia's body clenched at the same time, her nerve endings suddenly white-hot.

She fell against the side of the cage and slumped into a heap, curled up.

He walked some more. She could only stare at the far wall and listen to him stop. He clinked a lock. "Get out."

The twins gasped. One whispered, "She's pregnant."

Cherry walked in front of Amelia, shoved along by Nicholas. If he used that cattle prod on a pregnant woman . . .

Amelia gasped. A tear rolled from the corner of her eye onto the mat beneath her.

"No one leaves." Nicholas shoved the door closed, and the slam echoed through the room.

"Amelia."

She tried to move.

"Amelia."

"She isn't dead, is she?"

She needed all her strength to get her arm out from under her, push herself up, and lean back against the side of the cage, facing the twins.

Relief washed over Maddie's face, the cloth gag now around her neck. "Are you okay?"

Amelia shook her head.

"He killed Olivia." Maddie gasped. "He hit her so hard there was blood all over her face. He put her in his trunk."

Ella said, "He's going to kill us, isn't he?"

Amelia took a breath. "I'm not going to let that happen."

She tried to sound certain when she was anything but. Who knew what Nicholas was doing to Cherry outside of the room? And Olivia? Was the officer really out in the trunk of his car, nothing but a cold body with no life in her?

Amelia inhaled a shuddering breath.

"Ridge will find us." Maddie sat against the back of her cage, hands on her lap—still tied at the wrist. Ella was biting the ropes, trying to work herself free. Maddie said, "He'll be here."

A gunshot echoed through the house.

Maddie flinched.

Ella looked up from her ropes.

"Cherry." Amelia winced. She needed to keep her feelings— and her fear—in check, even while she cried. He'd murdered a pregnant woman?

Nicholas came into the room, a gun in his hand down by his side. He had something in the other hand and took it to the window. He stuck the thing on the bottom of the window frame. Whatever it was looked like what Elam had used on the windows at the bank to keep the police from coming through them.

As she watched, he drew out what looked like a marker and wrote *vibration sensor* on the window. Backward, so she couldn't read it. Like a mirror image—or something that could be read from outside. He bent and flipped a switch on the little thing.

He did the same with a couple of other windows in the room.

"Nicholas."

He didn't look at her.

"Nicholas, tell me you didn't kill a pregnant woman." She gasped. "Tell me you didn't do that, and I'll help you. We can leave here and run, and you can do whatever you want to me. None of them are involved."

She didn't know how to convince him.

God, help me. Please.

She needed a way to get through to him, but he was heading for the door again. He was going to leave, and she would lose her shot at convincing him to do the right thing for once in his miserable life.

"I love you!" She screamed the words as loud as she could. He wouldn't be convinced. She didn't even say it like she believed it.

He turned at the door. "You always were a liar."

"Don't leave me here. Take me with you."

His eyes flickered, as if he was actually contemplating listening to her.

He felt more than heard movement behind him, and someone slammed into his back. Nicholas stumbled forward, falling onto his knees.

Olivia wrapped her arms around his shoulders, her legs around his waist, and her teeth flashed. Gritted as she struggled with him. Blood had dried down her face from a knot on her forehead, and she had the glassy eyes of someone with a concussion.

Nicholas toppled farther, and the gun skittered across the floor.

He roared, grabbed her arm, and twisted around, rotating Olivia's arm the wrong way. Her knees buckled and she screamed. Bone snapped.

The twins screamed.

Nicholas dragged Olivia across the floor by her broken arm and kicked her into the cage. He padlocked her in.

Then he came to Amelia.

She backed up, huddled as small as she could.

"I suppose reinforcements will be here soon enough." He glanced around. "I'll have to speed this up."

He dragged more of those window things from his pocket and placed them on the locks for each cage—except hers. Nicholas retrieved his gun and unlocked the padlock securing her.

He backed up. "Get out."

"Did you kill Cherry?"

"She whined too much. It was annoying."

Amelia's whole body shuddered. He'd killed a mother and her baby.

"Get out!"

She scrambled forward. "Don't hurt them."

He dragged her off the floor. "Walk." Pressed the gun to her side. "When your boyfriend gets here, everything needs to be ready."

He thought Ridge was coming.

How would he know that? And how would Ridge know where to find them? "Don't hurt him!"

Nicholas laughed. "He's going to suffer most of all. He'll have to live knowing he's responsible for the deaths of you and his sisters. Sweet victory."

He wanted to hurt Ridge.

But he was going to kill Amelia—and all the rest of them.

"You're sick."

He dragged her to the hall and through the open front door, kicking it shut. "Open that bag." The duffel beside the door bulged with another of those devices, like the one Elam had used on the door.

"What is it?"

"Motion-activated detonation."

"You were going to kill my brother."

"That idiot deserves to die," Nicholas said. "He only cares about money." He told her what to do with the device, and she complied with shaky hands. "I get my sweet revenge, no one is left alive to come after me, *and* I get all the money."

Amelia turned to him. "That won't work."

"Of course it will. I've thought of everything." He smiled and his eyes gleamed. "This plan will work."

Before she could say anything, he dragged her down the hall, through this maze of a house. The twins were in danger, locked in booby-trapped cages. Olivia, the same, and she needed medical attention.

She swiped at her cheeks. "What happened to you? You were a firefighter. You protected people. How could you do this?"

"I'm not a firefighter anymore. Thanks to you, I'm nothing." He wrapped an arm around her, securing her to his side with a grip more powerful than anything she'd ever felt.

She struggled against him but couldn't get out of his grasp.

"I lost my job. My friends. My house. All of it, all because you say too much and people think too much who have no business questioning *me*." He slapped his gun hand on his chest. "It'll take that money of yours to set me up. Get me to Bolivia so I can start over."

"You don't have to do this."

Nicholas dragged her into a small room with a folding table set up and one plastic chair, the only furniture she'd seen so far. "I want to see the look on your boyfriend's face when he sees it's all gone. He'll know how it feels. What loving you does to a man, leaving him with nothing."

He shoved her at the table. "Sign that paper." Nicholas backed up, holding the gun on her. "Sign it, Amelia *Hilden*." He chuckled. "Think I would've liked your daddy. Sounds like he might've been my kind of guy."

She stared at the paper. A transfer of funds, everything filled out but the signature box.

"Tick tock, *sweetheart.* Everything needs to be in place when your boyfriend gets here."

Amelia lifted the pen and turned to him. "If I sign the money over to you, why don't you just leave? You'll have what you—"

He fired a shot. It went wide over her shoulder.

Amelia flinched, curling her shoulders in.

"Sign it!"

THIRTY-FOUR

HOW DO YOU KNOW IT'S THIS ONE?" RIDGE asked, leaning forward between the two front seats.

Kane pulled off the highway onto an overgrown lane through the wooded area around Last Chance County. "Power bill is still being paid."

Maria sat in the front passenger seat on her laptop, using a hotspot from her phone, scrolling through bank records. "This is the only one where utilities are covered. The rest are abandoned."

"Covered by who?"

"Actually," Maria said, "the same account that was pegged as being Amelia's, the one used to pay those men to endanger firefighters."

"Her brother was in jail. Is he still running his father's empire— or what's left of it—even now? Didn't seem like he was interested in anything but Dad's money." Ridge bounced one knee up and down, trying to keep it together.

Maria said, "The account was opened by Elam Hilden. Supposedly. But he was in jail at the time. All of it was put into her name, like a transfer of ownership moving the funds to Amelia—under her birth name."

"To set them both up?" Kane glanced over. "When was it opened?"

"A year ago."

Ridge said, "So he's been in town working on his plan at least that long."

They'd been to the town house and managed to get the cops to let them look around inside. Olivia had to have been subdued and taken and both the girls loaded into a car as well. But no one had used the front door, so he had nothing on camera but the edge of the driveway.

Nicholas, or so he presumed, had to have come in through the garage and taken the girls, then backed out. The feed on his doorbell cam had shown a car coming in. Less than fifteen minutes later, he'd left. Inside, furniture had been overturned, and someone had clearly dropped a glass, shattering it across the floor.

It didn't matter that the cops wanted to take evidence and test the blood on the glass for DNA. That wasn't what would find his sisters. Or Olivia.

Or Amelia.

Everything. His whole world apart from the two in this car. They were captive to a man twisted around with narcissism, who had nothing to lose and everything to gain if his revenge plan came to fruition.

But why take his sisters?

They were innocent. Dragged into this.

Ridge fought to control his breathing.

"Almost there." Kane pegged the gas and got them down the lane faster.

Branches clacked against the outside of the car, scratching the paint. The house that came into view was worse than the mansion. In fact, it made the mansion look small. He'd never have known it was here, hidden as it was in the woods. But it made sense that

Steven Hilden had multiple residences, places he could keep public while others remained private.

Ridge hadn't liked the guy as chief when he joined the fire department years ago, but he hadn't been stationed at Eastside until after the guy had been taken down. God had spared him from having to go up against that man where others hadn't been so fortunate.

He was going to lean on that favor and the fact he could remain steady. So long as he got his girls back safe and sound. He was going to use the temperament that God had given him to hold it together. With God's help, he'd be there for Amelia and his sisters so he could take care of them while they recovered.

Kane pulled to the side in front of the house.

Ridge got out, not even knowing what the plan was. Get in. Find them. Get them out. Subdue this Nicholas guy until the police got here. As soon as they knew for sure it was the right place, they would call the cops.

Kane made him stop long enough to put on a bulletproof vest, and Ridge put his jacket on over it. He ran to the house and spotted something written in huge letters on the front window, to the right of the door. Huge wood double doors with columns either side, stretching up two stories. This place was massive. It needed to be converted into a retreat center, or an annex of the local college.

Ridge got close enough to read *vibration sensors*.

Kane dragged his arm back. "What are you doing? You have no idea what situation you're walking into."

Ridge waved at the window. "We know something." He crept forward, able to see into the brightly lit interior. Across the bare wood floor was a row of . . . "Are those . . . they're cages!" He spotted Ella, then Maddie. Beyond them was another person, but he couldn't tell who the blonde was.

"Ella!" Ridge waved his hands.

"Don't knock on the window." Kane's tone didn't invite anything but following that order. "Even yelling could be risky."

Maria moved closer to the window, looking at the frame on the inside, right by the glass. "Probably the same stuff illegally purchased from the National Guard. We need a window or a door not wired to blow."

Kane said, "We have to assume they all are."

Ridge hadn't taken his attention off the window. *Come on, Ella. Look my way.* They needed to know where Nicholas had gone. And whether the person in that third occupied cage was Amelia or Olivia. What was happening in there?

And how were they going to get inside?

"I'll find one." Maria kissed Kane quickly, then jogged away, around the building.

"She'll find a drainpipe to climb up. I doubt he wired every window."

Ridge winced. He didn't like the risk. He waved his arms as big as he could. If Nicholas came into view suddenly, he'd have to duck down below the window without being seen.

Assuming the guy didn't already know they were here.

"Call it in."

Ridge followed the order since Kane was trained in this kind of stuff and Ridge was the local with local contacts. He dialed Aiden's number and put it on speaker, getting the police sergeant on the line.

As soon as he answered, Ridge said, "We found the girls and your officer." The cops would care about a fellow cop. Not that they didn't care about teens in danger, but having Olivia caught up in it meant an added layer they couldn't ignore. "But we can't get in the house. It's wired up like the bank."

Aiden said, "We just took the National Guard traitor into custody for illegal weapons sales. The ATF is about to show up and take over the investigation, and when that happens, we'll lose any shot at intel. So tell me what you need to know."

Kane leaned over. "A frequency that will jam the signal that alerts the detonator to a vibration."

"Copy that," Aiden said. "I'm sending units to your location. Wait for them to arrive. We'll get you a way in." The police sergeant paused for a second. "I know what it's like to have loved ones in danger. Keep it tight, Foster."

He hung up.

Ridge stowed the phone, searching the windows above the door, since Ella hadn't looked over. He didn't want to know why she was slumped against the side of the cage. Was she unconscious or simply dejected? Waiting for rescue.

I'm here. He wasn't going to let anything happen to his sisters if there was something he could do about it. But where was that Nicholas guy?

They were going to have a reckoning.

He glanced back at Kane, who said, "Copy that." Then he looked over and yelled, "Maria found something!"

Ridge waved him off.

He continued left while Kane ran right, going after Maria. Ridge scanned the exterior of the building, looking for a drain and a window that might have been missed. Like a tiny bathroom with frosted glass but big enough for him to crawl through. He had his multitool, so he could break glass. Risky, given the noise and how likely it was he'd be injured. But did that matter?

His family was inside this house, trapped with a guy who was prepared to do anything.

Revenge against Amelia.

But why involve the twins? Unless he wanted Ridge to suffer as well.

Olivia had probably been caught up in it, another victim. She might even be dead.

Ridge raced along the west side of the mansion and peered around the back. On the far side, he spotted car headlights, and maybe Kane and Maria, talking to someone else. He didn't know what was going on over there. It was too dark and too far to see.

Whatever it was, he needed to get inside and get to the twins.

And he knew exactly how he was going to do it—that second-floor balcony. Not the wide doors that led out to the back view. The window beside those.

If he sat on the concrete rail that protected someone on the balcony from falling, he could reach over and smash that window.

Ridge tugged on the drain that ran down the back wall, close enough he could get to the balcony. It didn't budge, so he started to climb.

When he was high enough to reach for the balcony, he saw that the door was slightly ajar. Abandoning the idea of smashing a window and crawling in, Ridge climbed over the edge. He stayed out of sight, behind the wall, and then peered around.

No one in the room. It looked dark though, so he couldn't see much but bare floor and shadows. Using his phone flashlight would reveal his presence immediately. But he wasn't going to go in without Kane knowing, so he went to the edge of the balcony and whistled quietly.

A long tone that got Kane's attention. Ridge waved from his position, and when Kane saw him, Ridge motioned to the door. *I'm going inside.* He wasn't going to stay out here and wait when lives were at stake.

He eased the door open enough to slip through, listening for someone hiding in the shadows. The door put up a fight. Enough that he frowned at how heavy it was. The door wanted to snap back and hit him.

He made sure the rock stayed where it was, wedging the door open so Kane could follow him.

Nothing jumped out at him as he crept through the room,

hands outstretched. Feeling for a door in front of him. His fingers hit the rail of wainscoting around the wall, and he traced it until he found the open exit into the hallway.

His boots echoed on the floor, so he switched up how he was walking. Trying to channel a little of Kane's stealth skills.

When the floor disappeared out from under his next step, he caught himself. Stairs.

Ridge stuck to the wall and made his way down. The staircase angled to the left and then opened up. He could feel the expanse of the room around him.

Like a huge entryway.

He heard an anxious intake of breath that didn't belong to him, and he couldn't pinpoint where it came from.

Halfway down to the ground floor, he started to see a glow from the side room where the twins were—a yellow strip across the floor, under the closed door.

Maybe it was his anxious breath.

The lights flipped on, blinding him for a second. Ridge froze, then looked around. Amelia stood at the edge of the balcony, which stretched around in a semicircle that overlooked the chandelier and the lobby below. The two staircases followed the wall down, and he headed down the left side.

On the outside of the rail, Amelia had somehow managed to stay put with her feet wedged back between the bars. She had fear in her eyes and a cloth over her mouth. About to fall to her death.

No . . . about to be hanged.

She had a rope tied around her neck that stretched up to the chandelier.

Ridge turned to run for her.

A man appeared at the top of the stairs holding a gun. Ridge froze.

The man's dark gaze narrowed on him. "Surprise."

"Let her go!"

"I don't think so." Nicholas shook his head. "Not if you want your sisters to live. Isn't that why you're here. To save them?"

"*All* of them."

He sneered.

Before Ridge could do anything, the gun exploded in a flash, and something heavy slammed into him. He toppled over onto the stairs and rolled.

Down.

Down.

He hit the floor at the bottom of the stairs.

Amelia screamed behind the cloth.

THIRTY-FIVE

NICHOLAS DRAGGED HER BACK OVER THE RAIL. Amelia wasn't sure it had been his intention to only make it *look* like he was going to hang her from the chandelier. She thought he probably would have killed her, depending on what Ridge had done in that moment.

She hadn't expected Nicholas to shoot him.

Kill him.

Her mind was a hot haze of questions, painful sensations, and the utter heartbreak of what she had just seen.

She stumbled onto the carpet and almost fell, dragged back to the rail by the rope around her neck. Nicholas untethered her with one cut of a knife he sheathed back on his belt.

I guess you've thought of everything.

This scenario was over. But the outcome had cost her everything she wanted.

Ridge.

Her mind spun at everything that had happened so far tonight. This whole thing was why it had taken so long for him to show up in her life, looking for revenge. The man had planned this thing on an elaborate scale. Maximum pain and maximum casualties.

There was no way he expected to get free of the situation. He was far more likely to be determined to kill himself along with the rest of them at the end of this cat-and-mouse game.

No one had noticed he was this far gone.

He certainly hadn't sought help.

Nicholas dragged her by the arm, her hands tied behind her back. Thankfully that had enabled her to grab the rail and keep from falling. That would have meant strangling herself on the rope he'd tied around her neck. But if he'd pushed her off the rail, she would never have been able to maintain her grip.

Ridge was dead.

The twins were going to be devastated—if they survived. He might've already killed them, though they'd been alive when he dragged her out, and he hadn't left her side since.

She couldn't make much noise behind the cloth tied around her mouth.

If she could, she would scream and not stop.

Nicholas needed to be admitted to a psychiatric facility for the criminally insane. There was nothing else, except for his death, that would keep him from hurting more people.

He froze.

She heard it too—voices.

He dragged her along the carpeted hallway, going faster until they were practically running, then into a room where he left the door cracked and stopped to listen.

She wanted to make noise. Scream.

Fight him.

All her strength had evaporated, leaving her without the will to fight him, even if she were able to succeed. Maybe he wouldn't shoot her, because that wasn't how he wanted her to die. But she knew he would make her suffer for trying to overpower him.

A low male voice drifted to them from somewhere down the

hall. "Nothing she said made sense. But as long as she's safe and out."

"I'm not so sure."

It was Kane and Maria.

Nicholas shifted, and she felt the barrel of the gun press against her ribs. Amelia sucked in a breath through her nose.

"This whole thing doesn't add up. Let's—Ridge!"

Footsteps pounded down the stairs.

A tear rolled down Amelia's cheek while she huddled in the dark with Nicholas. Her friends had no idea where she was. They weren't going to save her, and right now she didn't see how she could save herself.

Aren't You supposed to help me get out of things like this? Maybe it didn't work that way. Her grasp of faith was tenuous at best. *Can You help me? Ridge, the twins, and Olivia . . . They all need You. Get them out. If I don't make it . . .*

It doesn't matter.

She would rather die knowing they'd survived. But right now, she had no idea. They could just as easily be casualties of this whole thing.

His sick plan.

Nicholas dragged her from the room, continuing down the dark hall, away from that scene in the lobby. Where Ridge lay dead on the floor at the bottom of the stairs.

He shoved another door open, and her shoes hit wood floor. The temperature dropped drastically, and Nicholas stopped long enough to flip on a light. "Down the stairs. Now."

He was almost crazed with energy. The dangerous gleam in his eye was nothing she wanted anything to do with. But here she was. Trapped by her past mistakes.

It was a form of justice, keeping a balance to life, that she paid like this. People like Maddie and Ella should never be hurt because of her mistakes. There was nothing she could do about that.

Wasn't God all about vengeance as well as love?

About justice and things being fair.

Mercy.

Amelia figured she could use all of that right about now. And if she could, she would send it all to Ridge and his sisters. To Olivia, who had been helping out apart from her job and didn't deserve to be hurt.

She would give all the goodwill she had to them if it meant they would go on.

"Go." He pushed her toward the dark staircase.

She should fall on purpose, stumble down the stairs and go flying, injuring every bone in her body. Which would, of course, be excruciating, but it would also hopefully ruin whatever plan he had in place.

She couldn't bring herself to do it.

Walking down the stairs was dicey, her hands tied behind her back. The spiral wood staircase was steep and seemed to descend into darkness. She stumbled a couple of times but kept her balance by leaning against the side wall all the way down. Amelia was pretty sure she got a few splinters in her arm, but right now, that was the least of her worries.

His breath on the back of her neck.

The gun pointed at her.

Others in danger, and there was nothing she could do about it.

This was a nightmare she couldn't escape from.

Making everything she'd had with Ridge feel like a dream she would never have. It wasn't real. Not now that things had gone so wrong and she was certain they were all going to die in this house.

She stumbled off the bottom step and let out a relieved breath. *What are we doing, Nicholas?* She had a hundred questions she wanted to ask, but he'd silenced her ability to do that with this cloth cutting into the sides of her mouth. They were going some-where. Leaving the others behind.

Nicholas dragged her by the elbow, through a set of doors and into a garage, empty except for one car, a mid-size Toyota with the engine running. Their footsteps echoed on the concrete.

Amelia shivered. The air down here was frigid. She looked around but saw only a ramp that led up, which had to be how cars got in and out. Nothing else. Just a place to store cars.

There was something on the wall at intervals. She didn't quite understand what she was seeing, but it looked like what she'd seen in a training textbook.

About bomb disposal.

Amelia cried out behind the cloth and tried to get her arm from his grasp. He didn't let go.

Nicholas was going to blow the house.

He would detonate those charges he'd bought from someone in the military and collapse the building—destroy it all—and kill everyone inside.

She struggled more, blinded by the fear for her friends.

Nicholas held her arm with that punishing grip and shifted. Before she realized what he was doing, he kicked her in the thigh.

Pain exploded in her quad muscle. She collapsed to the floor, crying.

Across the concrete, she heard footsteps.

"Took you long enough." Cherry set a hand on her hip, one knee cocked in attitude and her other hand on her baby bump. "I was about to leave without you." She tipped her head back and laughed.

Amelia breathed hard behind the cloth. He dragged her up, and they stumbled toward the pregnant woman. The one Amelia had believed.

Felt sorry for when she'd shown up in town, on the run and destitute.

Grieved over when she thought Cherry had been killed.

Cherry glared. "Why is she here?"

Nicholas whipped around to her. "Shut up and get in the car. She's coming with us."

"I didn't sign up for that. She ain't part of the plan." Cherry huffed. "You get in the back and I leave, and no one knows you're in the car. That's what you said."

"Plans change." He pointed the gun at Cherry. "Do you want to die for real this time?"

Amelia could only stand there with no power and no idea what was happening to her friends upstairs. She didn't think the plan had changed at all. More likely, Nicholas had a number of ways this could go down and had prepared for every eventuality.

With the amount of time he'd had to plan, there was no way this wasn't exactly what he wanted.

"Fine." Cherry huffed a breath. She turned and sauntered to the driver's door, pulling it open so she could get in. "Just as long as I get paid."

"You get money when I get money. Got it?"

Cherry slid into the front seat.

Nicholas was taking her from here, leaving destruction in his wake. Cherry was the getaway driver. No one would suspect a pregnant woman—apparently not even Kane and Maria. They'd been suspicious of her but let her go. Which had turned out to be a good thing, considering they'd discovered Ridge at the bottom of the stairs. Left for dead.

If he could be saved, they would be able to do it.

Meanwhile, she would be long gone.

Nicholas opened the trunk of the car. "We're getting cozy for the ride. But I'm sure we'll both enjoy it."

Cold washed over her, and she shuddered.

But as long as her friends weren't the target anymore, wasn't this better? Not her preference for the outcome, but she could handle whatever Nicholas was going to do to her. What counted was that the twins got free of this situation.

Nothing that happened to her mattered.
Not if they lived.

THIRTY-SIX

RIDGE LEANED AGAINST THE DOORFRAME, GASP-
ing, trying not to collapse onto the floor. Maddie and Ella stared
at him from inside two cages. To their left was an empty one, and
beside that, Olivia Tazwell sat holding her arm to her chest.

"Is Ridgey okay?"

Of course Maddie was more concerned with him than with
her own situation.

Kane and Maria crouched in front of the cages and broke off
their discussion about how to defuse the device on the cage's padlock.

"I'm okay, Mads." He would be better when everyone was out
of here. Not just everyone except Amelia. "It hit the vest."

"You don't look okay," Ella said.

"He's okay," Kane said.

Ridge needed to reassure her but couldn't muster up the energy
to do more than stand here, using the doorway to hold himself up.
Bruised ribs and a gunshot that'd slammed into his chest? Yeah,
they were probably broken ribs now.

Olivia said, "I got shot once. It was a through and through."

"What does that mean?" Maddie glanced between him and Olivia.

The cop said, "It means the bullet went in the front and out the back. It was high enough on my shoulder that it missed anything vital."

"It went in and came out?" Maddie wailed.

Olivia shifted, gritting her teeth. "That's a good thing. A bullet is dirty. Wearing a vest? Even better."

Maddie said, "Where's Amelia?"

Ridge wanted an answer to that question but didn't have it in him to respond to Maddie.

Kane said, "Soon as you're out of here, we're gonna go find her."

Maria did something to the mechanism, then pulled it off the padlock, tossing it aside.

Ridge had lost a good amount of time lying on the floor, almost passing out. Able to hear Amelia being dragged away by Nicholas. He'd wanted to run after her but couldn't move, let alone be the one who rescued her.

If it was going to happen, it would be Kane who saved her.

Ella and Maddie raced to him. They took his weight, but he found he didn't have to lean on them. Maddie hovered on his injured side, her arm around his waist. Ella held up his other arm, and they all headed for the door while Maria helped Olivia.

Kane raced around them and opened the door, the device Maria had disarmed on the lawn where she'd tossed the pieces after rendering it inert.

It was all taking too much time. "We need to get Amelia." Ridge had to say it, even though they all knew it. Kane especially.

"Let's get you guys outside first." He held Maddie's arm. "I hear engines."

A second later, flashing lights breached the tree line on the lane. Multiple police vehicles raced toward them.

Ridge couldn't relax. This wasn't over—not even close.

"Where is she?" Maddie looked around.

Ella said, "Come on. Kane will get her."

He wanted to turn around.

A massive boom rocked the building, followed by another a second later and a third right after that. The floor under them rocked.

"Go." He stepped out, ignoring the pain. Bringing the girls with him. "Come on."

Kane said, "We need to get clear of the building, now!"

Amelia.

Ridge started to turn back.

Olivia yelled, "Run, Foster!"

He moved faster, getting the girls clear. Leaving Amelia in God's hands, even though it broke his heart to do that. She could be dying inside the house, or trapped.

Now it was falling down around them.

He picked up their pace, down the steps to the gravel. The house started to collapse on itself with a great crash. The sound of stone hitting stone. Cracking. Creaking.

It swelled in volume, like the loudest, longest peel of thunder he'd ever heard. The twins clapped their hands over their ears.

Kane got everyone back a little more.

The cop cars pulled up, but Ridge didn't look to see who had shown up for them. Too late.

Amelia was in there.

She was gone.

Ridge stared at the house as it was demolished by the force of the explosions. The structure collapsed, spraying dirt and glass into the air.

He backed the girls up a little more.

Tears ran down Ella's face. Maddie wrapped her arms around her sister. He wanted to pull them both close. Say something that would make things better.

But there was nothing that would make the nightmare of this evening better.

Maddie gasped, pointing at the house. "A car!"

Ridge spun around to see headlights lift and dip as the car traversed the grass in front of the house.

"That woman."

He turned to Maria. "What woman?"

"The pregnant one we saw behind the house."

Maddie yelled over the settling building, the car engine, and the residual noise, saying, "The pregnant lady is dead. Nicholas took her away and killed her!"

Maria shook her head. "We saw her outside, and she said she'd escaped him. She's pregnant, so there was nothing she could do to help you guys. She was going to save herself and her baby."

Ridge started toward the car. Picked up his pace. This woman knew where he'd find Amelia.

Kane tugged on his good arm and jogged in front of him.

"What's going on?"

Ridge knew that was one of the cops asking, but didn't stop to answer, and neither did Kane. He heard Maria and the girls launch into conversation with the officers, but Olivia told them all to shush, then took over.

Ridge tuned it out. He lifted one hand and waved. "Stop!"

Kane waved his arms overhead. "Stop!"

The car kept coming. The driver held the steering wheel with both hands and stared at them with wide eyes. *Cherry.*

They waved their arms more.

"Stop!"

Kane yelled, "Stop!"

One of the police cars fired up its siren for a second. The car jerked a little in front of them, as if her foot slipped off the gas. For a second, it looked like she was going to swerve around them and keep going, but Kane sidestepped and kept in front of her.

Finally, she skidded the car to a stop, spraying mud and grass behind her.

Ridge ran to the passenger side. Every step jolted pain through his shoulder. He needed to get stitched up by a doctor and all that, but not without knowing where Amelia was.

Kane opened the driver's door. "Step out of the car, ma'am."

Officer Thomas ran over. "I'll take over from here." He had his gun drawn. "Step out, please."

The pregnant woman, Cherry, climbed out slowly, grasping the sides of the door. Kane even held her hand for a second.

"Where's Amelia?"

Ridge didn't mean to yell it over the roof of the car, but now it was too late.

Officer Thomas shot him a look.

Cherry said, "I don't know anything. I can't be here. I have to leave, or my baby will be in distress."

"We can call you an ambulance, ma'am," Thomas said. "You don't need to drive yourself."

"But first you need to tell us what's going on." Kane folded his arms. "Where are Nicholas and Amelia?"

Another cop jogged over. "I see we still don't know if she's with these guys or innocent."

"Basuto." Ridge turned to him. "If I hadn't been shot by this guy while trying to save Amelia from being hanged in the lobby of that house, I'd punch you in the face."

"I'd arrest you." Basuto wanted to get in his face, but he didn't.

Maddie and Ella started crying.

Ridge glanced over and saw Maria put her arms around the girls. "Where is Amelia?" He turned to Cherry as he said it.

"He's a madman. I don't know where he went or what's happening. I'm not responsible for this!"

Interesting that she felt as if she needed to clarify. Because of Basuto's comment, or because of something else? Ridge said, "Where did he go?"

"Did he say anything to you about his plans?" Officer Thomas asked her.

Cherry shook her head. "I need to go. I can just drive myself." She looked at the rubble, what remained of the house. "I don't want to be here."

A small thump sounded from the trunk of her car.

Cherry launched into loud wails. "You can't keep me here! I'm a victim!"

Ridge opened the passenger door, spotted the button on the key fob, still in the ignition since she hadn't turned off the car, and hit the button to open the trunk. Basuto got there first.

Ridge spotted Amelia's hair color, and Basuto hauled her out of the trunk.

Kane said, "Watch out!" But his attention was on the back window.

Ridge looked and saw a dark figure crawl over the seats and hit the gas, throwing the car into Drive. Amelia fell out onto Basuto, her hands tied behind her back.

The engine revved.

Ridge went to her but glanced over at the car now careening down the grassy hill with the trunk open. The driver's door slammed shut.

Officer Thomas and a number of the other cops raced after the car with their weapons drawn. Aimed. Officer Thomas stopped, his feet apart. He squeezed off a shot at the car.

The volley of shots that followed was deafening. Glass splintered, and the engine whined. It swerved to the side and slammed into a tree.

The cops ran to it while Basuto grunted, shifting out from under Amelia. He got up just in time to see the other officers pull Nicholas out onto the ground.

Ridge turned to Amelia. Kane crouched and cut her hands free, then untied the cloth around her mouth. She looked about as haggard as Ridge felt, but she'd never been more beautiful.

Ridge wound his good arm around her and pulled her onto his lap while she let loose the tears. He held his arm around her, babbling nonsense that sounded reassuring.

Basuto hadn't moved from beside them.

Ridge looked up at the guy, and it nearly made him pass out. Okay, so maybe he needed to get seen by a doctor.

"Sorry I didn't believe you." Basuto lifted his chin. "Old wounds I didn't realize were still there."

"Do me a favor?" Ridge lifted his chin as well.

Basuto said, "What's that?"

"Grab Cherry before she flees. She was in on it with Nicholas."

The minute everyone had turned to the fleeing car, Cherry had tried to make a run for it. Trotting off like a person unaccustomed to exercise. Still, she was halfway across the yard already.

Basuto took off after her.

Amelia twisted around and looked in the direction he'd gone. "He needs to get you a helicopter to take you to the hospital, then he and I can call it even."

Kane came over and crouched. "Amelia, you okay?"

She nodded, sitting up a little. When Kane walked away, she turned to Ridge. "You were shot." Her body shuddered, her voice raw. "I thought you were dead."

He touched her cheek and leaned his forehead on hers. "I think I might be. It hit the vest, but it still hurts." Actual tears rolled down his face. He had to suck in a breath. "Don't let me pass out."

She shifted off his lap but sat facing him, close enough their hips were touching. "I've got you. Passing out might be a good idea. It'll stop hurting. The girls are good, right?" She moved her arm out of sight. "Everything is okay now. Because you were here."

She leaned over and touched her lips to his. "God brought us through it."

His eyes flared.

Before he could say anything, Maddie and Ella sat around them. "Ridgey?" Maddie bit her lip. Ella leaned against her sister.

"I'm good." He gritted his teeth and got the words out.

"You don't look okay," Ella pointed out.

"I've got the three of you," he said, holding her gaze with a steady stare. "I'm good."

THIRTY-SEVEN

WELL, IT SEEMS ODD TO SAY THIS, GIVEN HOW you look, but you're actually doing all right, Ms. Patterson." The nurse peeled off the blood pressure cuff.

Amelia glanced over at her from the bed in this tiny ER bay surrounded by curtains. The bay was barely big enough for the nurse to walk around the bed. They'd segregated all of them to check them out, but Amelia was going to jump off this bed in a second and go find the twins, Maria and Kane, and Ridge. She needed to know they were all okay.

Ridge had passed out right as they got to the hospital, and she hadn't seen him since they'd wheeled him away as soon as the helicopter touched down.

The twins must be scared out of their minds still.

"Your headache will go away when it's good and ready. Until then, you need to get as much rest as possible. So no rushing into buildings to save people. Leave putting out the fires to these guys for now." The nurse pulled back the curtain to reveal a huddle of turnout coats.

Bryce, Eddie and Zack, Zoe and Della. Izan, and even Chief James.

"Amelia!" Zoe rushed in, giving her a quick hug. "Are you okay?" She checked Amelia more thoroughly than the nurse had, turning her hands over so she could see the marks on Amelia's wrists where she'd been tied up. The old and new bruises on her neck. The knot on her head from being smacked by the butt of Elam's gun.

So many things had happened since the bank robbery. She had bruises from the truck exploding and flipping over, and even more from being taken by Nicholas.

"I'm gonna live." She tried to say it flippantly to lighten the situation, but the words caught in her throat, and to her horror, tears filled her eyes. "Is Ridge okay?"

Zoe's expression softened. "His family is going to tell us when they get an update. He went for X-rays, and they said he was sleeping, since the doctors gave him something."

"What about Warren?"

Zoe looked at Chief Macon, who said, "It's bad, but the doctor is hopeful."

The tears rolled down Amelia's face.

She half expected all the guys to rear back in shock, but they didn't. Izan came over to the other side of the bed, got in her space, and wrapped his arms around her. "You're okay, Amelia."

Her nose filled with his uniquely spicy scent.

Amelia wrapped her arms around her friend, returning the hug. When she drew back, she said, "Thanks, Izan. How is Olivia?"

He said, "Broken wrist. She's getting it bandaged, and she'll need a cast when the swelling goes down. But she's good. She's tough."

Amelia wondered if anyone else caught the possession in his tone, that *my girl* he didn't add but it was there. She saw it in his expression too. He'd been worried about Tazwell, but she was all right now.

"I need to apologize." His dark eyes tracked hers, those handsome Hispanic features warm and earnest now. He was a joker and sometimes didn't realize he should be serious, but that was gone now. "I'm sorry I wasn't more on it when you were in the training house. Even if that Nicholas guy messed with our system so the surveillance feed was off, I should've been paying more attention." He lifted his chin. "It won't happen again."

"Collins, I'm not your superior anymore. You don't report to me."

"I'm still sorry."

She touched his hand. "I forgive you."

God had shown up for her when she'd needed Him most. In her darkest hour, as they said. She figured that meant it was time to really figure out what this Christianity thing was all about. Learn more. Claim it for herself.

God was real. It had taken her long enough to figure that out. She had no time to lose now.

"Thanks." Izan scrunched up his nose, but he looked relieved. "You'll always be my lieutenant, Patterson. That's just the way it is."

She smiled.

"Okay." Macon elbowed through everyone else. "All of you clear out. Give Amelia some space."

Izan squeezed her shoulder and followed the others back into the hallway.

Chief James came over to the side of the bed. "How's your head?"

"It'll be good by the time I come back to work."

Ordinarily, she would have dismissed the injury for the sake of not being put on medical leave until she was healed up. Right now, she figured that wasn't what he was asking for. He wanted honesty. Besides, she was barely the same person who'd been called to his office and asked where her paperwork was.

She'd faced her greatest nightmare and lived to tell about it.

"What happened to Nicholas? And Cherry?" With Ridge

beside her and everyone out of the house, she had barely paid attention to what was happening around her.

"Both in custody." Macon stood at the foot of the bed. "They're trying to figure out how Cherry got tangled up with him and whether he is actually the father of her baby."

Amelia shook her head. "She was convincing. But at the end of the day, he wanted my father's money just like everyone else. And he was going to kill me, probably horrifically, out of revenge."

Macon's expression darkened. "He isn't going to hurt you anymore."

Amelia figured a good therapist could help her unpack all this. It would take time, but good things—and healing—usually did. Rushing it wasn't going to get her anywhere but back on her face, trying to figure out what to do with her life. She still wanted to sell the big house and ensure all her father's properties were offloaded. That might mean legally claiming her heritage, but it was a means to an end.

Like donating the house to a local women's shelter or a foster kids' organization so they could have bigger facilities.

Zack's wife Naya might be able to help her work out something that would benefit the local community.

"Nicholas is never going to get out of prison. Not for several lifetimes." Macon looked like he wanted to punch something.

"Good."

He nodded. "They already started looking through the rubble. Starting in a section that didn't collapse. They found a lot of evidence in the debris, surveillance photos of you. Equipment for bombs and explosives. He had all kinds of sick things planned."

"Seemed like he was constantly evolving the plan depending on what happened."

"He's not some criminal mastermind. Just a guy with far too much time on his hands and a sick obsession." Macon folded his arms across his chest. "But he's behind bars now, and he won't get bail if the cops have anything to say about it."

"I'll probably have to testify."

"If you do," he said, "I guarantee there will be a row of firefighters in the gallery to support you. You aren't going to have to face him alone."

She nodded, sniffing back more tears.

"Elam is behind bars. Who knows what the district attorney is going to do about your father's money in those accounts."

"Nicholas thought he could get me to sign it all over to him." Her mind was still reeling from everything that had happened.

"He also nearly killed you in the training house, strangling you with his bare hands."

If he'd been after the money the whole time, he probably hadn't planned to go so far as to kill her. He'd just wanted her weak and off shift so he could enact his plan.

Macon reached out and patted her foot under the blanket. "Get some rest. Get better. I'll see you back at work when you're ready, and not before. And I expect you to pass that lieutenant's exam after that, when you're back up to speed. Get your rank back, Patterson."

"Yes, sir."

He gave her a wave and left her by herself long enough for Amelia to slide out of the bed.

She'd convinced the staff she didn't need to change her clothes, so all she had to do was find her shoes. Her head swam while she moved around. Amelia could ignore it just enough thanks to the meds they'd given her—not much more than a basic over-the-counter painkiller.

In the hallway, she asked a nurse where to find Ridge and the twins.

The nurse lifted a brow. "Have you been discharged?"

"Not exactly. Yet. But I'm sure that's the next thing." She wasn't going to sit around for hours waiting. "I'll be back for the paper-work. I'm just going to check on my friends."

"I'm sure." She didn't like it, but the nurse told her where to find the Foster family.

Amelia approached the bay but spotted someone exiting the elevator at the end of the hall. Meg stepped off, followed by the twins and then Maria and Kane. All of them had Styrofoam bowls and plastic spoons. It looked like they'd gone out for ice cream.

The bay was empty.

Maddie came rushing over, Meg and Ella right behind her. Apparently they'd made friends with the woman who was the closest thing Amelia had to a sister.

Amelia hugged all three of them in turn, her head swimming anew with all the movement. She probably needed to sit down. "You went out for ice cream?"

"Only to the cafeteria." Meg sent an endearing smile to the twins.

Amelia wanted to ask Meg if they were okay but wasn't going to ask in front of them.

Ella bit her lip. "Are you okay?"

Amelia said, "Nothing a loaded baked potato and two weeks on the couch with the remote won't fix."

Maddie let out a loud whimper, then gave Amelia another hug. "You should stay with us again!"

"Whatever you want." For a while, at least. After what they'd been through, Amelia wanted to be close by so she could be sure they were all right. That they would continue to be all right. "Also, let's call Natalie. Macon's wife is a counselor. We're all going. Deal?"

The twins nodded. Ella sniffed. "I'm glad it's over."

"It is." Amelia pulled her over for a hug, catching both the girls in it. Meg put her arms around all of them.

Maria said, "Kane, it's a group thing. Get over here." She

slammed into them, and they all jolted. Amelia grinned, and one of the girls snorted.

"I'm good back here."

She looked over and saw Kane glance at his watch.

Ella let go with one arm and turned to Kane, motioning him over. "It's a group thing, you know."

Amelia sniffed, unable to keep from thinking about how far she'd come. Long days alone in her lieutenant's office followed by long days in her cabin. Living a solitary life.

Now she had firefighters who showed up to see if she was all right.

She had her best friend and this family, people she had connected with during tragedy. Brought together to be a kind of family.

Kane put his arms around all of them. "Later we should celebrate because Maria and I just got a job offer. Looks like we might be putting down roots in Last Chance County."

Maddie squealed, everyone else chuckled, and Amelia had to wipe away a tear.

"That's great news." She stepped back and saw a couple of hospital staff members wheel a bed out of the elevator at the end of the hall. "He's back."

Ridge lay on the bed, his arm hooked up to an IV. Kind of pale, with his eyes closed.

They backed up as the staffer wheeled him into the bay. "He should be awake in a few minutes."

Maddie grabbed Ella's hand and held it, going into the bay to be close to Ridge. Amelia glanced at Meg, who looked at her with an odd expression.

"What?"

Meg flushed. "Nothing. Just . . . something I was praying for."

"For me?"

Meg nodded.

"We should talk more about that." Amelia hesitated. "Maybe also . . . go to church."

Meg beamed. "Deal."

THIRTY-EIGHT

RIDGE BLINKED AND STIRRED AWAKE, VERY MUCH aware of the tightness in his chest. Three broken ribs, thanks to the bullet that had hit his vest and the tumble down the stairs. That was going to take some time to heal.

He tried not to move too much. Before he opened his eyes, he registered the bustle of the ER. He hadn't been admitted, but he had been given meds that were apparently his Kryptonite. He'd passed out under their influence and slept . . . he didn't know how long.

He blinked and the bay came into focus. Curtains on three sides. Only one person in the room with its low light. The usual brightness had been turned down to simulate night for the patients still here, and the staff were quieter than normal.

Amelia sat in the chair by his hospital bed, her head back against the seat and her eyes closed.

She was here.

He shifted so he was lying facing her, so he could take her in. Hopefully not in a way that she thought was creepy. Fact was, Amelia Patterson was the most amazing woman he'd ever known. She'd survived what would have destroyed a lot of people. She had left a horrible situation and saved herself so that she could fight another day.

Had all the conditioning she'd done over the years she'd been back in Last Chance County been not just about the job of a fire lieutenant but also about the belief that one day Nicholas would come back into her life? She'd withstood his plans when he took her from the fire truck. He hadn't won. Now he was in jail, and he wasn't getting out.

Right now, it was Ridge who needed to be reassured that the situation really was over.

He turned the other way and found his cell phone on the nightstand. Multiple texts from the twins, updating him on everything since they'd been released, because they might've been scared, but they hadn't suffered injury.

More texts from Kane, updating him that they were all at the town house, safe.

He sent a quick reply, able to move long enough to do that before he collapsed back to the bed.

"I'm not sure you're supposed to move."

Ridge's phone clattered onto the nightstand, and he found Amelia watching him, probably the same way he'd been watching her.

Her cheeks pinked.

"They gave you a clean bill of health?"

She nodded, very slightly, and touched the side of her head. "I'll be out of work at least a week. But that's time I can use to study for the lieutenant's exam."

"Think I'll be out longer."

Amelia shrugged.

"I'm glad you stayed."

"I didn't really want to go back to the cabin after everything." She shivered. "And your house is a bit crowded right now."

He smiled. Probably not the entire reason she'd hung around.

He lifted his fingers and motioned her over, even though it made the needle in the inside of his elbow pull.

Amelia got up and came over, sitting on the edge of the bed. "Are you actually okay, or are you just pretending?"

"Whatever they gave me that's making me feel like I could leap a tall building right now makes me think I'm okay."

Amelia chuckled. "Okay, Superman."

"Don't you forget it."

"Pretty sure I already knew." She held on to his hand. "You came to find me. And the twins."

"I'd have been there if it was only you. I was looking for you when the call came into the police department. Going crazy not knowing where you were or what was happening to you." It was enough to make his breath catch in his throat. "I'm glad you're all right."

"Because you came to save me." She leaned in and touched her lips to his.

Ridge wanted her to linger for more time, but she pulled back and said, "Thank you."

"You don't have to thank me." He shook his head.

"I want to. I get to say thank you if I want."

He pressed his lips together, then lifted their hands and kissed the back of hers. "You're welcome."

"I prayed." She ducked her head for a second. "In the heat of the moment, thinking Cherry and I were going to die. Thinking the twins were going to be hurt or . . ." Her breath caught. "I prayed for help. And you came."

"With Kane and Maria."

She nodded. "You're the one I saw. In the house, looking for me. You were the one who tried to save me."

"Sorry I didn't manage to get you out of that noose." Ridge couldn't get the image out of his head. He had a new set of nightmares to contend with now, waking up in the middle of the night in a cold sweat. The twins would as well, while they worked through what had happened and healed.

"Nicholas is the one to blame. You did what you could." She shook her head. "I can't believe that Cherry woman was in on it."

"There's a lot for the police to unpack. Like how Nicholas knew to contact Elam."

Amelia said, "He did a deep dive into my background and found more than he bargained for." She gave him a slight smile. "Jess came over and filled me in. She said Nicholas is talking, and they can't get him to shut up now."

Ridge shook his head. Evidently he thought telling them everything was in his best interest—or he was gloating.

"He realized he could get revenge and a payout, so he staged it all. Set Elam up with the robbery so that while everyone was focused on that, he'd be able to wire the explosive to the fire truck."

"Only a firefighter knows our rigs and our procedure well enough to pull that off and kidnap you in the aftermath."

She nodded. "Cherry was just someone who looked enough like me that he thought I'd be sympathetic toward her. It was just more mind games."

"It's over now."

"I think I'm starting to realize that. It feels like it hasn't fully settled in yet. Like I still need to keep one eye on my back, watching for him. Just in case."

Ridge sat up a little, or tried to. The ache in his chest exploded. Even with the meds, he could feel it. He groaned.

"Easy."

"You're safe."

"I know. I just need to convince my nervous system."

"I know what might relax you." He lifted his chin. "Come here."

Amelia burst out laughing. "I feel like maybe you have a one-track mind and there will be a *lot* of kissing."

It worked. He'd successfully distracted her. "You'll get used to the feeling of being safe. In the meantime, I'll be here when you do and when you don't. I'm happy to be of service."

"So selfless."

"I really am."

Amelia laughed again.

"You have a great laugh."

"I like your smile."

"Yeah?" He lifted his brows. "What else?"

"I feel like I'm going to be rolling my eyes a lot when I'm around you."

"As long as you're happy." He ran his thumb over the back of her hand.

"We technically can't date still, until we're the same rank. We'll have to keep it light and breezy until then. After I pass the test, we can make it official."

Ridge said, "That'll be good because by then I'll be all the way in love with you, not just falling for you."

He heard her breath catch in her throat. Her eyes widened, a whole lot of wonder in her gaze. Ridge was going to do his utmost to keep that look in her eyes as often as he could.

"You're beautiful," he said. "You're an amazing firefighter, a great boss, and the strongest person I know." If she brought that strength and intentionality to marriage and a family, her husband would be a blessed man. "You deserve the world. Everything you've ever dreamed of. And I want to be the one to give it to you."

A tear rolled down her cheek. She touched his cheek like she didn't even notice, then touched her lips to his. Ridge tilted his head to the side and captured her kiss, savoring it. Settling into the moment, like he had all the time in the world.

Maybe even forever.

Thank You.

God had drawn her to Himself, and He would continue to do that as Amelia chose to seek Him. He prayed she would even commit to following Him one day. Soon. That they could get married in front of God and their loved ones. Probably in the forecourt of the firehouse.

She leaned back a fraction. "I'm already in love with you. I have been for a while."

Ridge didn't want to seem *too* self-satisfied hearing that, but...

She rolled her eyes.

He laughed. "If someone as amazing as you can fall in love with me, then maybe I might be worth sticking around for."

She blinked, shaking her head like she couldn't believe he'd said that. "You have so much love in you. Your family is amazing, and everyone at the firehouse thinks you're great. You saved my life. More than once, actually. You go all out for the people you love. I never believed I'd have someone like you in my life. It feels like a dream. Something else I guess I'll have to get used to."

"We've got all the time we need."

She nodded, looking so beautiful he couldn't believe it.

He wanted to pull her against his chest, but that would be a bad idea. Instead, he settled for her snuggling up on the blanket beside him so they could hold hands and whisper about the future. Talking about anything and nothing, dreaming some more.

Because God had given them the desires of their hearts. Now it was time to dream even bigger.

EPILOGUE

One month later

AMELIA SLID THE BAKING TRAY OF COOKIES OUT of the oven in the firehouse kitchen. Ridge had taught her how to make his chocolate banana cookies, so cakey they were amazing. She was more than obsessed and figured she'd make them for the firehouse Thanksgiving party.

She set the tray down, and Eddie tried to snag a cookie. She smacked him with the potholder. "You'll burn yourself." Amelia spotted someone in the doorway. "Besides, your guest is here."

"Bia!" Eddie headed for his actress girlfriend. A woman no one would have expected to land in Last Chance County, but she had. The work they were doing together with local kids' programs was amazing.

Eddie and Bia went over to Zack, who had his arms around Naya—only a couple of months from her due date now.

Music played through the firehouse kitchen from one of Maddie's holiday playlists. The girl was obsessed with Christmas music, and that was just fine. Even if it was early.

The table had been covered with a fall-themed tablecloth, and the spread of food made Amelia feel full just looking at it. She'd been training hard the last few weeks and had finally taken the lieutenant's test last Monday. Now all she had to do was wait for the results.

Waiting sucked.

Bryce and Penny occupied the couch, with Kane nearby, talking to them.

The twins strode in from the front door, hauling bags that looked like presents. Ridge had a stack of wrapped gifts in his arms, which he tucked under the food table while the girls came over and gave Amelia hugs. Ella snagged one of the hot cookies, chewing appreciatively.

"How was your bizarrely early Christmas shopping trip?"

She'd asked Ella, but it was Maddie who said, "He's crazy. We had to go to three different stores and the mall just to find what he was looking for. All because Kane is *impossible* to buy for."

Amelia grinned because Ridge was adorable in his need to over-plan the holidays and get everything done way ahead of time.

Ella shrugged. "I got him an Alaska Air One Rescue T-shirt and a Midnight Sun Smokejumpers one."

Maddie twisted around. "That's a better idea than what I did!"

Amelia chuckled. "I'm sure he'll love whatever you got him."

"Yeah, but what Ridge got you is better."

Ella smacked her sister's arm, and Maddie flushed red.

"What did you tell her?" Ridge came over, holding a thin rectangular package that looked heavy. "Did you tell?"

The girls lifted their hands, snagged another cookie each, and scurried off toward Zoe and Della, who were laughing over plates of nibbles. Izan held out a fist and got a bump from both the girls.

Amelia wiped her hands on the towel she'd hung on the front of the oven.

Ridge held out the package. "This is for you."

"It's Thanksgiving." She frowned. "You're giving me a Christmas present on Thanksgiving?"

"Trust me." His brows rose. "You'll want to open this now."

Amelia gingerly peeled back the paper. When was the last time she'd been given a gift? And one from Ridge? She wanted to savor the moment, but soon enough, she got the paper peeled back and found a frame. Glass on the front. Metal bar for a hook on the back. Something to hang on a wall.

She turned it over.

Her breath caught.

In loving memory.

"I had the department give me the badge and name tag for your dad."

She ran her fingers over the name Matthew Curtis Patterson, too choked up to say anything.

"I think we could hang it on the wall in your office. If you'd like." He shifted, as if nervous about how she'd receive it.

Amelia hugged the memorial display to her front, lifted up on her toes, and kissed Ridge in front of everyone. He was so certain she'd pass the lieutenant's exam. She had started to dream big, but life was still life. When had it consistently gone in her favor? But now that she had God in her life, she had someone to whisper her worries to. A place where she found peace and hope.

Someone whistled—probably Izan. He was bizarrely on board with their relationship.

She heard a throat clearing. *The chief.* Amelia lowered her heels to the ground and looked over at him in the doorway, her face flaming.

"Special delivery." The chief split what was in his hand, holding out two white envelopes. One toward her, and the other to Bryce.

She went over and grabbed the envelope. Bryce did the same. Penny came over and hugged his side.

"Three, two, one, go?" Bryce said.

Amelia grinned. "Race you." She tore open her envelope.

He did the same.

Amelia slid out the paper, her stomach flipping over. Unfolded it. "I passed."

"Duh." Izan wrapped an arm around her shoulders. "*Lieutenant.*"

Having the paperwork to prove it . . .

She looked at Bryce. "Well?"

He looked at Penny. "I passed. I'm a captain now."

Amelia cheered with everyone else.

Macon said, "Sounds like it's time for Frees to clear out his office and go full-time from city hall."

"The guy should just run for mayor." Zack snagged a handful of cheese cubes from the table, and the room erupted into conversation.

Ridge slid his arms around Amelia from behind and whispered in her ear, "I knew you'd do it."

Amelia stared at the paper. "I did it." And now she could prove it. No one could take her victory away from her.

"Guess I'll have to move out of your office."

Amelia laughed. "No way. Bryce's is bigger. If he's moving into Frees's office, I get his."

Ridge tickled her side, and Amelia broke into louder laughter.

He spun her around and kissed her.

Someone yelled, "Happy Thanksgiving!"

THANK YOU!

Thank you so much for reading *Rescued Dreams*. We hope you enjoyed the story. If you did, would you be willing to do us a favor and leave a review? It doesn't have to be long—just a few words to help other readers know what they're getting. (But no spoilers! We don't want to wreck the fun!) Thank you again for reading!

We'd love to hear from you- not only about this story, but about any characters or stories you'd like to read in the future. Contact us at www.sunrisepublishing.com/contact.

Spend the festive season with your favorite first responders in *Last Chance Christmas*!

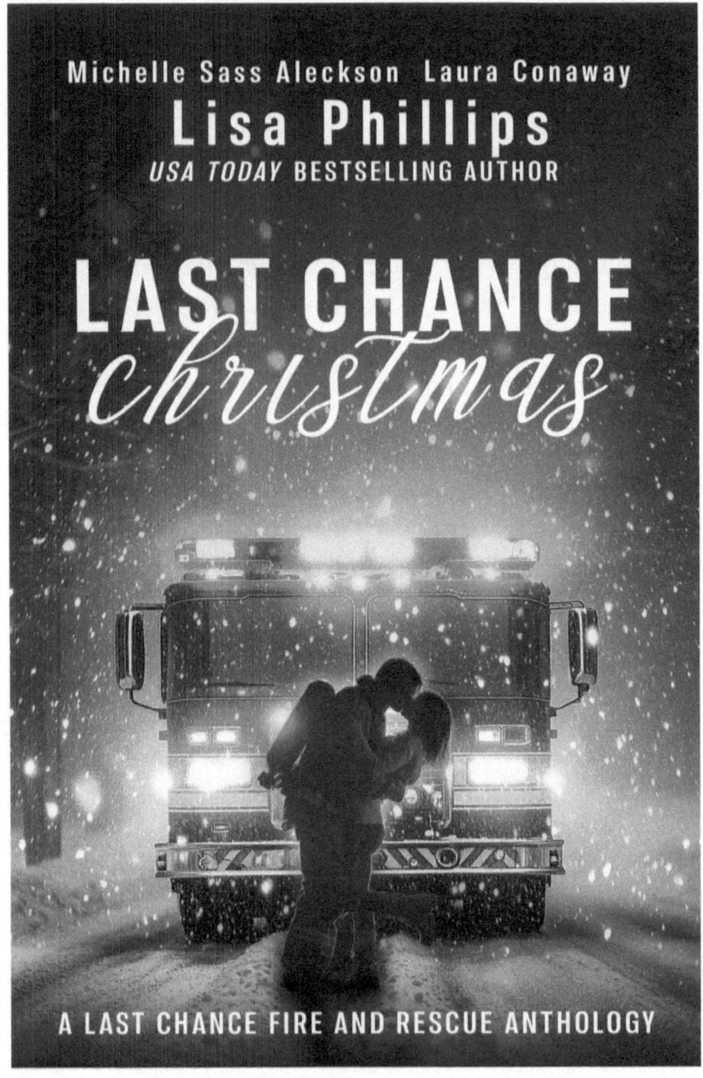

Christmas was supposed to be peaceful in Last Chance County—until escaped killers turn their winter wonderland into a deadly hunting ground.

When a catastrophic blizzard causes a prison transport crash, hardened criminals scatter into the frozen wilderness. With roads impassable and temperatures plummeting, Last Chance County's bravest first responders must abandon their holiday plans for the most dangerous manhunt of their lives.

But in the heart of winter's fury, love is the light in the storm…

Firefighter Izan Collins has waited months to win guarded cop Olivia Tazwell's heart, but when a cartel killer targets his family during a church event, their first date becomes a fight for survival.

Officer Anthony Thomas never believed in Christmas magic—until protecting fierce firefighter Della Nixon from a vengeful serial killer shows him that some gifts are worth any sacrifice.

K-9 Officer Cole Stuart has hunted his nemesis for two years, but partnering with determined EMT Kianna Russell in a deadly mountain pursuit teaches him that some battles are meant to be fought together.

Three couples. Three heart-stopping chases through winter's deadliest storm. Three Christmas miracles that prove love conquers all.

ONE

OFFICER OLIVIA TAZWELL GRIPPED THE STEERING wheel and swung the squad car around a turn onto Rutland Boulevard. She'd broken her wrist a couple of months back, but it had healed since. The memories? Not so faded.

Her partner, Officer Junior Ramble, sat in the seat beside her. "Are we in a hurry for some reason?"

"Just keeping my skills sharp." Truth was, she was restless in a way that she hadn't been since college. That had caused her all kinds of trouble, getting in with the wrong crowd. Hooking up with the wrong kind of guy. Getting her heart broken and the downward spiral that followed.

She didn't want to go back to that dark place.

Not just because she was a cop now and had been for four years. She lived on the right side of the law rather than skirting the dividing line and hoping she didn't get caught. Thankfully she never had been. Otherwise a career as a cop would have been out of the question.

The last thing she wanted now was to get fired and have the people of Last Chance County think she had never deserved their respect.

"How's your mama?"

Olivia blew out a breath, rolling her eyes. The usual reaction anytime he brought up her mom. "Ornery as usual. Complaining that the night manager hates her. She wants to get switched back to the day shift so she can get back on a cash register."

"We should swing by. Say hi." He checked his watch.

"Too early for lunch break."

"It's after midnight."

"Exactly. We should wait at least another hour, or you'll start complaining at four, and you'll be miserable until we get off at seven."

Junior liked to grumble under his breath.

Mostly she ignored it since he was a solid partner and he'd never tried to hit on her. They were more like brother and sister and had settled into a friendship that had developed over the last few years working together. Since they'd both graduated from the same academy class.

He'd been born and raised in Last Chance County. She'd grown up in Benson, Washington, and the minute she'd been able to leave, she'd gone. Olivia had persuaded her mom to come with her, and they'd left that town in the rearview—with Olivia eighteen and driving because her mom had been wasted at the time. These days she had periods of being sober and on the right track, then rocky weeks where she needed some help.

The fact both of them loved Christmas in a way that bordered on obsession was about the only thing they agreed on.

Their radios came to life at the same time, the sound by her left shoulder, where the unit was clipped to her uniform shirt.

"All units, robbery in progress. Bridgewater Café."

"Finally." Junior grabbed his radio. "This is unit twelve, responding."

Olivia flipped on their lights and hit the gas. "Finally?"

"Not that hanging out with you, driving around doing nothing but shooting the breeze isn't fun and all…"

"You're a man of action?" Olivia chuckled. She took the next corner at speed, fast enough Junior grabbed the handle at the top of the door, which made her grin.

He muttered, and she thought she heard the name "Meg" in the middle of it.

Olivia turned another corner, passed a truck that had pulled over to the side of the street, and hit the gas again. "How are things going with Meg?"

"They aren't." Junior shifted in his seat.

"What?"

"I'm working on something else."

"Since when?"

Junior shrugged. "Saw a woman at church. Introduced myself. I'm making progress." Sounded like he was talking through gritted teeth. "Meg is history."

But he still cared about her, and if she was in the café, she might be in danger.

They'd learned the hard way not to process what might be happening at a scene before they even arrived. Right now they had no idea who might be in the café and what the situation was. There was never any point speculating about whether someone was hurt.

Olivia saw his knee start to jog up and down and drove faster, pulling up outside the café. Junior was out of the car, the gun in his hand down at a low angle, before she'd even rounded the hood with her own weapon drawn.

He went in the front door of the café first. "Doesn't look like the lock is busted. Maybe someone left it open."

"Her security system should have called it in, but this seems more like someone reported an intruder." She frowned. "Let's clear the place quick, then call in and find out." After all, someone could be hurt.

Inside the café was dark, but she knew the layout. Junior and Olivia both clicked on the flashlights that attached to the barrels of their guns. Junior worked his way through the tables, calling out as he went. "Police department! Is anyone here?"

Olivia listened and heard a rustle followed by a crash in the back. "Police department!"

Junior picked up his pace and went first down the hall. He looked through the circular window before he pushed open the swinging door into the kitchen. And then stopped to laugh.

A low, throaty chuckle.

"What? What is it?"

"A trash panda." He holstered his weapon and bent forward to laugh some more.

Olivia slid her gun into its holster but had to pause. "A what?"

The back door to the café was open.

"A raccoon."

"A trash panda?" She shook her head.

"You've never heard that?"

Olivia went to the back door and looked around outside. She saw a car pull up, a little blue compact. Meg climbed out of it. Probably also alerted by her security company that there had been a break-in. Olivia waved so Meg would know everything was all right. "I'll get dispatch to send animal control."

Junior sized up the animal, currently over by a set of wire rack shelves, reaching for dry goods just above its head. "I can take it."

She grabbed his shoulders and steered him to the back door. "You speak with the owner. I'll take care of your trash panda."

He made a noise in his throat but didn't get the chance to say anything before Meg stepped in the back door from outside. "Meg, hey. Everything's okay in here."

"Junior." Meg cleared her throat. "Good to see you."

Olivia heard him start explaining what it was and stepped into the kitchen. The raccoon had a package of cookies open and was enjoying his treat. She grabbed her radio and called in the need for animal control.

"Understood, unit twelve. Hang tight and I'll get you an ETA."

"Thanks. Twelve out." She stepped out of the kitchen, back into the hall.

Meg let out an adorable sound, like a giggle but more mature. It had a light quality to it.

When Olivia laughed it sounded like a choking snort, so she tried not to laugh aloud if she could help it. Most times she settled for a grin. But when was there all that much to laugh about?

It wasn't like her life had been fun and games, with her mom working all hours to take care of her and trying to manage being a somewhat-functional alcoholic at the same time. The community in Benson had treated them like white trash, and the churches her mom sent her to—so she could get free childcare—hadn't exactly been welcoming. The other kids hadn't played with her. Not even when their moms weren't around.

Olivia found a chair and wedged the kitchen door shut so the raccoon couldn't escape. Animal control needed to remove the thing and release it somewhere it could thrive. With Junior and Meg still making awkward small talk, she went to the front window and looked out.

From here she could see a few streets over, where the roof of Eastside Firehouse stretched above the new gas station roof. Her own kind of addiction, proving she wasn't so different from her mother. She had things she wanted that weren't good for her.

Olivia's life was about keeping things tight. Maintaining control at all times so that no one could look at her or treat her like people had when she was growing up. The less people knew about who she was and where she'd come from, the better.

Her radio crackled. "Unit twelve, this is dispatch. Animal control will be to your location in ten minutes. Advise the owner to clear out and secure the structure."

Olivia wanted to ask why but wasn't going to interrupt.

The dispatcher continued, "Reports of shots fired and a traffic collision on highway, mile marker six."

And they were closest.

She spun around. "Junior!"

"I heard it."

Olivia grabbed her radio. "Unit twelve responding."

"Confirmed, twelve. Dispatch out."

She heard him giving Meg instructions, and then he appeared in the main café room. "She's going to wait in her car."

"Good." Olivia caught the door and held it open for Junior. She made sure it was shut, and they raced to the squad car.

Junior got to the driver's side first and climbed in.

They peeled out, lights and sirens going. Olivia said, "Shots fired and a traffic collision?" That would mean more than just them responding. Probably the fire department, though it would be up to Olivia and Junior to contain the situation.

Not that she knew if Izan was even on duty tonight.

She might not see him at all.

But there was a big difference between what Olivia Tazwell wanted and what she usually got.

ACKNOWLEDGMENTS

It's bittersweet to see the Last Chance County series come to an end. I'm a very blessed author, and I'm sad to see Last Chance County hit the rearview mirror. At least for now. It's been an amazing journey through multiple series, seeing how the stories have branched off into others like Chasing Fire and Benson First Responders. A huge thank you to the readers who have loved these stories and fallen hard for the characters the way I have.

Happy Reading,

Lisa

Lisa Phillips is a USA Today and top ten Publishers Weekly bestselling author of over 80 books that span Harlequin's Love Inspired Suspense line, independently published series romantic suspense, and thriller novels. She's discovered a penchant for high-stakes stories of mayhem and disaster where you can find made-for-each-other love that always ends in happily ever after.

Lisa is a British ex-pat who grew up an hour outside of London and attended Calvary Chapel Bible College, where she met her husband. He's from California, but nobody's perfect. It wasn't until her Bible College graduation that she figured out she was a writer (someone told her). As a worship leader for Calvary Chapel churches in her local area, Lisa has discovered a love for mentoring new ministry members and youth worship musicians.

Find out more at www.authorlisaphillips.com.

LAST CHANCE
FIRE AND RESCUE

USA Today Bestselling Author

LISA PHILLIPS

with **LAURA CONAWAY**, **MEGAN BESING** and **MICHELLE SASS ALECKSON**

The men and women of the Last Chance County Fire Department struggle to put a legacy of corruption behind them. They face danger every day on the job as first responders, but the fight to become a family will be their biggest battle yet. When hearts are on the line it's up to each one to trust their skill and lean on their faith to protect the ones they love. Before it all goes down in flames.

We solve the problem of what to read next.   Available on Amazon

ELITE GUARDIANS: SAVANNAH

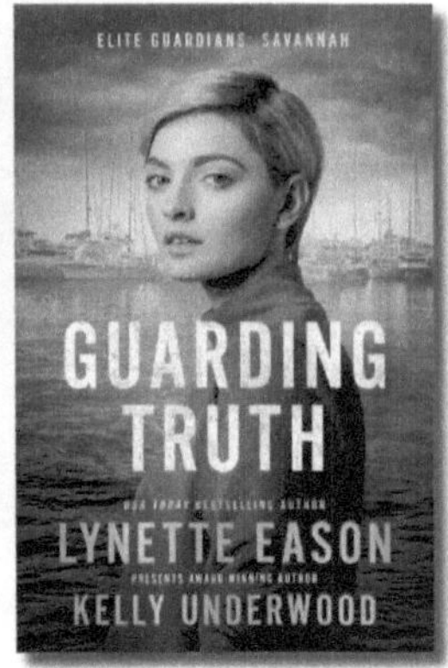

With mystery, pulse-pounding action, and swoon-worthy romance, this edge-of-your seat series is totally addicting from start to incredibly satisfying finish.

FROM USA TODAY BESTSELLING AUTHOR

LYNETTE EASON

with **Kate Angelo**, **Sami A. Abrams**, and **Kelly Underwood**

We solve the problem of what to read next.   Available on Amazon

SUMMER RANGERS

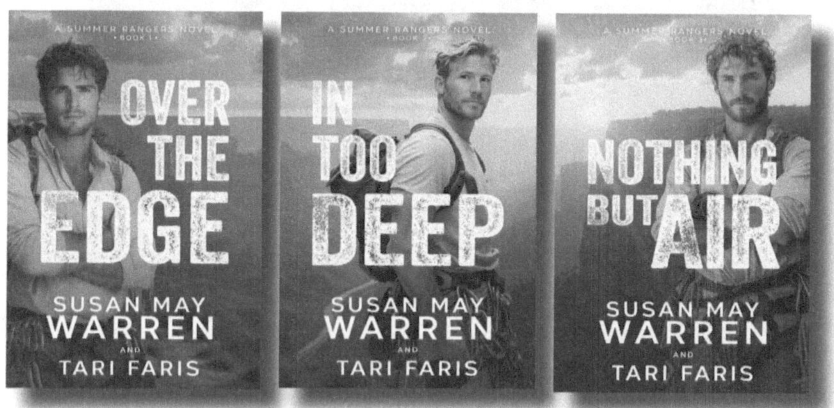

Where heart-stopping adventure meets breathtaking romance in America's most dangerous playground.

FROM USA TODAY BESTSELLING AUTHOR

SUSAN MAY WARREN
AND TARI FARIS

We solve the problem of what to read next.

Available on Amazon

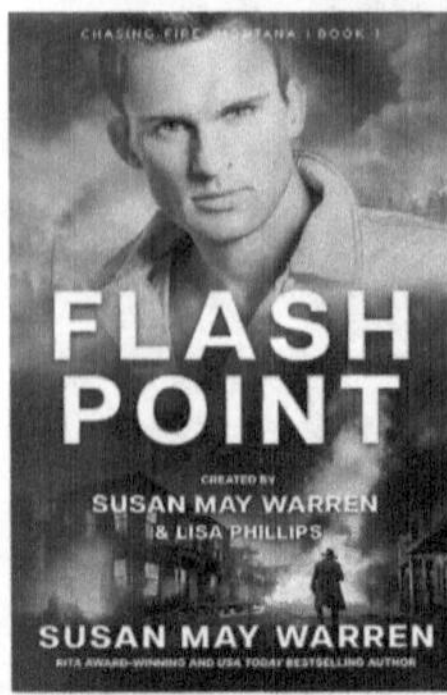

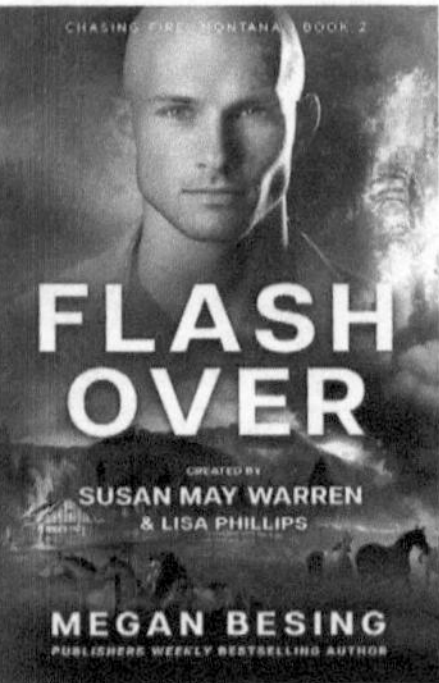

CHASING FIRE:
MONTANA

Dive into an epic series created by

SUSAN MAY WARREN
and LISA PHILLIPS

We solve the problem of what to read next.

Available on Amazon

WE THINK YOU'LL ALSO LOVE...

Fire Department liaison Allen Frees may have put his life back together, but getting the truck crew and engine squad to succeed might be his toughest job yet. When a child is nearly kidnapped, Allen steps in to help Pepper Miller keep her niece safe. The one thing he couldn't fix was the love he lost, but he isn't going to let Pepper walk away this time.

Expired Return by Lisa Phillips

Stunt double Vienna Foxcroft's stunt team are the only ones she trusts. Then in walks Sergeant Crew Gatlin and his tough-as-nails military dog, Havoc. When an attack on a film set sends them fleeing into the streets of Turkey, Vienna must face the demons of her past or be devoured by them. And Crew and Havoc will be tested like never before.

Havoc by Ronie Kendig

When an attempt is made on Grey Parker's life and dead bodies begin piling up, suddenly bodyguard Christina Sherman is tasked with keeping both a soldier and his dog safe... and with them, the secrets that could stop a terrorist attack.

***Driving Force by Lynette Eason
and Kate Angelo***

We solve the problem of what to read next.

Available on Amazon

SUNRISE PUBLISHING

**WHERE EVERY STORY IS A FRIEND,
AND EVERY CHAPTER IS A NEW JOURNEY...**

Subscribe to our newsletter for a free book, the latest news, weekly giveaways, exclusive author interviews, and more!

@sunrisemediagroup

@sunrisepublish

@sunrisepublishing

Shop paperbacks, ebooks, audiobooks, and more at
SUNRISEPUBLISHING.MYSHOPIFY.COM